ATTACK ALARM

One of the author's first novels, *Attack Alarm* was written when Hammond Innes was a young gunner stationed on a Battle of Britain aerodrome in 1941, living through the shattering experiences he so accurately describes. Because the book was written 'under fire' on a gun tower in 1941, the urgency and intensity of the times are communicated by the young author.

As well as a thrilling adventure story of fifth-column activities, the book is an authentic, hair-raising account of the long summer of 1940 when England hung on the brink of disaster and only a handful of fighter planes could prevent total defeat.

Attack Alarm

HAMMOND INNES

COLLINS

fontana books

First published 1941
First issued in Fontana Books 1963
Second Impression, September 1963
Third Impression, April 1964
Fourth Impression, March 1966

Printed in Great Britain
Collins Clear-Type Press
London and Glasgow

CONTENTS

TO DOROTHY

*Here at last is the book I have been promising you.
If it is scrappier than usual, you must blame the
circumstances in which it has been written. At the
same time, I hope you will find the material interesting. Within the framework of a thriller, I
have endeavoured to give some idea of the atmosphere of a fighter station during the Blitz. And
since it has in it so much of my life since we have
become separated, it has, in the fullest sense, been
written for you.*

Chapter One

GROUND PLAN

The atmosphere of the place was stifling. The air was hot and full of smoke, and the lamps, which had just been lit, glowed dimly. From where we sat at the entrance it was barely possible to see the beer counter at the far end. And between ourselves and the bar was a sea of faces, sweat-glistening and animated—like masks seen vaguely through curling tobacco smoke. This was our only recreation. This was Thorby in mid-August.

It had been exciting enough at first. A fighter station at the beginning of the Blitz was exciting. But after only a week in the place, the excitement had palled; it had become a strain. The inevitability of concrete runways and brick and concrete buildings, the din of revving engines and the dust had asserted themselves. Dust and noise—that epitomised Thorby. And not even the excitement of action could dispel my sense of depression.

It wasn't just the dust and the noise that made me depressed. Thorby was better than some stations. It had been built in 1926, and those who had planned it had had the grace to give the roads grass borders and to plant trees. At certain strategic points there were even flower-beds. God knows, I longed for the fresh green of the country, but it wasn't that that made it impossible for me to join the others in celebrating their first action. It was the atmosphere of the place. It was tense—tense and waiting. Even in the few days I had been on the site, Thorby had changed. France had fallen in June. The Luftwaffe was just across the Channel now. Invasion was in the air. The coast and the fighter 'dromes felt it most, for they had become the front line. All around the 'drome barbed-wire entanglements were springing up. Trenches were being hastily dug at vulnerable points and brick and concrete pill-boxes built to cover the landing-field as well as the outer defences. Civilians had been brought in to help the Army. Thorby was like a town preparing for a seige. And it had the same atmosphere. Every one was waiting, waiting with nerves taut.

That atmosphere of tension was nowhere more noticeable than in the big Naafi tent at the edge of the square. There was no leave now—not even local leave. There was no relaxation from the strain of waiting, except to come here and drink and sweat.

God! how stifling it was! At the table opposite ours a sapper struck up "Tipperary" on a mouth organ. In an instant half the tent had taken up the song. Why did we have to fall back on the last war for our songs? I was thinking with distaste of those abortive efforts of the early days—"Run Rabbit Run" and "We'll Hang Out our Washing on the Seigfried Line"— when somebody touched me on the arm. I looked up. It was Kanly Furle. "What are you drinking?" he asked, leaning across the table to make himself heard.

I shook my head. "No more for me, thanks."

"Oh, but, my dear man, you simply must. We've got up to sixty-five. One more round and we'll have seventy-five. That will be a new high for the troop."

I stared at the array of bottles. Whilst I had been lost in my thoughts, the others had collected our litter of bottles and arranged them in columns of threes. They stretched from one end of the table to the other and overlapped on to the next.

Kan pointed to the one bottle of brown ale which had been stood out in front. "Oggie," he said. He had risen to his feet and his slim body was swaying slightly. "You know—our little man—Ogilvie. You're drinking a pale ale."

And with that he went off up the gangway and pushed his way in amongst the crowd at the bar. He was a tall, slim boy, rather too narrow in the shoulders to be well-built, but graceful in his movements. He

8

was an actor and an obvious devotee of Gielgud. This and the fact that he affected a silk scarf beneath his battle blouse made him rather an outstanding personality even in a varied troop like ours.

He returned bearing ten bottles. When he had distributed them, he sat down in the seat opposite me.

" Well, here's to those famous last words of yours, Kan—' Look at those Blenheims ! ' " said Sergeant Langdon. He was our detachment commander.

" Blemins !" exclaimed Micky Jones. " Blemins ! Were they—hell ! I'd like to kill every bleedin' Jerry wiv a baynet. Cold steel ! that's what they want. The beggars can't take it. Cold steel, mate ! They can't take that, can they, John ?" he asked Langdon and buried his face in his glass. He was a scruffy little man, with a dark, round face, hardly any teeth and very close-cropped brown hair.

" It certainly was pretty funny," said Bombardier Hood. " There we were, standing around chatting, and suddenly you yell, ' Look !' with dramatic outflung arms. ' They're Blenheims.' And the next minute they go into a dive over Mitchet."

" And when they dived—did you 'ear what 'e said when they dived ?" put in Micky. " He said : ' They're going to land.' He said that, didn't 'e, John ? You was wrong there, mate. They was bloody dive-bombing the place."

" And then you began to cry," said Hood. He had the grace to take the edge off his remark with a laugh, but I felt it was a bit much as he was drinking Kan's beer.

" Well, I must admit we thought they were Blenheims too," said Philip Muir. He was the sergeant from the other three-inch site on the far end of the 'drome. He had come from one of the discount houses and was rather older than most of us. " I had the glasses on them. I knew Junkers 88's were like Blenheims, but I never really knew how like until I saw those blighters."

9

"Can't think why we didn't get a proper plot."

"I must say I was certain they were hostile as soon as I saw them." This from Bombardier Hood.

"He's always right," Kan said to me in a stage whisper that carried the length of the table.

Hood darted him a quick glance. "What would eleven Blenheims be doing in a fighter area anyway?" he added defiantly.

"Could you see the markings?" Muir asked John Langdon.

"Yes, quite plainly. I had the glasses on them all the time."

"Glasses! You could see 'em wiv the naked eye, mate. Bloody great crosses. The bastards!"

"Guess it'll be our turn next."

"I thought they were coming for us to-day."

"They must have unloaded all their bombs on Mitchet."

I couldn't help thinking what a story it would have made in peace-time. And now it would be dismissed in a paragraph. *Enemy aircraft make a dive-bomb attack on an aerodrome in the south-eastern counties.* Or more probably there would be no mention of it at all. It seemed incredible when such a fuss was made about things like railway smashes in peace-time. And how much more spectacular this attack on Mitchet was!

We had taken post at about 16.30 hours. The plot had been an unknown number of hostile aircraft approaching from the south-west. Nothing happened until just after five. Then suddenly the gentle hum of engines sounded in the still summer air. It was absolutely cloudless and we scanned the azure bowl of the sky, waiting as the sound grew louder until it was a dull throb, like the beat of blood against one's eardrums. It was Kan who saw them first. They were coming almost out of the sun, and for an instant one of them glinted, a silver speck, as it banked slightly to maintain formation.

They were to the east of us and at between fifteen and twenty thousand feet. Slowly they came lower. They passed to the north-east of the 'drome at little more than ten thousand feet. It was then that Kan said they were Blenheims. They certainly looked like it with practically the same taper on the leading and trailing edges of the wings. They continued past Thorby towards Mitchet, still dropping.

And then suddenly the leader banked. The other two in the first formation followed suit. For a second it really did look as though they were circling to land at either Thorby or Mitchet. But the leader rolled right over on his port wing-tip and then began to fall nose first; the other two followed. And then one by one the others tipped over and went down. Nobody in the pit said a word. We held our breath, waiting for the bombs. It was the first time I had ever seen a dive attack. The downward plunge had the inevitability of a preying hawk. There was no ack-ack. Not one of our fighters was to be seen. It made me feel sick. Mitchet lay defenceless on the floor of the plain between us and the North Downs. It was murder.

"There they go," Bombardier Hood had said suddenly. From beneath the first plane several bombs fell in a cascade, their metal showing white for a second as they caught the sun. Almost immediately bomber and bombs parted company as the former flattened out of its dive. The others seemed to follow right on his tail. I thought the stream would never cease. And before the whole formation had completed its attack my eyes were drawn to the ground. It was misty with heat. Nevertheless I could make out Mitchet hangars and the criss-cross of the runways. And right in the midst of it great fountains of earth and rubble shot into the air. An instant later came the sound—dull, heavy crumps that seemed to make the earth quiver beneath our feet.

Then somebody said, "They're turning this way." And sure enough they were coming out of their dive into formation again and banking towards Thorby, climbing all the time. For a moment my heart was in my mouth. And then all sense of fear was lost in the excitement of action. They came back straight over the 'drome at about ten thousand feet. My impression of what happened is blurred. I remember the ear-splitting crack of the first shot. I had been warned that the three-inch was one of the noisiest guns. But even so, I was not prepared for the loudness of it. It was like hell let loose, with the flash from the muzzle and the flames flung backwards round the breech ring as the gun kicked back. I remember handing a shell to Micky Jones, who was loading. I remember, too, a brief glimpse I had of the planes when they were right overhead. My impression was of a perfect formation, of big black crosses on light-green wings and of little white puffs where our shells were bursting. Langdon's "Cease fire!" left me with a shell in my hands and a feeling of the keenest disappointment that we had not brought anything down.

"Hallo, boys!" I looked up. Tiny Trevors' big bulk loomed over the table. "I see by the parade-ground effect that everybody is drinking pale ale. How many is it—ten? Would you like to get them for me, Micky? I had a sort of premonition I should find you all here." Trevors was the Troop Sergeant-Major and very popular at that. He was like a great big playful boy, and he could be charming when he wanted to be.

"Really, Tiny, I don't think I want any more," said John Langdon. "I ought to get back to the site."

"Oh no, you don't, John. The occasion demands a drink. Besides, I want to have a chat with you and Philip." His roving eye fell on two Waafs standing near the bar. "Ah, there's Elaine. I promised I'd meet her here. I'll be back in a second. Make it thirteen, will you, Micky?" He tossed ten bob on to the table in front of Micky Jones and went up to the bar.

"Who's Elaine got with her?" asked Philip.

"Don't know," replied one of the older members of the troop from his site. "Must be new. I haven't seen her around before."

"A new batch arrived last week," said another from the same site, whose name I did not know. "I saw them going through the gas chamber the other day."

"Fair smasher, ain't she," said Micky as he got to his feet. "Puts me in mind of a tart I met down at Margate one August bank holiday. She had fair hair an' all."

"An' all," Muir repeated in the general shout of laughter. "Sure she had 'an' all'?"

"Who's coming wiv me to help carry these drinks?"

Two fellows got up. I didn't notice who, for my attention had wandered to the two Waafs talking to Trevors. They were both very attractive. The shorter, whom I took to be Elaine since Trevors was talking mainly to her, was small and dark, with rather round features and a short straight nose. It was the other, however, who attracted my gaze. She was tall and slim with straight fair hair beneath her peaked cap. There was a certain distinction about her. The movement of her hands when she talked was expressive, and though her face was too long and her mouth too wide for beauty, she was undoubtedly attractive.

Trevors nodded in the direction of our table and they came down the gangway towards us. Elaine seemed to know every one. "Meet the Artillery, Marion," she said. Some she introduced by their surnames but mostly she used their Christian names. She stopped at me and said, "I'm sorry, I don't know your name. I don't think we've met before."

"Hanson," I said, "Barry Hanson."

"Barry Hanson," the other girl repeated. "You're not by any chance a journalist?"

"Why, yes. How did you guess?"

"On the *Globe*?"

"That's right."

"Oh dear, it's a small world, isn't it? I was on the *Globe* too."

I stared at her, puzzled. "I'm sorry," I said, "but I don't ever remember seeing you around."

"No, I don't think we ever met. I was at the City office. Norman Gale's secretary. You probably remember me as Miss Sheldon. You used to ring me up periodically to get industrial unemployment statistics. Remember?"

"Good God! Yes. Of course I remember. Strange! You were just a voice on the telephone and now we meet in this dump. Come and sit down."

Kan made room for her on the bench beside him. She pushed her gas mask and tin hat under the table and took off her cap. Her straight hair fell practically to her shoulders. She had blue eyes and a way of looking directly at the person she was talking to.

Trevors pushed past behind me. "Come and sit down over here, Elaine," he said. "I want to talk to these two boys. He sat down next to Philip Muir. The drinks arrived and were distributed. Marion Sheldon and I began discussing the paper and the various personalities on it whom we had both known.

"It's funny that you never came up to the office," she said. "You were quite a friend of Norman Gale's, weren't you?"

I explained that I usually met him either down in the Street or else at one of the City haunts. "I can't think why you wanted to join up," I said. "You had a very good job and a very interesting one. And I should think Norman was a very good fellow to work for."

"The best," she smiled. I liked her when she smiled. "But the City notes got smaller and smaller. I began to feel I wasn't pulling my weight. Life seems a bit dead when you're spending six hours at the office and there's only about an hour's work. And that's how I came to join the Air Force."

"What's your job?" I asked.

"Well, I've been rather lucky. I only joined up about six weeks ago and I've managed to get into Ops. It's really very exciting plotting the movement of all these raids. I came here about a week ago straight from the training course."

"Funny! We've both been here about the same time." I was just going to ask her how she took to life on an aerodrome when I realised that every one else had stopped talking and was listening to Trevors.

"The trouble is," he was saying, "they don't know how they got into the agent's hands. Either the agent himself got into the place or else somebody gave him the information."

"Well, it's easy enough to get into it," said Muir. "A bloody sight too easy. The police at the main gates seem to let any one in uniform through without question."

"And there are all these workmen coming and going," put in Hood. "Any one of them might be a fifth columnist. If I know anything about British organisation, they haven't been checked up on very carefully."

"It's not only the workmen," said John Langdon. "It might just as well be someone in the Services. Nobody bothered to find out whether I was a Fascist or if I was pro-Nazi when I joined up. Germany has had seven years in which to prepare for this. You can bet your life their fifth-column organisation won't be confined to the civil population."

"In fact, the trouble is that it might be any one who has access to the 'drome," said Trevors. "It might be somebody in this troop."

"Westley, for instance," said Hood. Nobody liked Westley, and he was known to have belonged to the B.U.F. at one time. "He was sitting shivering in the pit when we went into action this afternoon, as though he was scared out of his wits we'd bring something down."

"Anyway, Oggie is going to give us all a little lecture to-morrow on the British Empire and our duties as soldiers of the Crown," Trevors went on. "They're checking up on all the workmen. And we're all going to be issued with special passes so that it won't be so easy for any unauthorised person to get into the camp."

"What's it all about?" I asked Kan. "I missed the first bit."

"Intelligence have found a complete ground plan of the aerodrome in the hands of a Nazi agent, so Tiny says."

"What would the Germans want with that?" I asked. "I mean, you'd think they would have got all routine information of that nature long ago."

"Oh, but it isn't as simple as all that," Kan pointed out. "I mean, things change from month to month. Take it that they intend to make fighter aerodromes their Number One objective. They well may. If the fighter aerodromes were immobilised for even twenty-four hours the invasion would succeed. Only two months ago this place was defended by six Lewis guns—two manned by the R.A.F. and four by another troop in this battery. Now there are our two three-inch guns, two mobile Bofors and one Hispano, quite apart from all the ground defences. Information about all those new defences would be vital to a successful attack on the station."

"I see." It was obvious, of course. Whatever the views of the High Command two or three months ago, I knew that the Air Ministry had never been under any delusions as to what would happen if the main fighter 'dromes were immobilised for even the shortest period.

The table seemed to have fallen strangely silent after the first outburst of speculation. Thinking about it in the light of what Kan had said, I felt an unpleasant sinking sensation inside me. It might be the routine collection of information by the German espionage system. But the news that Germany wanted detailed plans of the ground defences came too soon after the bombing of Mitchet for me to regard it as other than an indication that they were out for the fighter 'dromes, and that we were on the list.

I think it was then that I first realised that Thorby was an enclosed space imprisoning us. There was no getting away from the place. Here we were and here we had got to stay whatever was in store for us.

"It's a horrid thought, isn't it?" said Marion at last. "I mean, the idea that they want the position of every gun, every trench and every piece of barbed wire."

She gave a wry smile. "You know, when I came here," she said. "I thought it was all so interesting. It excited me to see the 'planes taking off. There was the call to readiness on the Tannoy and the revving up at the dispersal points. Then the gathering for the take-off, engines roaring at the start of the runway. I loved to see the leader of each flight of three drop his hand as he signalled the take-off. It thrilled me. One minute they were on the ground and the next they were dwindling specks in the sky. A few minutes later they might be engaged in a desperate fight in defence of Britain's shores. And it was fun to be at the pulse of the whole thing in Ops., plotting the raids as they came in." She shrugged her shoulders. "Now I've lost my girlish thrill. The novelty has worn off, leaving a rather tawdry picture of dust and wire and noise. Partly one is tired, I suppose. But also I'm beginning to realise that air defence is not a big adventure, but war, just as brutal and wearing as it was in 1914—different, that's all. I get no kick out of being at the pulse of the whole thing now. Just a primitive joy in helping to bring our own machines into contact with the enemy."

"Your reaction to the place seems much the same as mine," I said. "At first I thought it exciting. Now I'm not sure it isn't too exciting."

"I think you've got something there," said Kan, looking past me towards the entrance of the tent.

I turned. One of our fellows was coming in. He had his gas mask at the alert and his tin hat on, and he was in a hurry. He paused to peer through the smoke of the tent and then made straight for our table. "Take post!"

"Oh, hell!" said Trevors.

"Anything exciting?"

"Just the usual visitors. There's one overhead now."

"Come along now, lads—drink up." Trevors imitation of the Naafi girl at the supper canteen caused a shout of laughter as every one scrambled to their feet, gulping hurriedly at their beer.

Chapter Two

NIGHT ACTION

We tumbled out of the tent into the square. It was dusk. The barrack blocks stood in black silhouette against the long stems of the searchlights, which weaved a pattern against the stars. Some of us had bicycles. Kan and I began to run. The intermittent throb of a Jerry could be heard overhead. Somewhere up there in the half-darkness of the night a 'plane was moving swiftly towards London. And to the north came the sound of the Thames barrage, and occasionally we could pick out the little star-like burst of a shell.

At the far end of the square we were picked up by a Bofors tow-er, which dropped us at our gun pit. We ran into the hut and got our steel helmets and gas masks. The place looked bare and deserted in the light of two hurricane lamps. The table was littered with the remains of supper and amongst the dirty plates was a half-finished game of chess. The cards still lay on a bed just as they had been dealt for a hand of bridge. Everything was just as it had been left when the detachment on duty had gone out to take post.

Outside the night seemed darker. The searchlights had moved to the north, clustering as they followed the passage of the plane. Against their light the pit was just visible as a black circle of sandbags with the thick barrel of the gun pointing skywards. And inside the circle tin-hatted figures moved restlessly to and fro. As we went across to the pit we met Micky Jones, panting. He had been less fortunate in the matter of a lift. "Some people 'ave all the luck," he said. "Cor, I ain't 'alf puffed. Run all the bloody way. And there's Bombardier bloody Hood strolling along as cool as you please. Any one would think there wasn't no war on."

As we came into the pit, John Langdon, still sitting on his bike, was talking to Helson over the sandbagged parapet. Eric Helson was the lance-bombardier in charge of the detachment on duty. "Was that Micky who just went into the hut?" Langdon asked us.

Kan told him it was, and Langdon said : "All right then, Eric. That completes my detachment. You people come on again at one o'clock and then we'll take over at stand-to. That gives us three hours each between stand-down and stand-to. You might explain this new arrangement to Hood."

"I will," said Helson. "And I think I'll turn in now and get my three hours. Are you coming, Red?"

"Like hell I am." He was chiefly remarkable for his flaming red hair, and as he climbed off the layer's seat, he pushed a big hand through it. "Can't remember when I last went to bed at this time, knowing that I could count on three hours uninterrupted sleep."

"Don't count on it," said Langdon. "We may get a preliminary air-raid warning or I may decide it's necessary to call the whole detachment out."

"Oh, you wouldn't do that, Sarge."

"I'll try not to," said Langdon with a grin.

The detachment that had been on stand-to began to drift off. Langdon looked round the pit. "What about layers? Chetwood, you'd better be Number Two, and Kan, you can take the elevation side. Micky will take his usual place as Number Four. Is that you, Micky?" he asked, as a figure appeared from the direction of the hut. "You're firing. Fuller and Hanson ammunition numbers. Fuller, you'll hand the shells to Micky. And you'd better be responsible for the phone," he added to me.

So began one of the most exciting nights of my life. For the first few hours it was much the same as every other night since I had been at Thorby. It was warm and we took turns at dozing in the three deck-chairs. Every few minutes an enemy plane came up out of the south-east. The first indication would be a white criss-cross of searchlights far away over the dark silhouette of the hangars. These would usher the 'plane over their area and pass it on to the next group. By the movement of the searchlights you could follow it right in from the coast, across the 'drome and on over London. It was a definite lane they had found. There seemed to be no heavies anywhere along it. It was like a bus route.

Mostly they came in high and the searchlights wavered helplessly, unable to pick them out. Sometimes Gun Ops. gave us plots for them, but more often not. Occasionally they dropped flares. They seemed to be no more than armed reconnaissance, for they seldom dropped any bombs. And by the way they dropped flares to light the way into London it seemed as though experienced pilots were showing youngsters the way in.

It was actually just a coincidence that their route led them straight over Thorby. But it gave us all the feeling that we were the objective. Once I was quite convinced we were for it. There had been a period of comparative quiet when the sky was strangely blank. The only searchlights to be seen were away to the north-east, where a steady stream of raiders was coming into London by way of the Thames Estuary.

Then suddenly Micky said : " Here 'e comes again—the bastard."

A little knot of searchlights showed far away to the south-east. And at the same moment the phone rang. I picked up the receiver. " Calling all guns. Calling all guns. One, two, three—three?—four." " Four," I said. " Five, six. Are you there now, Three?" " Three," said a voice. " One hostile approaching from the south-east. Height ten thousand feet."

I repeated the message to Langdon. " That sounds more hopeful," he said, getting out of his deck-chair. " All right. Layers on." Kan and Chetwood got on to their seats. The gun swung round, its muzzle nosing in the direction of the 'plane as though it would smell it out. The searchlights came nearer. Others flickered into action as the 'plane approached until those across the valley were in action too, their dazzling white beams showing up every detail of the landing field.

The muzzle of the gun slowly elevated. We strained our eyes upwards to the point where all the beams converged. " There it is," said Kan suddenly in an excited voice. A speck of white showed in the beams. But it remained stationary and the searchlights moved away from it. " Sorry," he said, " it's only a star."

Then the Tannoy broke the expectant stillness. " Attention, please ! Attention, please ! See that all lights are out. All lights to be put out at once. Enemy aircraft are directly overhead. Take great care to show no lights. Off."

" What's the betting they turn on the flare path now?" said Fuller.

" I wouldn't be surprised," replied Kan. He turned to me. " You weren't here when they did that, were you, Barry? It was last week. They actually turned it full on for a Hurricane coming in when there was a Jerry right overhead. And were we scared ! The fellow couldn't help seeing it was a 'drome."

" Look at that silly bastard !" said Micky. A car had turned out of the officers' mess, which was on the far side of the 'drome near our other three-inch pit. Its headlights, though dimmed, showed white against the dark bulk of the hangars. " If I was over there I know what I'd do. I'd tell 'im to put them out. An' I wouldn't give 'im no more than one chance. If he didn't put them out, I'd shoot 'em out. I would an' all—officer or no bloody officer. The silly fool—endangering every one's lives !"

Micky had a phobia about lights. He was a queer mixture of bravery and cowardice in the same way that he was a queer mixture of generosity and selfishness. In the hut at night he was a perfect curse until the lights were put out. Every night he would go round the blackout. If there was the slightest chink showing he made a nuisance of himself until it was stopped up. He'd even been known to complain about the light showing through cracks in the floor boards at the side of the hut. And if he was on guard you couldn't enter or leave the hut without the warning, "Mind that light!" spoken in that gruff rather aggressive voice of his.

In this particular case, of course, he was more than justified in his outburst. He had barely stopped speaking when from across the aerodrome we heard, faintly, the shout of, "Put those lights out!" Immediately they vanished, and not a glimmer showed from any part of the 'drome. Yet it was lit by the surrounding searchlights as though by a full moon. I felt we must be visible at ten thousand feet. I waited, tensed, for the whistle of the first bomb.

But nothing happened. The 'plane passed slightly to the west of us, maintaining a steady course for London. Not once had it been picked up by the searchlights.

Chetwood climbed stiffly off the layer's seat. "Any one want a cigarette?" he asked.

"Don't you go lighting a cigarette, mate," said Micky. "Do you want to get killed? I tell you it's bloody silly."

"Oh, shut up, Micky," snapped Chetwood.

"He'll see you, mate, I tell you. An' don't you talk to me like that, see? I ain't your servant even if you have got a lot of brass. What's more, I'm senior to you. I bin in the Army since the beginning of the war."

Chetwood ignored him. "Cigarette, Langdon?"

"No, thanks, old boy." Kan didn't smoke, but Fuller and I took one. "You be careful," Micky muttered. "You bin lucky so far. But one day he'll see you and he'll drop one right on this ruddy pit."

"Don't be a fool." Chetwood spoke quite pleasantly, but I could tell by the restraint in his voice that he was on edge. "That one has gone over. And the next one is right down on the horizon. How can any Jerry see a cigarette when he's miles away?"

"Well, I'm warning you. You ain't the only one that's going to get killed if a bomb falls on this pit. You want to think of others sometimes. You're in charge, John. You didn't ought to allow it."

"Well, as long as they're careful it's safe enough, Micky."

"All right, but they'd better be careful. I ain't in no hurry to go to Heaven."

Chetwood lit his cigarette under the folds of a gas cape. We lit ours from the butt of his. It seems incredible, but we were really very careful about cigarettes, smoking them in cupped hands even when there was nothing overhead. The trouble with light ack-ack is that mostly you're posted right on the vital point. We often envied the heavies who could fire at planes with a sense of impunity. On a V.P.—especially an aerodrome—there is always the knowledge that you may be the objective. The frayed nerves that were revealed by a craving for cigarettes and a tendency to be short with one another were, I am certain, due more to this than to lack of sleep.

After that 'plane had passed over no one seemed inclined to doze again in a deck chair. I felt very wide awake. We all stood around the gun, tensely watching each cluster of searchlights as they ushered 'plane after 'plane across the 'drome. They all seemed to be coming in from the south-east and going out of London by way of the Thames Estuary, where the barrage was incessant. Several times we saw one caught in the beams of the searchlights. But they were all a long way away, and even through the glasses showed as no more than a tiny speck of white in the centre of criss-cross beams.

The second of these was quite invisible to the naked eye. But I happened to be looking at the various clusters of searchlights through the glasses. "There's one," I said. I experienced the excitement of a fisherman who has at last got a bite. It was coming out of the Thames barrage and flying south-east. It was nose down for home and travelling so fast that I felt it must be a fighter.

Micky was at my side as soon as I reported it. Let's have a look, mate." I hardly heard him. I wanted to see whether it would turn in our direction. "Come on, give us the glasses. Other people want to 'ave a look besides you."

"In a minute, Micky," I said. "I don't want to lose it. It's very faint." But the 'plane held its course, and in the end I let him have the glasses.

"Gawd, it's a Jerry all right. You can see the double fin."

"That's more than I could," I said. "You can barely see the 'plane itself."

"Well, it's a Jerry anyway."

"How many times have I told you, Micky, that not all Jerries have double fins and not every 'plane with double fins is a Jerry," said Langdon. "Here, give me the glasses."

It took some persuasion even for Langdon to get the glasses from him. And when he had them Micky muttered something about sergeants having all the fun.

"Well, whose glasses are they?" asked Langdon tolerantly. Young though he was for a sergeant—he was only twenty-two—he had a fine understanding of the handling of men. Inevitably your first impression was that he was slack. And he was slack in things dear to the tradition of the Army. He had no hard-and-fast rules. His site was often rather untidy. He allowed his men tremendous licence. Yet no one, not even Micky, took advantage of it. He was cool and efficient in all things that he thought mattered—things that would lead to greater accuracy in firing. His men liked him, and unhesitantly obeyed those commands that he did give. He never upbraided a man. Yet I never heard any one, not even Bombardier Hood, question his authority. They obeyed him because he was a born leader and not just because he had three stripes.

Faced with Langdon's tolerant friendly smile, all Micky's pugnacity vanished in an answering grin. "I know, mate. I know. They're yours, ain't they. Anyway, I seen all I want to of the ruddy thing."

For some time we stood watching the cluster of searchlights moving south-east. "Cor, love old iron, I'd like to have a crack at it, wouldn't you, mate?" Micky asked me.

"Yes, I would," I said. "I'd like to send it crashing to earth. Funny how war changes one's outlook. One gets a war mentality. I never thought I'd exult in killing. Yet here I am wanting with all my heart to kill three men. I suppose one develops the mentality of the huntsman. All one thinks about is the excitement of the chase. One doesn't give a thought for the poor devil of a fox. And yet inside that 'plane are three human beings, much the same as you or me. Probably none of them wanted war. They've come over just obeying orders. There are shells bursting all round them. There's probably a smell of burnt cordite in the cockpit. They're all probably feeling pretty frightened."

I had been speaking more to myself than to Micky, for I did not really believe that he would understand what I was talking about. And when he spoke I knew that he hadn't. " 'Course they wanted this war. Machine-gunning women and children, that's what they like. The cowards! Look at the way they're running out of the barrage. They can't take it, mate, I tell you." Then suddenly he gave me a sidelong glance. " It's a bastard kind of war," he said. " Cold steel, that's what I like. I don't mind 'em when we're firing at them. But I can't stand just having them coming over and not doing anything. The infantry—that's what I wanted to join. Did you know I volunteered for the Buffs? But they said there wasn't no vacancy. I'd have to wait a month. And I couldn't wait—straight, I couldn't. I wanted to get at 'em right away. They said I could go straight into the R.A. That's how I came to join this bleeding outfit."

He hesitated, watching me out of the corners of his eyes. I said nothing. "You think I'm silly about the lights an' all, don't you? You think I'm a coward because I keep my gas mask and tin hat on when there are Jerries about. Well, I ain't, see. Give me a baynet and I'd go over the top with the best of 'em and never give a thought to the fact that I might get killed. But I can't stand this inaction. This place is driving me nuts."

" I understand," I said. " I haven't been here long, but the atmosphere of the place is too tense to be pleasant."

" Remember when that formation came over Wednesday? I was scared stiff, mate, I tell you. They seemed to fill the sky. It didn't seem as if they could miss. And then we started firing at them an' I wasn't a bit afraid, was I?" And when I made no comment, he said: "Funny! I can talk to you."

"I know how you feel," I said. "It isn't cowardice. It's frustration. I feel the same myself, but it doesn't show in the same way."

"Gawd! I'd give anything to get out of the place. I'd like to go to Egypt. There'll be fighting in Egypt—real fighting. Hand to hand, mate—that's the way to fight. Not like this."

"It's nearly one," Langdon said. "Will you go and wake the others, Fuller?"

Fuller had barely left the pit when Chetwood suddenly said: "Have a look at that bunch of searchlights away to the north, John. Looks like a 'plane."

Langdon swung round and put the glasses to his eyes. "By God! You're right, Chet," he said. "And it's coming this way."

I followed the direction in which his glasses were pointing. The criss-cross of searchlights showed quite plainly beyond the downs. And in the centre of it I saw—or thought I saw—a speck of light. I couldn't be certain. Your eyes play you funny tricks after you've been straining them into the dark for some time. One minute it was there and the next minute it wasn't. But the searchlights came steadily nearer, and I could see little pin-points of shell-bursts very near the centre of the criss-cross.

Soon the searchlights on the ridge of the downs were in action and there was no doubt about there being a 'plane in the beams. It was quite visible now to the naked eye and growing more distinct every second.

"It's only about eight thousand feet and seems to be coming lower," said Langdon. "I should say it's been hit." We watched it, breathless, expecting it any moment to see it turn off its course. But it continued to come straight on towards Thorby. "I think," said Langdon slowly, "we're going to see some action."

His voice was very cool and calm by comparison with my own excitement. I remember thinking how young and boyish he looked, standing there, his tin hat tilted on to the back of his head and his eyes intent on the 'plane. There was no ack-ack now. But the searchlights held it, and faintly over the still night air came the throb of its engines. I could see the shape of it now, the wide spread of its wings all silver in the dazzling beams.

"All right, layers on," said Langdon. "Fuse nine—load!" I handed the shell to Micky. He lowered the breech and rammed it home with his gloved hand. The breech rose with a clang. "Set to semi-automatic."

Fuller came running back into the pit. The 'plane was at about 5,000 feet now and still heading straight for us. The layers reported, "On, on!" Langdon waited. The throb of the engines beat upon the air.

Suddenly came his order : "Fire!"

A flash of flame and the pit shook with the noise of the explosion. I found I had another round in my hands. I held it for Micky to ram home. The gun crashed. Fuller came up with another round. I have a vague impression of that bright spot in the midst of the searchlight; the flash of our own shells and those of the other three-inch exploding just to the right of it. And then it seemed to fall apart in mid-air. I stood stupefied, with the next shell ready in my hands. The port wing crumpled and the nose dropped, so that we could see the big double fin of a Dornier. And then it began to fall, the wing bending back and separating itself from the rest of the 'plane.

"My God!" Kan cried. "It's coming down. Oh, my God! This is too exciting."

It fell very quickly. And as it fell it grew much larger, so that I suddenly realised that it was coming right down on the edge of the 'drome. I had a momentary glimpse of the big black cross on its one remaining wing. Then it hit the ground. One searchlight had followed it right down so that we actually saw the nose strike into the ground among some bushes to the north of the 'drome. The tail snapped off as it struck, and the whole plane appeared to crumple. An instant later came the sound of the impact. It was a dull thud splintered by the noise of rending metal. I remember being surprised that the sound of the crash should come after the 'plane had hit the ground. There was something almost supernatural about it, as though it had spoken after it was dead. I noticed this apparent phenomenon many times afterwards and, though I knew it to be quite natural since sound travels slower than sight, it always surprised me. There was something rather horrible about it. It was one of the things that always made me feel sick inside.

Immediately the 'plane had crashed, the searchlight swung upwards. For a moment I could see no sign of the 'plane, though the light of the searchlights showed up the edge of the 'drome quite clearly. Then suddenly I saw a pin-point of light. It grew. And then flung outwards in a flash of orange. A great umbrella of flame leaped upwards to a height of several hundred feet. And when it was gone, the light from the blazing wreckage showed a perfect ring of smoke drifting slowly skyward.

"God! It's horrible!" Kan was standing up and his thin æsthetic face was working as though he himself were in the blazing wreck.

"What d'you mean—horrible?" demanded Micky.

"They're human beings just the same as us," replied Kan, his hands pressed tight together as though in prayer and his eyes fixed on the blaze, fascinated.

"Bloody murderers—that's what they are, mate, I tell you. You don't want to waste no sympathy on them bastards."

"Look!" cried Fuller, pointing up into the beams of the searchlights. "It's a parachute. Two of 'em."

Our gaze swung from the wreckage up into the point in the searchlights where two white umbrellas of silk swung lazily earthwards. It was possible to see the men dangling from the parachutes as though held there by magic.

"Who got it—us or the other site?" It was Bombardier Hood.

He was still only half dressed. The rest of his detachment, in various stages of undress, were streaming out behind him.

"We did," Micky replied promptly. "An' a bloody good shot it was, I tell you."

"It was impossible to say;" Langdon said. "Philip's gun was in action. I saw two bursts. One was away to the right and the other seemed close beside his port wing-tip. It was quite impossible to say which was ours. Confoundedly lucky shot anyway."

At that moment the troop van drew up at the gun pit and Tiny Trevors got out, a big grin on his face. "Congratulations, Johnnie," he said. "Damn good shooting."

"There, I told you so," said Micky.

"It was our shot, was it?" asked Langdon.

"I don't think there's any doubt about it. Though, of course, Site One are quite convinced they brought it down. But Philip's first shot was definitely to the right. He was firing fuse twelve, and he never had time to alter it. Your first shot was definitely short. You didn't change your fuse, did you?"

"No. We fired three at fuse nine."

"Then it must have been yours. The Jerry ran right into it." He looked round the pit. "You're second detachment are due to take over, aren't they? All right then, the others can pile into the van and we'll go and have a look at the good work."

We needed no second invitation. We were as excited as a bunch of school kids. We scrambled over the parapet of sandbags and into the back of the van, all talking at once. When we got to the north end of the 'drome, the wreck was still burning. Several bushes had caught adding to the blaze. Ground defence guards had already arrived, but it was impossible to get nearer than fifty yards owing to the intense heat. It hit one in the face as though one were standing in front of the open door of a blast furnace. Every one stood about helplessly, their faces ruddy in the glow and their eyes fascinated by the flames. The 'plane was just a twisted mass of steel framework that stood out black against the flames, except here and there where the steel was white with heat and dissolving into molten metal.

It seemed incredible that a few minutes ago this mass of writhing steel had had power and a will of its own, and had been proudly flying through the night sky. I couldn't believe that the transformation from a beautiful deadly weapon of modern warfare to this ugly mess was entirely due to the six of us—six ordinary men manning a gun.

There was a sudden shout and every one's gaze lifted skywards. Almost directly above us a parachute showed a dull orange in the glare. Slowly it descended, drifting silently through the still air. We watched it in silence. The only sound was the roar and crackling of the flames. Soon it was low enough for us to see the face of the man who dangled from it, swinging gently to and fro on the thin cords. His face was without expression. It was like a mask. It seemed a symbol of mass-production, and I immediately thought of the hordes that were pouring over Europe. Had all these men who had goose-stepped down the Champs-Elyées the same expressionless features? Was this the face of the new Germany—Hitler's Germany?

It was surprising how long it took for him to reach the ground. Yet when he hit the tarmac on the edge of the 'drome he seemed to be falling horribly fast. He managed to land with his feet first, and attempted to break his fall by rolling over. But at a distance of nearly a hundred yards the thud of his body striking the tarmac was sickeningly loud.

We all ran towards the spot where he had fallen. I was one of the first to reach him as he staggered to his feet, his face white and set with pain. He did not attempt to reach for the revolver in his belt or to raise his hands in surrender. He did nothing. There was nothing he could do. One arm hung limp from the shoulder and he swayed unsteadily as though at any moment he must fall. But he kept on his feet and his face was no longer expressionless. Hate and mortification struggled for mastery of his features.

A guardsman seized the revolver from his belt. The German forced himself to attention. "*Wo ist ein Offizier?*" he snapped. There was bitterness and contempt in his voice, which bore the stamp of the Prussian Junker class. "*Ich verlange den meinem Rang gebührenden Respekt.*"

None of the others understood what he said. I looked quickly round. There was no officer in sight. A crowd of men, mainly soldiers, were pressed round in a circle. "*Ich bedavere, es ist noch kein Offizier gekommen,*" I said. I had spent some months in our Berlin office and knew the language quite well. "So it's an officer he's wanting, is it?" said a Scots Guard with a sour, lined face. "Ye've got a nerve, laddie. Ye had no mercy on the women and children over the other side. Ye had no mercy on us on the beaches of Dunkirk. Yet as soon as you're down, ye start squawking for an officer."

The sights those men had seen of the bombing and machine-gunning of terror-stricken refugees in Belgium and France had left their mark.

The German did not flinch in the face of the hostile circle of men. He stood stiffly erect, his face set. He was a tall, well-built man of about thirty. He had well-groomed fair hair, and his most noticeable feature was a very square jaw which gave him a sullen look. He had a row of ribbons on his flying suit.

He looked round the crowd of faces. "You've shot me down," he said, speaking in German. "But it won't be long now. Soon you will collapse like the cowardly French."

"You'll never invade this country successfully," I replied, also in German.

31

He looked at me. I think he was too dazed with shock to realise what he was saying. "You English! You are so blind. It is all planned. The day is appointed. And on that day your fighter aeroplanes will be taken from you and you will be left defenceless to face the courageous might of the *Luftwaffe*."

I suppose I must have looked at him rather foolishly. But it was so reminiscent of our conversation in the Naafi that evening. Through a gap in the encircling crowd I saw a big R.A.F. car slither to a standstill. The C.O. Thorby and several other men got out, including the ground defence officer. Quickly I said, "I don't believe you. It's not possible."

"Marshall Goering has a plan," he said heatedly. "We shall succeed with England just as we have succeeded with the other plutocratic nations. You do not understand the cleverness of our leaders. Thorby and your other fighter stations will fall like that." He clicked his fingers.

"You can't possibly know anything about Goering's plans," I said. "You talk like that because you are afraid."

"I am not afraid and I am not a liar." Two angry spots of colour showed in his white cheeks. "You say I know nothing of the Marshal's plans. I know that on Friday Thorby will be heavily attacked by our dive-bombers. You will not think me a liar on Friday. And when——" He stopped suddenly, and I thought I saw a look of surprise tinged with fear in his blue-grey eyes, though his face remained as wooden as ever.

I turned to find Wing-Commander Winton just behind me. But it was not on the C.O. that the German pilot's gaze was fixed, but upon Mr. Vayle, the station librarian. The man's mouth seemed to shut like a clamp and he said no more. The last I saw of him was as he was marched away between two guards to the C.O.'s car. He seemed suddenly to have become dejected and weary, for he staggered along, his head bent and his every movement betraying a listlessness that I could hardly believe due solely to reaction.

32

Chapter Three

OUT OF TOUCH

A detachment of Guards had been detailed by Major Comyns, the ground defence officer, to keep people a hundred yards from the burning wreck. No attempt was made to put out the flames. The authorities feared that there might be unexploded bombs. The rest of our detachment moved to the nearest point from which they could watch the spectacle, which was the edge of the roadway that circled the landing field. The blaze seemed to fascinate them. Subconsciously their reaction to it was the same as mine had been—amazement that they were responsible for it. Both Wing-Commander Winton and Major Comyns had spoken to Trevors and Langdon before they left and congratulated them on the detachment's success.

But though I stood with the rest and watched the flames consuming the mass of twisted steel, I was barely conscious of what I saw. And when a second German was brought to the roadway to wait for a car, I only noticed that he was very young, that his face was covered with blood from a big cut on his forehead, and that he was crying—great uncontrollable sobs that seemed to shake his small frame. I could not crowd round like the others to gape at him in his boyish misery. My mind was occupied with my own problem.

"The navigator must have been trapped in the 'plane," I heard Trevors say as an R.A.F. car took the boy away. "Only two were seen to come down."

"Perhaps his parachute failed to open," said a sergeant of the Guards.

"Perhaps," Trevors agreed. "In which case his body will be found in the morning. Poor devil!"

"What do you mean—poor devil? If you'd seen what I'd seen in France you wouldn't be saying poor devil!"

I lost the rest of the conversation. I was trying to figure out whether the pilot with whom I had spoken had really known something or whether he was just bluffing when he had talked of a plan. It was so difficult to be sure with a man in his condition. I tried to place myself in his position and consider what I should have felt like, and what I should have done if I had had his training and background.

Obviously he had been bitter at the loss of his 'plane. A pilot, I felt, must acquire for his machine at least some of the affection that a captain does for his ship. He would want to hit back at the men who had transformed it from a winged thing, full of life and beauty, to a blazing wreck. I remembered the circle of hostile faces showing in the light of the flames. He could only hit back in one way and that was by frightening them. I could speak German and so it was through me that he had had to hit back.

And yet what had made him tell me that they had a plan for getting control of British fighter 'dromes? What had made him give me such specific information about an attack on Thorby? Was that just bravado?

It seemed hardly credible that a mere pilot would know about a plan to seize our fighter stations. Such a plan would for obvious reasons be kept a closely guarded secret and be known only to the higher officers of the *Luftwaffe*. But it was of course possible that the rumour that such a plan existed had permeated the messes. Or it might be just a case of wishful thinking. Obviously it was highly desirable that the fighter defences of this country should be immobilized if invasion were to succeed. For this reason, German airmen may have come to the conclusion that their High Command had a plan to achieve this end. Alternatively, he may just have thought that they ought to have such a plan, and in his moment of bitterness had produced it as a fact in the hope that it would assist the state of fear into which he would almost certainly imagine the British had been thrown by the collapse of France.

And yet he had seemed so sure of himself, so definite.

And was he really in a condition to think up the idea of a plan if he was not aware that one existed? It was all very complicated.

His statement that Thorby was to be dive-bombed on Friday was understandable. A pilot might quite easily know the date on which a certain target was to be attacked. And I could well understand his use of that information to add conviction to a statement that was untrue. If I reported the conversation—and I knew that I should have to—the authorities might well regard the idea of a secret plan with scepticism. But if his prediction of the raid on Thorby turned out to be accurate, it would add considerable weight to his first statement.

But there were two things that puzzled me. First, that he should have wasted his bravado on a mere gunner. He must have known that in a very short while he would be interviewed by an Intelligence officer. Surely that would have been the time to release his information if it was to have its maximum effect? The second was, why had he closed up on me the moment he saw Vayle? I could have understood it if it had been the C.O. who had caused him to stop in the middle of a sentence. But Vayle—a man in civilian clothes! It seemed rather extraordinary—almost as though he knew the librarian.

In the end I gave it up. My brain had reached a state when it was impossible for me to argue my way to a solution one way or the other. There seemed so much to suggest that the idea of planting the information about a plan in my mind was dictated by the instinct for revenge, and yet so much to suggest that it had slipped out in the bitterness of the moment when he was too dazed to control his tongue.

I edged my way to where Tiny Trevors was talking to Ogilvie, who had just arrived on the scene. I waited. At length Ogilvie went across to speak to a Guards officer. Trevors turned and saw me. " Hallo, Hanson," he said. " You haven't waited long to get your first 'plane. There was something I wanted to speak to you about. Oh, yes.

35

You were talking in German to that pilot. What did he have to say?"

"Well, I was just coming to speak to you about it," I said. And I gave him the gist of the conversation.

"I think you had better see Mr. Ogilvie," he said. "There may be nothing in it, but, as you say, the man was pretty shaken. Though I can't believe a pilot would have information of that kind." He looked across at the group of officers that Ogilvie had joined. "Hang around for a bit and when the Little Man is free I'll take you—— Better catch him now." I followed him along the edge of the roadway and we intercepted Ogilvie just as he was entering the Guards officer's car.

"Just a minute, sir," said Trevors. "Hanson has some information which seems interesting."

Ogilvie paused, one foot on the running-board. "Well, what is it?" he demanded in his sharp staccato voice.

He was a man of small stature, inclined to stoutness, with a round, uninteresting face and horn-rimmed glasses. He lacked a natural command of men. And in place of it he had built an air of aloofness about himself. This did not make him popular. I think he had been in the insurance business before the war. At any rate he was not an O.C.T.U. product, but had obtained his commission in the Territorials. It was perhaps unfortunate that he was in command of a unit in which most of the senior N.C.O.'s were socially his superiors. Inevitably, it resulted in his standing on his dignity to an extent that was unnatural. His staccato manner, which was not, I am sure, natural to him, was the noticeable result.

I gave him an account of my conversation with the German. But when I came to my views on the reliability of the information, he cut me short. "Quite. I understand. I'll pass on your information to the proper authorities. Good-night, Sergeant-major." And with that he climbed into the car and left us.

I watched the car disappear with a feeling that the responsibility of bringing the conversation to the notice of men who would know how to assess its value was still

36

mine. The proper authorities to whom Ogilvie referred were obviously the C.O. Thorby or the Intelligence officer attached to the station. In due course a report on the matter would reach the Air Ministry. But, in all probability, it would be part of the routine reports and would be filed away without even being brought to the notice of those higher officials who were best able to judge its importance. On the other hand, I knew the assistant director of Air Ministry Press Section, and I felt that I ought to write to him giving him the details of the conversation.

I mentioned this to Trevors. But he said, " For God's sake don't do that. You'll only get yourself into trouble. You're in the Army now, and in the Army there are formalities to be considered. Any report has to pass through your Officer and thence via Battery and Regiment to Brigade. You can't go direct to the fountain head."

" I suppose you're right," I said. " But if there is anything in this idea of a plan it is vitally important."

" If there is anything in it, then no doubt Intelligence know all about it," he replied. " In any case, the responsibility is no longer yours."

But I didn't feel that way. As a journalist I had seen too much of the delays of red tape not to feel some misgivings as to what would happen to my information in its passage through the official channels. My main concern, as I lay awake in bed that morning, was to decide whether or not the German pilot had really known something and let it slip in the heat of the moment. But the more I thought about it, the more uncertain I was. And if I was uncertain, I knew that whoever was responsible for reporting the matter to the Air Ministry would be disinclined to make much of it. Everything depended on the result of the examination of the prisoner.

In this knowledge I fell asleep, dead tired. We were on again at four, a very tired detachment. The events of the night seemed like a dream. But at the north end of the 'drome the burnt-out wreck of the 'plane stood as a monument to our achievement. We were relieved at seven, but instead of going to the mess for breakfast most of us went straight back to bed. The next thing I remember is being wakened by the sound of engines revving in the dispersal point near our hut. The din was terrific and the vibration made my bed shake.

I heard somebody say, "Sounds as though there's a flap coming." I did not open my eyes. But I had scarcely turned over when the Tannoy broke in on my sleep. "Attention, please! Attention, please! Tiger Squadron scramble! Tiger Squadron scramble! Scramble! Scramble! Off."

"All right, we'll come quietly," I heard Chetwood say. "No peace for the wicked." His bed creaked as he got up.

I waited, unwilling to wake up, yet my nerves fully awake. The engines roared as the 'planes left the dispersal point for the runway. I waited, dreading the inevitable patter of feet that would mean leaving the comfort of my bed. It came almost immediately—the sound of running feet, the bursting open of the door and the cry of "Take post!"

My limbs reacted automatically. But my eyes were still tight shut as I reached blindly for my battle blouse. "What's the plot?" I heard someone ask. "Twenty hostile south-east, flying north-west at twenty-five thousand feet," was the reply.

I opened my eyes as I felt under my bed for my canvas shoes. Sunlight was streaming into the darkened hut through cracks in the blackout curtains. Outside I found a clear blue sky and a haze over the ground. It was already beginning to get warm, for the air was very still. As I reached the pit the last flight was just taking off. The leading flight of three was already disappearing into the mist, flying south-east and climbing steeply.

"Attention, please! Attention, please! Preliminary air-raid warning! Preliminary air-raid warning!"

"A bit much, don't you think," said Kan. "I mean, it's so frightfully early in the morning for this sort of thing."

"Funny how he always comes at meal-times," said Helson. "He missed breakfast yesterday, but he was over for lunch and tea."

"All part of the war of nerves," said Langdon.

"What's that up there?" Micky's outstretched arm was pointing high up to the east. A 'plane glinted in the sun for a second. Langdon raised his glasses.

But it was only our own Hurricane squadron circling. We saw no sign of the enemy and eventually Gun Ops. reported that the raid had been dispersed. The Tannoy gave the "All Clear," but it was some little time before we were allowed to stand down. When we were, it was past nine and our detachment was on duty.

I should explain that throughout the day we were at that time working in two-hour shifts—an exception being the first period, which was of three hours. The idea of this constant manning was, of course, to guard against surprise attack. With twelve men on the site and no leave, it was possible to have six in each detachment, which was ample for manning. During the day, however, those off duty had to man as soon as a "Take Post" was given. But at night we only manned on an alarm. Since I had been on the site, night alarms had been fairly constant. Hence the new arrangement whereby the duty detachment only manned on a night alarm unless there was a preliminary air-raid warning, or the detachment commander thought it necessary.

The other detachment went off to breakfast. Having had none ourselves, several of us produced chocolate. For myself, I was not hungry. The sleep I had had, which, though it was only three and a half hours, was the longest since I had been on the site, seemed only to have made me more tired. Moreover, my mind was once again occupied with the memory of my conversation with the German pilot in the early hours of the morning.

In the pleasant warmth of the sun his words seemed much less important. Yet I suddenly remembered what Trevors had told us in the Naafi. Was there some link between the attempt to secure a plan of the ground defences of the station and the idea that the Germans had a plan for immobilising all our fighter 'dromes? It all seemed very melodramatic. But I remembered stories of the last war. War was melodramatic. And the German was fond of melodrama. The whole history of the Nazi rise to power was the crudest melodrama. We were not used to it in England. But on the Continent melodrama had become commonplace.

The 'phone rang. Langdon answered it. As soon as he had replaced the receiver, he turned to me. "You're to report to the orderly room immediately. Mr. Ogilvie wants to see you." It took me back to my schooldays—"The headmaster wants to see you in his study."

The orderly room—or troop headquarters, as Mr. Ogilvie liked it to be called—was at the south side of the landing field, a part of the station headquarters block. When I got there, I asked Andrew Mason, the office clerk, what Ogilvie wanted to see me about. He said he did not know, but added that an R.A.F. officer had been in just before he had been told to 'phone for me.

Mason opened the farther door and announced me. I went in, walked up to the desk at which Ogilvie was seated, saluted and stood to attention. The office was a mixture of tidiness and disorder. The corner by the window was taken up with stores—boxes of gas equipment, a heap of battle dresses, steel helmets, gum boots. The sergeant-major's desk, which was against the wall opposite the door, was a litter of papers, note-books and passes. There was an old-fashioned safe in the corner next to it. The falling plaster of the walls, which were distempered a rather sickly shade of green, was adorned with copies of standing orders, aircraft recognition charts, and posters of big-chested men in peculiar postures illustrating the more elementary physical training exercises.

But the corner of the room occupied by Mr. Ogilvie's desk was homely by comparison. Orderly batches of papers lay beside the yellow blotter and the desk itself rested on a strip of red carpet. The walls behind were practically intact. And beside the desk was a bookcase with a clock and the polished case of a three-inch shell.

Mr. Ogilvie looked up as I saluted. "Ah, yes, Hanson," he said, leaning back and taking his pipe from his mouth. "About this conversation you had with the German pilot. I have just had a visit from the Intelligence officer who interrogated him this morning. I had told him what the pilot had said to you. The man didn't deny it. In fact, he repeated it in the most truculent and boastful manner. But when questions were put to him about the nature of the plan, he could give no details at all. He spoke at length of the might of the *Luftwaffe* and how Britain's fighter bases would be annihilated and our resistance crushed. He spoke darkly of a plan. But he said nothing that convinced the officer that there was in fact any specific scheme for destroying the bases other than a general plan that they should be destroyed."

He produced a box of matches and relit his pipe. "On the subject of the raid on Thorby," he continued, "it does seem probable that he knows something. He was very evasive about it, said it was no more than a rumour and he couldn't remember what day it was. The Intelligence officer had the impression that he was covering up. It is possible, of course, that it is a false scent. The German Air Force have apparently done that sort of thing before. They give the pilots false information, so that if they get shot down and are inclined to be talkative they won't be giving anything away. However, I have been assured that all necessary steps will be taken to protect the station on Friday. I thought you would like to know as you were instrumental in bringing the matter to the notice of the authorities."

I thought it was nice of him to give me such a full account of the position. But I was troubled. It seemed to me that the German pilot had been inconsistent. I said so. "There is only one motive he could have had in telling me the plan," I said. "Bitter at the loss of his plane, he wanted to frighten us. Now, either this plan was a pure fabrication or else there really is a plan and, knowing of it, he used his knowledge in the heat of the moment to achieve his aim."

"Come to the point." Ogilvie's voice was staccato again.

"Well, sir, if it was a pure fabrication he wouldn't have hesitated to invent details." At that moment the whole thing seemed suddenly crystal clear to me. "My own view is that in the heat of the moment he let slip something he should not have done. He was in a very dazed condition. When the Intelligence officer questioned him about the plan, he knew it would only increase his suspicions to deny having said anything about it to me. Instead he repeated his statement, and when pressed for details made vague and grandiose claims that he knew would throw doubt on the whole thing. But about the proposed raid on Thorby he covered up in an obvious manner. Apparently he achieved his object in drawing the officer's interest away from the plan to the raid."

Ogilvie clicked his pipe stem up and down against his teeth. "Well, I'm afraid the Intelligence officer doesn't take that view at all. He is experienced in these matters. I think you may take it that he is right."

But the Intelligence officer had not seen the German pilot close up like a clam in the middle of a sentence as his eyes met Vayle's. That seemed to be the key to the whole problem. "Could you tell me, sir, whether the Intelligence officer is making a report to Air Intelligence on the matter?" I asked.

"He didn't say anything about it. I imagine it will be included in the daily report to the C.O."

It was just as I had feared. "I think a report on the matter should go to A.I. without delay," I said.

"I'm afraid what you think or do not think, Hanson, is of little importance," Ogivlie said curtly. "The matter rests with the R.A.F. and their Intelligence officer has formed his own views." He hesitated. "If you like, you can make out a report and I'll send it in to Battery."

I saw I was up against a brick wall here. Though I knew it was pretty useless, I said I would make out a report. He gave me paper and I settled down at the sergeant major's desk. It took me some time to write it out. It had to be brief, yet comprehensive. There was always the chance that it might get to somebody who would take the same view of its importance that I did.

By the time I got back to the pit it was nearly ten-thirty. Micky, who could never restrain his curiosity, immediately asked me what Ogilvie had wanted to see me about.

" My grandmother has just died," I said. " He's given me a week's compassionate to see her decently buried."

" A week! No kidding. You ain't got a week? Just because your grandmuvver's dead? This is a lousy battery. You people all hang together. If it's one of the nobs and he just happens to feel tired, why, give 'im leave, give 'im leave. A week because your grandmuvver's died! Cor, stuff me with little green apples! If it was one of the roughs like me and Fuller, it would be go chase yourself. It ain't right, mate. It wouldn't happen in the real Army. Not bloody likely. Infantry, that's what I ought to be in."

Micky was very class conscious. But he was unintelligent about it. He saw privilege where there was none. This and his constant grumbling over nothing made him very annoying at times. He was always hardly done by, yet in point of fact he got away with more than any one else.

" Oh, don't be a fool, Micky," said Langdon. ' " He hasn't got leave. He's just telling you politely to mind your own business."

" Oh, I get you." Micky was all smiles again. " Sorry, mate. I didn't rumble it."

Langdon had started examination of equipment, which was carried out on our gun every morning between ten and eleven. As there were already quite enough on the job, I sat down on the bench by the telephone. I was still worried. Most men, I suppose, would have considered the matter closed. If the Intelligence officer was satisfied, why should I worry? But journalism makes it instinctive in one to follow up a story to the bitter end. The Intelligence officer might be right. But what worried me was the way the German had broken off as soon as he saw Vayle. It was almost as if he

43

had been caught saying something he should not have said. That alone explained the abruptness with which he had ceased speaking. And that suggested that he knew Vayle— that Vayle was, in fact, a fifth columnist.

When we were relieved at eleven by Bombardier Hood's detachment, I got hold of Kan as he left the pit. "You've been here some time, Kan," I said. "Do you happen to know any one in the station who can tell me anything about Vayle—you know, the librarian?"

He gave me a quick glance. But he did not ask me why I wanted to know about Vayle. "There's an R.A.F. lad we used to meet in the airmen's Naafi—that was before they put the marquee up. I think his name was Davidson. Anyway, he was assistant librarian. We got to know him because Vayle used to take those who were applying for commissions in trig. A dear fellow, he used to help us no end. I expect he's still here."

"Could you introduce him to me?" I asked.

"Why, of course, dear boy. Any time you like."

"Now?"

"Now?" Again that quick look. For a second questions were on the tip of his tongue. But all he said was, "Right-o. I want to go down to the square to wash. I'll take you in on the way."

I thanked him. "I'd be very glad if you didn't mention this to any of the others," I said. "I'll explain some time."

"All right," he said. "But if you're free-lancing, be careful. Though God knows I shouldn't have thought there was a story in poor little Vayle."

"Why ' poor little Vayle '?" I asked.

"Oh, I don't know. He's rather precious, don't you think? Oh, I don't suppose you've met him. He once told me that what he really wanted to be was an actor." We went into the hut and he got his washing things out of his suitcase. As we set off past the dispersal point, he said : "I've often wondered why he became librarian at a place like this. He's been here nearly four years, you know. And he's a clever man. I should think he would have done well in your own profession."

Four years! That made it 1936. "Do you know what he did before he came here?" I asked.

"No, I don't know, old boy. He didn't come from another station, I'm certain of that. I should think he'd been a schoolmaster. He was very interesting when he was holding those trig. classes. Occasionally, when we had finished the routine work, he would talk about aerial tactics. I believe he's writing a book about it. Perhaps that's why you're interested in him? I should think he's travelled pretty extensively. At any rate, he's studied internal continental politics. He told us a lot that I didn't know about the Nazi rise to power and the behind-the-scenes activities in French politics. He didn't exactly prophesy the collapse of France, but after what he had told us of the internal situation I wasn't surprised when it happened."

This was interesting. Vayle, with his pale face and grey hair, was beginning to take shape in my mind. Everything depended on what he had been before he came to Thorby—or, rather, where he had been.

Kan could tell me nothing more about him that was helpful. The impression I got from him, however, was that Vayle was no ordinary station librarian. He appeared to have a very wide knowledge of European affairs. And why, if he was such a brilliant student of contemporary affairs, had he been content to remain for four years at the station?

The library shared a block with the Y.M.C.A. just behind Station H.Q. It was, in reality, an educational centre. Kan took me in and introduced me to Davidson, a thin wisp of a man with reddish hair and freckles. I told him I had come to see what the chances were of another trigonometry course. But when Kan had left, I led the conversation round to Vayle. Davidson, however, could tell me little more than I had already learnt from Kan. Though he had been working with Vayle for

45

more than eighteen months, he did not know where he had been before he became librarian at Thorby.

He admired Vayle greatly. He thought him a brilliant man. "His talents are wasted here," he said, his rather watery eyes fixed on my face. So it came back to the same thing—why had Vayle been content to stay at Thorby?

Then he began talking about the night's action. "Mr. Vayle told me all about it this morning," he said. "He talked to both the prisoners, you know." He was full of information. "The younger one was only a boy—just turned seventeen. But the other was over thirty, with masses of decorations, including the Iron Cross, first and second class. It must be interesting to be in a position like Vayle now that there's a war on," he added reflectively. "Being a civilian he's not subject to the restraint of rank. He's very highly thought of by the C.O. I think he often consults him about things. He knows everything that goes on here, and I wouldn't be surprised if he doesn't have a say in the strategy we adopt. What he doesn't know about aerial tactics isn't worth knowing."

"Did he actually talk to the prisoners?" I asked.

"Oh, yes. He's a great linguist. I think he knows five different languages. He'd be able to talk to them in German. And I bet he got more out of them than the Intelligence Officer."

"Did he tell you what they said?"

"Oh, he said the older man was very truculent—a proper hard-boiled Nazi, I gather. The boy was still in a terrible state of fright."

"When did he see them?" I asked.

"As soon as they were brought in, I think. He said he and the C.O. were with them when the M.O. was dressing their wounds."

This was incredible. Yet because it was incredible, I felt it must be true. The whole position was once again as clear as it had seemed when I had been talking to Ogilvie. One thing had been puzzling me. That was whether a man of the type I had judged the pilot to be was sufficiently astute to divert the Intelligence Officer's attention from the plan to the projected raid. If Vayle were a secret agent, that was explained. He had told the airman what line to take. True, the C.O. and the M.O. had been present, but the probability was that neither of them understood German.

I left Davidson in a very thoughtful mood. A horrible feeling of responsibility was growing on me. I knew only too well how a journalist's enthusiasm for sensation can run away with his discretion. Yet I felt there was something here that I could neither forget nor ignore. But I knew I must tread warily. If I went to the authorities, I should only get into trouble without achieving anything. Vayle was in a very strong position in the station. My suspicions, based solely on conjecture, would be laughed at. And it would be little consolation, when the place was in German hands, to be able to say, " I told you so."

There was only one thing to do. I must find out Vayle's background prior to 1936.

The square was hot and dusty in the glare of the sun. It was past twelve and the Naafi tent was open. I felt in need of a beer. It was stiflingly hot in the marquee, although there were few people there. I took my beer to a table near an open flap. The liquid was warm and gassy. I lit a cigarette.

Suppose I 'phoned Bill Trent? He was the *Globe's* crime reporter. Bill would know how to get hold of the information I wanted. But it would be folly to 'phone from a call box in the camp. They went through an R.A.F. switchboard. I couldn't be sure that the operator would not be listening in. I had no idea how strict the censorship was in the station. The nearest call box outside the camp was in Thorby village. To go down there would be breaking camp. This was too dangerous.

I suddenly remembered that we were on again at one. I ought to get my lunch. I was not very enthusiastic. One of the things I disliked about Thorby more than anything else was its messing arrangements. I suppose the airmen's mess had originally been built to seat about four or five hundred. It now had to accommodate about two thousand. It would be hot and smelly. The tables would be messy and there would be the inevitable queue. And there would be beans. There had been no other vegetable for weeks.

I had just finished my beer and was getting up to go when Marion Sheldon came in. She looked fresh and cool despite the heat of the day. She saw me and smiled. Before I knew what I was doing I had ordered beer and we were sitting down at my table together. Then suddenly I realised that here was the solution to my difficulties. The Waafs were billeted out and were allowed considerable freedom. Moreover, I felt she was the one person in the camp I could really trust.

"Look, will you do something for me?" I asked.

"Of course. What is it?"

"I want to get a message through to Bill Trent. It's rather private and I don't want to 'phone from the 'drome. I wondered if you'd put a call through to him from the village. I can't do it myself. We're tied to the camp."

"I would with pleasure. But I don't think it's much use. Several girls have tried to get through to London this morning. But they're only accepting priority calls. I think the lines must have been put out of action by that raid on Mitchet yesterday."

This was a bit of a blow. I could write, of course. But that meant delay. "What about a wire?" I asked.

"I should think that would get through all right," she replied.

I hesitated. A wire was not quite so private as a 'phone call or a letter. But it seemed the only thing. "Will you send a wire, then?"

"Of course. I'm off duty till this evening."

I scribbled it down on the back of an envelope. "Please obtain full details Vayle librarian Thorby since thirty-six stop May be of vital importance stop Will phone for results early Friday." I wasn't too happy about it. It would have been so much more satisfactory to have spoken to him.

48

I could only hope that he would read between the lines and realise just how important it was. I handed it to Marion. " I hope you can read it," I said.

She glanced through it. There was a slight lift to her eyebrows. But that was the only sign she gave that it was unusual. She asked no questions. And I was not inclined to explain the situation. Now that it came to committing myself on paper I felt too uncertain to risk any discussion of my suspicions.

She slipped the envelope into her pocket. " I'll send it off as soon as I've had my lunch," she promised.

" That reminds me," I said. " I suppose I ought to go and have mine. I'm on again at one."

" Then you haven't much time—it's twenty to already."

I got up. " What about a drink this evening?"

" I'd love to. But I'm on duty at eight."

" That's fine," I said. " I come off at seven. I'll meet you here as soon after as I can make it. That is, of course, Hitler permitting."

" I hope he will." She smiled. It gave me a sudden sense of confidence, that smile. It made me want to stay and talk the whole thing over with her. But I had to get my lunch, and so I left her there, sipping her beer.

The afternoon went slowly. There were no alarms and I had plenty of time for reflection. When we came off at three we tried to get some sleep. This afternoon siesta was now a daily ritual. Without it, I am certain, we could never have kept going. It was easy to see who were the town dwellers and who were accustomed to working in the open air. Micky and Fuller went to sleep on their beds in the hut, not bothering to take off anything but their battle blouse and with at least one blanket over them. The rest of us stripped down and lay out in the sun.

Though I had plenty on my mind, I had no difficulty in going to sleep. We were wakened at a quarter to five. As usual, I felt worse after my brief sleep. It would probably have been more intelligent to rest under cover, but the sun attracted me too much. The sense of leisure was infinite. The thought of the hot, dusty streets of

London made Thorby seem for a brief period a holiday camp.

I did not bother to go down to the mess for tea, even though it was the last good meal of the day. The sun had made me very weak and the idea of putting on battle dress and walking down to the square was quite repugnant. What several of us did was to make tea on the site. This was a much better proposition in every way, for the tea in the mess was really quite undrinkable. Then in the evening we would get food in the Naafi.

We were off again at seven and I went straight down to the canteen tent. It was already crowded. Several of the lads from the other site were there. I looked round, but could see no sign of Marion Sheldon. In the end I got myself a drink and went over and joined the others.

I kept a close watch on the entrance, but she did not come. At first I thought she must have been delayed. But by half-past seven I was wondering whether she had forgotten all about it. I began to feel rather peeked. Trevors had joined us and the whole of our detachment was there. The number of bottles on the table mounted rapidly. The place was insufferably hot and beginning to get noisy. I felt out of tune with it and very tired.

Shortly after eight Elaine came in and joined us. I didn't know how friendly she was with Marion, but I thought she might be able to tell me what had happened to her. But it was rather awkward. She was sitting at the end of the table with Trevors and the two sergeants. I waited, trying to pluck up courage to approach her. But I fought shy of the laughter that my concern about a particular Waaf would certainly evoke.

Then one or two began talking about going to the supper canteen for food, and when they got up I joined them.

As I passed Elaine I said: "What's happened to Marion to-night?"

She looked up at me over her shoulder. "Oh, she's got herself into trouble over something. Four days fatigues. Shall I give her your love?" There was a wicked gleam in her eyes.

I felt a sudden emptiness inside me. "What's she in trouble over?" I asked.

"She was very secretive about it, my dear." Again I was aware of that gleam in her eye. I felt uncomfortable. "You're not by any chance the cause of it, are you? You didn't seem to waste much time last night."

I didn't know what to say. I had a horrid premonition. And because I feared that she might be right, I felt tongue-tied. I was suddenly aware that the whole table was silent, listening to our conversation.

She squeezed my arm in a friendly gesture. "It's all right. I'll give her your love." And she gave me a sugar-sweet smile.

I replied with what I fancy must have been a very sheepish grin and went with the others out of the tent. As we crossed the square to the big block of the Naafi Institute, behind which was the supper canteen, Kan said : "She's a little bitch, isn't she?"

"Oh, I don't know," I said. "I was a bit vulnerable, wasn't I? I'd arranged to meet Marion there at seven and she didn't turn up."

He laughed. "She's still a little bitch. You don't know Elaine. She can be really sweet, though her 'my dears' are a bit reminiscent of the cheap side of Piccadilly. At other times she's just a cat. Tiny thinks she's a paragon of all the virtues. He's very simple. But she's as promiscuous as it's possible to be in a camp. She just naturally wants every man she sees."

I said nothing. What was there to say? I didn't care a damn about Elaine. What was worrying me was why Marion had got into trouble.

"You're very moody, old boy," Kan said. "You're surely not worrying about your girl friend. I mean, a few fatigues are nothing in any one's life."

"I'm just a bit tired, that's all," I said.

The canteen was already pretty full. We took the

51

only table that was vacant. It was against the wall nearest the kitchen. The heat was almost unbearable. We all ordered steak and onions. Whilst we waited for it we had more beer.

"Well, here's to our night's bag, Kan," said Chetwood, raising his glass to his lips.

"What do you mean—your night's bag?" demanded Beasley, a youngish lad from the other site.

It started quite good-naturedly. But it soon became heated.

"Well, what fuse were you firing? Fuse twelve? Well, listen, ducky, that 'plane crashed on the edge of the 'drome. It couldn't have been more than three to four thousand yards away when you opened fire. Fuse twelve would have been well beyond the target."

"My dear fellow, I saw it burst just by the nose of the 'plane."

"Well, John had the glasses on it and he says ours burst just outside the wing. And it was the wing that crumpled. Anyway, you were a layer, weren't you? How the hell could you see? I was laying too, and I could see nothing. The flash was absolutely blinding."

The argument was interminable. It seemed rather pointless. The main thing was that the troop had brought the plane down. At last we got our food. I had just started eating when I saw Andrew Mason come in. He stopped in the doorway to look round the room and then made straight for our table. He looked agitated.

"You're wanted at the office at once, Hanson. Mr. Ogilvie wants to see you."

He sounded urgent. I found I had my fork suspended half-way to my mouth. I put it down. "Oh, hell!" I said. "What's he want to see me about?" But I knew already. And I felt like a cub reporter facing his first awkward interview with the editor.

"I don't know," said Mason. "But Wing-Commander Winton is with him. I've been looking for you everywhere."

I got to my feet. "Don't be a fool—finish your supper

first," said Kan. I hesitated. "I think you'd better come now," said Mason. "It seemed to be urgent and I've already been some time trying to find you."

"All right," I said. I put my cap on and followed him out of the canteen. I felt nervous. Something must have gone wrong over that wire. And if it had, I was in a proper mess. It was hardly likely that Ogilvie would understand my explanation. Thank God Vayle didn't hold a King's commission. His civilian status made a lot of difference.

Mason took me straight into the inner office. Wing-Commander Winton was seated in a chair beside Ogilvie's desk. They looked up as I entered. I saluted. "You wanted to see me, sir?" I was rigidly at attention.

"Did you give a Waaf named Sheldon a telegram to send for you to-day?"

So I was right. I nodded. "Yes, sir."

"Is that the telegram?"

He handed me an inland telegram form. The message I had scribbled on the back of an envelope in the Naafi that morning was written on it in a clear feminine hand. "Yes, sir, that is the telegram."

"It's incredible, Gunner Hanson—quite incredible. You realise that by implication you are accusing Mr. Vayle of something that you don't dare to state? What are you accusing him of?"

"I was not aware that I was accusing him of anything," I replied.

"Then why do you write to your friend asking for full details about him? You must have had some reason for it."

"It was a purely private communication to a colleague on my newspaper, sir."

"Nothing is private once you are in the Army. You are fortunate at this station in that there is no censorship as such. But this telegram was so startling that the postmistress at Thorby thought it wise to ring up Station H.Q. to find out whether the Waaf in question had

53

authority to send it." He paused and glanced across at the Wing-Commander. " Perhaps you would like to question the man, sir."

The C.O. Thorby was a big heavy-jowled man with steady, alert eyes. He came straight to the point. " As Mr. Ogilvie says, this telegram of yours accuses Mr. Vayle by implication of something that you are evidently unwilling to put down on paper. You require from your friend details of Mr. Vayle's life prior to 1936. You say it may be of vital importance. Perhaps you would explain."

I hesitated. Winton was easier to talk to than Ogilvie. Probably because he had had more experience of men. But I was uncertain what line to take. In the end I decided on frankness. " I sent that wire because my suspicions had been aroused, sir," I said. I then went on to explain how the German pilot had stopped talking the moment he saw Vayle, how I had learnt that Vayle had spoken to the pilot before he went before the Intelligence officer, and how I was doubtful whether the pilot would have taken the line he did without guidance. " I could find out nothing about him prior to 1936, sir," I finished. " So I decided to wire my colleague and see whether he could discover something of Mr. Vayle's background. I was bearing in mind the fact that a plan of the ground defences of the aerodrome had already found its way into enemy hands."

" I see. In other words, you suspected Mr. Vayle of being a Nazi agent?"

The C.O.'s heavy brows were drawn downwards over his eyes and he spoke very quietly. I sensed a menace in his words. But I could do nothing to stave it off. I said, " Yes, sir."

" You realise that the proper course would have been to explain your suspicions to your commanding officer or alternatively to have asked him to arrange for you to see me? If you had done so I should have been able to tell you that Mr. Vayle came to this station from a well-known public school, and that we have the most complete confidence in him. Instead, you start a little personal investigation without any authority to do so." He gave me a suddenly keen glance. "What were you before you joined up?"

"Journalist, sir."

He glanced at the address on the telegram. "*The Globe*?"

"Yes, sir.

"And this man Trent—what is his position on the paper?"

"Crime reporter, sir."

"I see. A sensation-seeking paper and a sensation-seeking man." I was conscious of a very unpleasant feeling of loneliness. "I regard this matter very seriously." His voice was cold, distant. "The reasons for your suspicions seem to me quite inadequate. Apart from that, however, your communication with your newshound friend might have had very unfortunate repercussions. Mr Vayle, though of British nationality, was for a number of years lecturer at a Berlin University. Being of Jewish extraction, he was forced to leave in 1934. As I have said, we think very highly of him at this station. Had your wire not been intercepted, I can well imagine what a stunt article your friend would have written."

He got up abruptly. "I leave you to deal with this man, Mr. Ogilvie. You know my wishes. I want no repetition of this at my station."

Ogilvie got to his feet. "I'll see that it does not occur again, sir."

I hesitated.

But as the C.O. moved to the door, I said: "Excuse me, sir."

He paused with his hand on the door. "What is is?" he said, and his tone was not inviting.

"In the first place," I said, "Trent would never have used any information he obtained without my permission. Secondly, because I have joined the Army I have not forfeited my right as a citizen to take any steps I think proper in the interests of my country. My suspicions were flimsy. I knew that. It was out of the question at that stage to raise the matter with any one in authority. I took the only course open to me to attempt to satisfy those suspicions one way or the other."

"The interests of your country would have been best served by your bringing your suspicions to me, not to a newspaper." He still spoke quietly, but there was a tremor of anger in his voice.

I suppose it was foolish of me to pursue the matter. But I said : "Had I done that, without first seeing whether there were any grounds for my suspicions, I could hardly expect the matter to be taken any more seriously than my views about the information of a plan for immobilising our fighter 'dromes given me by the German pilot."

"The headquarters staff of the station is better able to judge the importance of information than you are. I think it would be wise if you forgot that you'd ever been a journalist and remembered only that you're a gunner in the British Army." He turned to Ogilvie. "Whatever you decide, I look to you to see that this sort of thing does not occur again."

"Very good, sir." Ogilvie opened the door for him. When he had left, Ogilvie went back to his desk and lit his pipe. "You haven't made it any easier for me by taking the line you did, Hanson," he said. "Wing-Commander Winton expressed a desire that I should have you transferred to another troop or even another battery, so long as you did not remain at this camp any longer than necessary. However, I am not prepared to go as far as that." He took his pipe from his mouth. "You will be confined to your site for twenty-eight days, and you will only leave it to get your meals and to wash. All letters and other communications during that period will be delivered to this office for me to censor. I will instruct Sergeant Langdon accordingly. All right. Dismiss!"

Chapter Four

NOT SINGLE SPIES

I think I was very near to tears as I came out of the office. The sense of frustration was strong in me. I felt lonely and dispirited. I was cut off from the outside world. I felt like a prisoner who wants to tell the world he didn't do it, but can't. Thorby was a prison and the barbed-wire bars had closed with a vengeance.

Seated on a bench outside the office building were Fuller and Mason. They fell silent as I emerged. I did not speak to them. I felt so remote from them, as they sat there enjoying the pleasant warmth of the gathering dusk, that I could think of nothing to say. I wandered slowly up the road and across the asphalt in front of the hangars. The peace of a late August evening had settled on the place. The revving of engines, symbol of war in a fighter station, was no longer to be heard. All was still. Faintly came the strains of a waltz from the officers' mess.

It was quiet. Too quiet. To me it seemed like the lull before the storm. To-morrow was Thursday. And Friday was the fateful day. If the proposed raid was to prepare the way for an air landing on the 'drome, any time after Friday might be zero hour. I was in a wretched position. Technically I had done all I could. Yet how could I leave the matter where it stood? Vayle had been a lecturer at a Berlin university. Winton might know him to be sound and my suspicions might be entirely unfounded. Yet the fact that he had been in Berlin at the time the Nazis came into power only served to increase my suspicions. British he might be, but there were Britons who believed in National Socialism. And there was certainly nothing about him to suggest the Jew.

As I approached our site I knew that somehow I had to go through with it. I had to find out whether or not

I was right. But how—how? Easy to make the decision, but what was there I could do, confined to my gun site with all my communications with the outside world censored? And anyhow, wasn't it far more likely that Winton was right? The headquarters' staff, as he had said, was far better able to judge the reliability of the pilot's story than I was. And as regards Vayle, Winton had known him intimately for several years, whereas I knew no more of the man than I had been told. It seemed absurd to proceed, when there was so little cause.

When I went into the hut, I found most of the other members of our detachment had already returned and were making their beds. It was nearly nine. I felt nervous. I thought every one must know what had happened and would be watching me to see how I took it. I went straight over to my bed and began to make it. Kan looked across at me. "Well, what did the Little Man want?" he asked.

"Oh, nothing," I said.

He didn't pursue the matter. At nine we went out to the pit and relieved the others. Fuller hadn't yet turned up. There was only Kan, Chetwood, Micky and myself. "Where's Langdon?" I asked. It was unlike him to be late for stand-to.

"He had to go down to the orderly room," Kan told me.

I was silent, gazing out across the 'drome. The sky was very beautiful in the west—and very clear. Soon the nightly procession would start.

"Got any fags to sell?" Micky demanded of the gun pit at large.

There was a shout of laughter. "Not again," said Chetwood despairingly. "Why don't you buy some once in a while?"

"Once in a while! I like that. I bought ten only this morning."

"Then you're smoking too much."

"You're right there, mate. Do you know how many I smoke a day? Twenty!"

"Good God!" said Kan. "That means we're supplying

you with seventy a week. Why don't you buy yourself twenty at a time instead of only ten?"

"I smoke 'em too quick, that's why."

"You mean, you don't smoke enough of ours."

"Well, as long as you're mugs enough." He grinned in his sudden mood of frankness. "I tell you, I wouldn't starve—not as long as there was a sap left in the world."

"All right, we're saps, are we? We'll remember that, Micky."

"Well, give us a fag anyway. I ain't got one—straight I ain't—an' I'm just dying for a smoke."

His request was met by silence. "That wasn't very well received, was it, Micky?" Chetwood laughed.

"All right, mate." He produced an old fag end. "Give us a light, someone."

"Oh, my God, no matches either!"

"Would you like me to smoke it for you?" This was Fuller, who had just arrived in the pit. He tossed Micky a box of matches.

At that moment the sirens began to wail. Micky paused on the point of lighting his cigarette and glanced up at the sky. "The bastards!" he said.

"You want to mind that light." It was John Langdon, who had just come up on his bike.

"Well, be reasonable, John, it ain't dark yet."

"All right, Micky, I was only kidding you." He propped his bike up against the parapet and vaulted into the pit. He produced two bottles of beer from beneath his battle blouse. He tossed one to Micky and the other to Chetwood.

"I thought you went to the orderly room," said Kan.

"I did," he replied. "But I stopped off at the Naafi on the way back."

I was conscious that he glanced in my direction as he spoke. He went over to the gun and looked at the safety lever. The other four settled down on the bench, drinking from the bottles. The first 'plane went over high, faintly throbbing. The searchlights wavered uncertainly. Langdon came over to where I stood leaning against the sandbags. "You seem to have got yourself into a spot of trouble, Barry." He spoke quietly, so that the others should not hear. "You understand that you are confined to the site for the next four weeks, and that all letters and other communications must be handed in to me so that I can pass them on to Mr. Ogilvie to be censored?"

I nodded.

"I don't want to pry into your affairs," he added, "but if you care to tell me about it, I'll see what I can do to get the sentence mitigated. Ogilvie's no fool. He knows the strain we're living under."

I hesitated. "It's very nice of you," I said. "I may want to talk it over with you later, but at the moment—well——" I stopped, uncertain how to explain.

"All right." He patted my arm. "Any time you like. I know how you feel." I don't know what he thought I'd done.

It was then I realised that the four on the bench were casting covert glances at me. They were leaning forward listening to Fuller, who was speaking softly. I heard the word "Friday" and I guessed what they were talking about. I remembered that Fuller had been talking to Mason when I came out of the orderly room. Micky looked up and met my gaze. "Is that true, mate?" he asked.

"Is what true, Micky?" I said.

"Bill here says that that Jerry pilot told you this place was going to be wiped out on Friday."

"I didn't say 'wiped out'," put in Fuller.

"You said a raid, didn't you? What's the difference?" He turned to me again. "You can't deny you was talking to the feller. I saw you wiv my own eyes. Chattin' away in German you was like a couple of old cronies. Did 'e really say we was for it on Friday?"

There was no point in pretending he hadn't. I said, "Yes, that's what he told me."

"Did 'e say Friday?"

I nodded.

"Cor blimey, mate, that's practically to-morrow—an' I was going to 'ave a haircut on Saturday."

"Do you think he really knew anything?" asked Kan.

"I don't know," I said. "It was probably just bravado. He wanted to frighten us."

"Well, he ain't succeeded," put in Micky. "But, blimey—to-morrow! It makes ye think, don't it? And we got to sit 'ere and just wait for it. Wish I'd joined the ruddy infantry." His brows suddenly puckered. "Wot you confined to the site for?" he asked.

The directness of the question rather disconcerted me. That was like Micky. One was always being faced with the problem of replying to remarks which other men would never think of making. I made no reply. There was an uncomfortable silence. Langdon broke it by asking about my conversation with the pilot. I told them what he had said. He made no comment. The others were silent too.

"How come you speak German?" Micky asked suddenly.

"I worked in the Berlin office of my paper for some time," I explained.

He turned that information over in his mind for a moment. Then he muttered, "An' you got yourself into trouble. Wasn't anything to do with what you said to that Jerry, was it?"

I said, "No." Perhaps I denied it a little too quickly, for I sensed a sudden atmosphere of suspicion. I realised that I was not the only one who had been thinking over the fact that someone had attempted to get details of the ground defences of the aerodrome to the enemy. I sensed hostility. Jaded nerves did not make for clear thinking, and a newcomer is never easily absorbed into a community of men who have been working together for a long time. I felt the loneliness of my position acutely. If I was not careful I should be in difficulties with my own detachment as well as with the authorities.

"Ever met the fellow before?" It was Chetwood who asked the question.

Perhaps I read suspicion where none was intended.

But as soon as I said, "Which fellow?" I knew I had attempted to be too off-hand.

"The Jerry pilot, of course."

"No," I said.

"Why did he talk so freely?" asked Chetwood. And Fuller said, "Are you sure he told you nothing else?" I hesitated. I felt at bay. Kan, with his easy manner, would have turned the questions with a wisecrack. But I was more accustomed to writing than to conversation—it tends to make you slow in repartee. Micky followed up the other questions by asking, "Sure you told him nothing else?"

I felt bewildered. And then quite suddenly the conversation was turned from me by Kan saying, "Funny that Westley should have asked for special leave on Friday."

"What for?" asked Micky.

"Oh, it's his uncle's funeral or something."

"His uncle's funeral!" Micky snorted. "Just because his father's an orderman in the City he gets given leave. If me muvver 'ad died they wouldn't give me leave. I tell you, that sort of thing wouldn't happen in the real army."

"Well, has he been granted leave?" asked Chetwood.

"Yes, he's got twelve hours."

"That should keep him out of danger on the fateful day. It does seem a bit clever, doesn't it?"

"I bet it was him that gave that information to the enemy."

"You shouldn't make statements like that unless you know them to be true, Micky," Langdon cut in. His voice was patient but quite final.

"Well, you must admit it's a bit of a coincidence," said Chetwood.

"Coincidences do happen," said Langdon. "If you want to discuss the matter, do it in front of him so that he can answer your charges."

"Oh, I wasn't making no charge," muttered Micky. And then added defiantly, "A bloke's got a right to 'is suspicions, though, ain't 'e?"

I wondered where Vayle would be on Friday. And whilst my mind was occupied with this the conversation drifted to the arrival of the new squadron. They had come in that afternoon. They replaced 62A squadron, who had gone for a rest. Every one had been sorry to see 62A go. They had put up a grand show. They had been a month at Thorby—and a month at a front-line fighter station at that time was a long while. In that month they had shot down more than seventy enemy 'planes. But they had had a bad time, and if any one deserved a rest, they did. The relieving squadron was 85B. Like its predecessor, it was equipped with Hurricanes. But we knew nothing about them. Langdon, however, who had been in the sergeant's mess that evening, said that they had had a good deal of experience in France and had been taking a well-earned rest up in Scotland. "The squadron-leader is apparently one of our crack fighter pilots," said Langdon. "D.S.O. and bar and nineteen 'planes to his credit. Crazy devil and always sings when he goes into a fight. Funny thing, his name is Nightingale."

It was an unusual name and took me straight back to my schooldays. "Do you know his Christian name?" I asked.

"No. Why? Do you know him?"

"I don't know. We had a John Nightingale at school. He was crazy enough. His most spectacular feat was to put two—pieces of crockery, I think they were called— on top of the Naafi marquee at Tidworth Pennings on his last camp. I just wondered whether it was the same fellow. It's rather an uncommon name, and he took one of those short-term commissions in the R.A.F. when he left school."

"What sort of a show did the squadron put up in France, do you know?" asked Kan.

"Pretty good, I gather," replied Langdon. "Anyway, they have a high opinion of themselves." ·

"Well, I hope they're not over-estimating themselves —for their sakes as well as our own," said Chetwood.

"I heard of a relieving squadron over at Mitchet who thought they were pretty good. They had come down from Scotland too. But they hadn't any experience of dog-fighting their way through big formations. They acted mighty big in the mess their first night. And the next morning they went up and flew straight into a hundred and fifty Messerschmitts over Folkestone. They lost nearly half the squadron without bringing down a single Jerry. I don't think they did much crowing after that."

Micky held a bottle of beer out to me. I don't think he was consciously trying to be friendly. It was just that his mood of suspicion had passed. The rest of stand-to passed pleasantly. Few 'planes came over. We were relieved at ten and went straight to bed. It was already clouding over.

I was woken up to be told that the "All Clear" had gone about quarter of an hour ago. The hut was full of the soft stir of men breathing. It was five to one. I was the first guard of our detachment. I scrambled into my clothes and went out to the pit. It was still cloudy, but the moon had risen and the night was full of an opaque light.

"Anything interesting happened?" I asked Helson, who had been left on guard by the other detachment.

"Nothing while the alarm was on," he replied. "They were coming over in an endless stream and several flares were dropped away to the north. Can't think why they suddenly dried up. Harrison told me something rather exciting, though. He's just come off Gun Ops. The squadron leader of 85B has taken a Hurricane up to intercept. Apparently he got annoyed at hearing them coming over without any attempt being made to stop them, so he asked the C.O. if he could take a 'plane up. But the C.O. wouldn't allow the flare-path to be put on for him. So he said that wouldn't stop him, all he wanted was one landing light at the far end of the runway. But even this wasn't allowed, so he said lights or no lights, he was going up. He went out from the dispersal point here. We saw him take off and wondered what he was up to.

It was a crazy thing to do. It was as black as pitch at the time. But he got up all right."

"Did you see him at all?" I asked.

"No, I tell you, it was like pitch. There was a bit of a mist over the field. Well, that's all the news. Enjoy your guard."

He handed me the rifle and torch and left me to my thoughts. They were pretty chaotic, for I was dopey with sleep. My guard passed slowly, as it always does when you are sleepy, but daren't go to sleep. It seemed unnaturally quiet. Occasionally I heard the movements of one of the guards patrolling the barbed-wire on the slope below our hut. Otherwise there was not a sound.

It was twenty to two—I had just looked at my watch —when I heard the sound of a 'plane. It grew rapidly louder. It was very low and travelling fast. The 'phone bell rang. I picked up the receiver. My heart was in my mouth. I expected a plot and I knew it would be on top of us before I could get the gun manned. Leisurely, Gun Ops. went the round of the sites. Then the voice at the other end said, "One Hurricane coming in to land." At the same moment the flare-path went on, a blinding swathe of light along the runway facing into the wind.

Then the plane appeared through the cloud with its navigation lights on. It came diving down at high speed straight for the gun. At not more than two hundred feet it flattened out. It passed right over my head and banked slightly on to the flare-path. The sound of it passing through the air rose to a scream. I could see the flame of the exhausts each side of the nose. And then it was lit up by the light of the flare-path and it began to roll over. It seemed very leisurely and easy. The 'plane went right over in a superb victory roll, scarcely losing any height. It was a mad, lovely piece of flying. For an instant it shone silver as it rolled and then the night beyond the flare-path had swallowed it.

I could have shouted for sheer joy at that superbly executed symbol of victory. It lightened my spirits. I took it as an omen. It was one of the very first occasions on which one of our 'planes had shot down a Jerry at night. I picked the 'plane up again circling leisurely to the south of the 'drome. It passed behind me and came in beyond the flare-path, two pin-points of light, one red, one green. Then suddenly there it was gliding along the flare-path, its brakes squealing as it slowed up. At the end of the runway it turned and taxied back across the field to the dispersal point a hundred yards to the north of our site.

A few minutes later I saw the pilot walking slowly along the road. I got the glasses out and watched him. He still had his flying suit on and I could not see his face. But I would have recognised that lithe yet curiously shambling gait anywhere. It was John Nightingale— no doubt about it. He was walking on the same side of the road as our pit and would pass within a few yards of me. It was strange to see him alone after having accomplished something so big. I felt that the least the C.O. could have done would be to come out and meet him in his car.

As he came abreast of me I said, " Squadron-Leader Nightingale?"

" Yes." He stopped.

I saluted. " It's John Nightingale, isn't it?" I asked.

" That's right. Who's that?"

" Barry Hanson."

" Barry Hanson?" he repeated. Then, " Good God! Barry Hanson—of course." And he came over to the parapet and shook me by the hand. " What strange places one does meet people now." He grinned.

I could see his face in the diffused light of the moon. I should never have recognised him by his face, it was so changed. When I had last seen him he had been a fresh-complexioned lad of eighteen. Now his face was tanned and leathery, there were little lines at the corners of his eyes and he wore a small moustache along the edge of his upper lip. There was a white scar across his chin and the left cheek was disfigured by a burn. But his smile was the same. He smiled with his eyes as well as with his lips, and there was the old flash of gaiety and recklessness in it.

He vaulted to a seat on the parapet. " So you're a gunner now? What were you doing before the war?" I told him. ". Well, well—so you didn't like the insurance business. That was where you went from school, wasn't it?"

" Yes," I replied, " but it was too dead for me." And I told him how I'd cut out on my own. Then I asked him about himself. He had done his five years and then been accepted for permanent service. He had been promoted to squadron-leader shortly after war broke out, and had led his squadron in France.

" What about your escapade to-night?" I asked. " That crazy roll you did when you came in meant, I suppose, that you'd shot one down?"

" Yes," he said with a careless laugh. " I was lucky. There's only a thin layer of cloud at about two thousand. Above that it's bright moonlight. I went up to twenty thousand, which is the height at which they were coming over. I figured that, as they were using a definite route, if I hung about right over the 'drome I'd be sure to see one of them sooner or later. I hadn't been up more than fifteen minutes when a Heinkel blundered right into me. I very nearly crashed it. I twisted on to his tail. I simply couldn't miss him. He was like a great silver bird in the moonlight. Absolute sitter. After getting him, I hung about for a further half-hour in the hope of picking up another, but I had no luck, and in the end I had to come down. I gather they had stopped coming over."

Then he went on to talk of old school friends that he had met. He was full of news of those who had joined the Services. And as we talked I was turning over in my mind whether to take him into my confidence and tell him of my suspicions about Vayle. It seemed such a heaven-sent opportunity. R.A.F. officers were given plenty of freedom. He probably had a car. He would have plenty of chances to 'phone a wire from some exchange at a reasonable distance. He might even be going up to Town the next day, in which case he could 'phone Bill Trent direct. And yet I was chary of getting myself into further trouble. Not that he was the sort of fellow to report anything I told him—but I did not know how discreet he would be.

At length he said, "Well, I must be getting along, I suppose, or they'll be sending out a search party."

I looked at my watch. It was just on two.

"You've passed my guard nice and quickly for me," I said.

"Good." He got down from the parapet. "Look, you must come and dine with me somewhere soon and we'll have a really good talk over old times."

I laughed. "I should like to," I said regretfully. "But I'm afraid it's not possible. We're not allowed outside the camp, and at the moment I'm confined to my site."

"Oh, have you been getting into trouble, then?"

I hesitated. And then I told him the whole thing— or rather, not quite all. I didn't mention the plan for immobilising fighter stations. I didn't want to run the risk of being thought too credulous again. But I told him about the pilot's story of a raid on Friday and how the man had shut up like a clam as soon as he saw Vayle. I told him what I had learnt about the librarian and the attitude Winton had taken when it was discovered I had been wiring a colleague for information about Vayle. I explained, too, that a plan of the ground defences of the aerodrome had been found on a Nazi agent.

"Yes, I heard about that," he said. "It's rather extraordinary, because it was more than just a plan. It gave the approximate number of rounds on each gun site, and a complete plan of the wiring of Ops., Gun Ops. and the runway lights. The plan was made out by someone who had access to a great variety of information that is not usually available."

"That points to someone in authority," I said. "Vayle could get details like that. But I've got nothing on Vayle— nothing definite at all. It's just that I'm suspicious, and I

68

shan't be satisfied till I know for certain whether my suspicions are justified or not."

"Is this fellow short with a rather fine head and iron-grey hair?"

"Yes," I said. "Long, almost sardonic features."

"That's right. I met him to-night at the Spinning Wheel. It's a sort of farmhouse turned night club up on the other side of the valley. He was there with a Waaf."

"Did he talk to any one?"

"Oh, he said cheerio to a number of pilots. The place practically lives on flying officers. Yes, he did have a chat with two fellows from Mitchet. But most of the evening he spent with this girl Elaine."

"Elaine?" I was interested. I remembered what Kan had said. Promiscuity might be very useful to an agent.

"Look," I said. "Can you get a message through to a fellow called Bill Trent on the *Globe*?"

"Well, you know the 'phones are very difficult and I believe there's great delay on telegrams." He hesitated, and then he said : "But I might run up to Town to-morrow evening. I could 'phone him then, if that's any use to you. Mind you, I can't promise. But I should be free. Anyway, I'll do what I can. What do you want me to tell him?"

"Just ask him to get all the information he can about Vayle. Tell him it may be of vital importance. You needn't worry about him being indiscreet."

"O.K. I'll do it if I can. What's his home number?" I told him. "Right. Well, I'll be seeing you." He raised his hand in salute and strode off towards the officer's mess. I went across to the hut and called Chetwood, who was my relief guard. It was two-fifteen. In a few minutes he came out and took over. I was so concerned about the steps I had taken to contact Bill Trent that I forgot to tell him anything about John Nightingale's escapade. The atmosphere in the hut smelt stale behind the blackout curtains after the fresh night air. But I was too sleepy to worry about it as I tumbled into bed.

I woke to the clatter of workmen as they entered the

hut just after seven-thirty. There were two of them. They had come to put in some panes of glass that had been broken when the hut was built. Strange and incredible are the ways of Government workmen. The hut had been erected about a month ago, and as soon as the roof was on the workmen had disappeared, though panes were missing from the windows, no interior boarding or decoration had been done, and the promised electric light had not been installed. And because the tents, though camouflaged, had been thought too conspicuous from the air, these had been struck and the whole gun team had had to move into the bare and half-completed hut.

Now, out of the blue, these two workmen came clumping in without any consideration for the fact that the occupants were trying to sleep. They were met by a liberal dose of invective. This had no effect on the elder of the two, a hatchet-faced man with a white, leathery skin. But his mate, who was little more than a boy, had the grace to say, "Sorry to disturb you lads."

I was slow to arrive at full consciousness. But suddenly I realised it was Thursday. I shall always remember that Thursday. Until then I don't think I had realised quite what I was up against. Subconsciously it had been something of a game, a diversion from the monotony of constant raids. But on that Thursday I discovered how far removed I was from a David in search of a Goliath, and by that evening I was almost sick in the face of a fear that came at me from every quarter.

It began rather better than most other days since I had been on the site. No alarm disturbed our breakfast. In fact, there was no alarm until just after eleven, and then it was only half a dozen hostile and did not last long. For once we were able to get washed and shaved in comfort. But inevitably there was no ease in the lull. A lull had become unusual. And jaded nerves were suspicious of the unusual. Every one seemed strangely reluctant to enjoy the blessed comfort of not having to take post. It meant something worse to come—that's the way they looked at it. There was no false optimism. We listened eagerly every night for the ever-mounting number of German 'planes shot down. But though the proportion of British to German losses exceeded all expectations, we knew only too well what it was costing us in worn-out pilots and unserviceable machines.

It was not long before somebody mentioned my talk with the Jerry pilot, and instantly every one saw in this lull the preparation for a raid on Thorby. That, of course, was ridiculous. They would not hold off for one day just to prepare for a raid on a single aerodrome. But the fact that they were holding off looked ominous. A big attack against a number of fighter stations might be followed almost immediately by an actual landing, since it seemed reasonable that they would strike while conditions in the aerodromes were chaotic. In a moment I was the centre of tense speculation. Questions were hurled at me right and left, and I was again conscious of that undercurrent of suspicion. I was the rooky who knew more than they did. That in itself inspired a subconscious hostility in most of them. At the same time, balked by any certainty about the morrow, they felt that I must be holding something back.

" Have you told Mr. Ogilvie?" asked Bombardier Hood.

" Yes, he knows about it," I replied.

" What's 'e goin' to do about it, eh?" Micky's face looked white and strained. Anticipation is so much harder to bear than reality.

" Don't be a fool, Micky—what can he do about it?"

" Well, they could have an umbrella of fighters up." This from Chetwood.

" Yeah, a squadron—that's what they'd give us, mate. An' wot the hell's the good of a squadron. You saw them when they came over Mitchet. Bloody fousands of 'em there was, wasn't there, Kan?—bloody fousands."

" Well, we did see as many as thirty odd of our fighters in the air at once the other day."

I said : " I was assured that every precaution possible was being taken."

" Oh, you was assured, was you, mate? You've got a

bloody nerve, you 'ave. Who started all this?—you just tell me that. An' you say you been assured it's all O.K. Well, I'm scared, mate, I don't mind telling you. Give me a baynet. Cold steel, that's wot I like. But this waiting to be bombed! It ain't war—not by rights it ain't. I oughta have bin in the infantry. I would've too, only——"

"Only the Buffs were full up," said Chetwood. "If you don't like ack-ack, apply for a transfer—otherwise shut up."

"You don't speak to me like that, mate," Micky grumbled on to himself, but he didn't do anything about it.

"Well, thank God we have some defence here," said Helson, "even if it is only the much-despised three-inch. I shouldn't like to have to sit around at a place like Mitchet with nothing but Lewis guns, waiting for an attack."

The conversation became general again, but every now and then a question was hurled at me. And always it was the same question put in a different way—hadn't the pilot told me anything else? I felt helpless. There was nothing I could say that would satisfy their need of more information about what might be expected next day. God knows, I was anxious enough about it myself. But, perhaps because my mind was occupied with troubles of my own that centred around something that I felt was so much vaster than a raid on the aerodrome, it did not seem so very important.

I was saved at last from further questions by the air sentry, who opened the door to say that there was a Waaf outside asking for me. I went out to find Marion standing by the pit. It did me good to see her smile as I came up. "I'm sorry," she said. "I hear you've got into trouble over that wire." Her grey eyes met mine and there seemed a bond of sympathy in the glance.

"It's I who should be sorry," I said. "I'm afraid I've got you into trouble. A pity it was all for nothing."

"Oh, but it wasn't. You see, when the postmistress had read through the wire, she gave me one of those searching looks and asked me the rank of the sender. I had to hedge then. I knew she'd smelt a rat, and though she said she'd send it off, I had my doubts. Then as I was wandering down the street, I met a pilot officer I know. He gave me a lift back to the 'drome. He was just going up to Town, so I asked him to 'phone the message through to your friend. I don't think he'd let me down."

"That's marvellous," I said. I did not tell her I had got John Nightingale to do the same. It was all to the good. If Bill got both messages he would realise the urgency.

"Do you know anything more?" she asked.

I told her "No." But I hesitated. There might be something in it. "Is Elaine a particular friend of yours?" I asked.

"I haven't been here long enough to have acquired any particular friends. I don't make friends as easily as that." She smiled. "But she's fun and we have quite a lot in common. Why?"

"She was dining with Vayle at a sort of country club known as the Spinning Wheel last night."

She nodded. "I know the place."

"I wondered, if she were a particular friend of Vayle's, perhaps you could find out something from her."

"Yes, but what?"

I shrugged my shoulders. What did I want her to find out? "I don't know. Anything you can that might help. Oh, yes, one thing—whether Vayle is going to be here to-morrow or not."

"I'll do what I can." She glanced at her watch. "I must be running along. I have my chores to do."

"Fatigues?" I asked.

"Yes. But it's not much really—just ironing."

"I'm sorry. It's wretched to be landed for a thing like that by doing something for someone else."

"Don't be silly." She laid her hand on my arm. "It was rather fun. Anyway, I ought to have been more careful." She hesitated, and there was one of those

73

awkward pauses. I thought she was going. But instead she suddenly said : " You know, if there really is something in your idea, then I don't think your friend will be able to find out much for you. An important agent has his tracks covered up much too well."

" Yes, but what else do you suggest?"

" I don't think you'll discover much outside this aerodrome. If there is anything, it's here."

I pondered this for a moment. But though I started to try and reason it out, I knew instinctively that she was right. If this were one of the 'dromes to be attacked then the whole plan was here to be unravelled on the spot. And suddenly I had an idea. It was not a brilliant one. But it did constitute some sort of action—and it was action I needed. " Can you find out whether Vayle is going to be in this evening?" I asked. And then I stopped. " No. That's asking too much. You're involved enough as it is."

" Nonsense," she said. " I'm as interested as you are. But what did you think of doing?"

" I understand he lives over the Educational Institute. That's right, isn't it?" And when she nodded, I said : " I was thinking I might have a look through his rooms. I mean, it seems the only thing to do. Probably I shouldn't find anything, but——" My voice trailed off. It seemed such a hopeless thing to do.

" That's rather dangerous, isn't it?"

I was pleased at her concern. " Can you suggest anything else?" I asked. " I've got to do something positive. I can't just sit around waiting for something to turn up. It's just a chance and I can't think of anything else."

" He obviously wouldn't leave anything incriminating about."

" No, but there might just possibly be something there that would make sense to me."

" I shudder to think what would happen if you were caught. You'd be charged with stealing, you know."

I shrugged my shoulders. " What's it matter?" I said. " To-morrow a bomb may land on this pit and blow me into little bits. Anyway, I hear there's a waiting list for the Glasshouse." I was very conscious of the fact that she hadn't vetoed it as useless. "If you can find out his movements, I think I'll have a shot at it," I said.

She seemed on the point of raising some objection. But all she said was : "I'll do my best. I'm on duty at eight. If I find that he's going to be out, I'll stroll up as far as your pit before going into Ops. If I can't find out anything, or if I find he may be in, I won't come. It might be thought rather odd if we were seen talking to each other twice in one day."

"Good idea," I said. "I'll be watching for you. It's sweet of you to do all this."

She smiled. "Good luck!" she said. "And don't forget to let me know what happens."

I stayed a moment watching her slim figure walking down the roadway. She didn't look back, and I turned and went into the hut with a queer feeling of having burned my boats. I found myself hoping that she wouldn't discover that Vayle was going to be out that night. Otherwise I was committed to an escapade that might seriously affect my life for the next few months.

The hut was seething with argument about food. John Langdon had come back from the orderly room with the news that as from lunch that day the three-inch teams would feed on their sites, the food being brought out in hay-boxes by the troop van. Most people seemed against the new arrangement. Partly it was the usual conservatism. Partly it was the prospect of being confined even more than before to the site. This was my own objection. But then my case was peculiar. It meant that I could only get away from the site to wash. Normally, however, I should have welcomed it, as I hated the queuing for food and the hurried, crowded eating that was inevitable in the over-full mess.

"Soon we'll be confined entirely to the site like Hanson here," said Chetwood.

"With a well-meaning old dear coming round with a canteen twice a week to dispense tea."

75

"But do you mean to say, John, that we've just got to hang around here until the van comes along with the food?" said Kan. "It's absolutely fantastic. It's bad enough in the mess. But getting the stuff half cold will make it quite impossible. I shall just go down to the mess as before. I mean, it's frightful being stuck up here for meals as well."

"No, you can't do that," said Langdon. "It's a good idea really. It means we can all get food without leaving the site only half manned."

So the argument went back and forth. It was so delightfully mundane, by comparison with my own thoughts, that I enjoyed it. And when the lunch actually did arrive, every one found it much better than they expected. It came with a table and benches and masses of plates. What is more, it was hot.

Pleasantly full, I lay back on my bed to smoke a cigarette. For the moment I felt at peace with the world—tired and relaxed. God! how quickly that fleeting mood was shattered.

I had barely finished my cigarette when Mason came in. He fluttered some papers in his hands. "New aerodrome passes for old," he said.

They were the new passes issued to make it more difficult for unauthorised persons to gain entrance to the 'drome. Our old ones had to be handed in in exchange. I took my Army pay-book out of my battle dress, which was lying on top of my suitcase beside my bed. From a pocket at the back I drew out my old pass. As I did so another folded slip of paper fell to the ground. I bent down from the bed and picked it up. Curious to know what it was, since I could not remember having put it there, I opened it.

When I saw what it was a cold shock of horror ran through me. Had it been my death warrant I could not have felt more frightened. I stared at it, stupefied. It was strange. That single sheet of paper with the two clear-cut creases where it had been folded was so completely damning.

Chapter Five

SUSPECT

" Hallo, what have you found?" A quick movement of my hand turned the paper face downwards. The action was automatic, secretive. I glanced up. I felt that my very movement betrayed me. It was furtive. Chetwood was standing over me. " Just a letter," I said hurriedly.

As I said it, I knew even my own voice betrayed me. It was too hurried.

" Funny sort of letter," he said.

I opened my mouth to make some explanation about an old diagram. Then I shut it. Thank God I had that much sense. He could think what he liked. I gazed up at him, hot and tense. He seemed on the point of making some further remark. But Mason came up and asked for his old pass, and he forgot about it.

I handed in my old pass and was given my new one in exchange. I folded it and slipped it into the pocket of my Army pay-book. And all the time the crumpled paper in my hand seemed to burn my flesh. I felt every eye in the room must be watching me. Yet when I stole a quick glance round every one seemed busy examining and putting away the new passes, and Chetwood was hanging up his battle dress.

I got up as nonchalantly as I could and went out to the lavatory at the back of the hut. I was conscious of each movement of my tensed limbs. I felt they must be watching me. In the seclusion of the lavatory I smoothed out that wretched piece of paper and examined it once again with the aid of a match.

There was the landing ground with the criss-cross of the runways—the hangars, mess, quarters, gun-sites, everything was marked. It was neatly drawn in common blue ink. Everything of interest to the enemy was indicated in fine hand print, even to the field telephone wiring and ammunition stores at gun sites and at the armoury. The information was precise and the drawing accurate. In view of the fact that such a document had recently been found in an agent's hands, it would have meant that if I had been searched weeks of interrogation would have followed.

I felt sick at the thought of what I should have had to face if I had not discovered it in time. And it was with a sense of immense relief that I watched the flames consume it as I set a match to it.

But the sense of relief did not last long, and I sat there in a state of numbed fear at the thought of what it meant. For it meant, of course, that I was a marked man.

I had no longer any doubt about the reliability of the pilot's information. I knew that I was right about Vayle. This was something big. There could be no other possible explanation of such elaborate steps being taken to dispose of a mere gunner. And I was horribly aware of the danger of my own position.

Press men, I know, are supposed to be tough. There is a firm belief that they are always adventurers capable of getting out of any situation. That is true of some, especially the free-lance foreign correspondents. But nothing could be further from the truth in the case of most newspaper men. The majority of them have a job that involves mainly office work. That job is to collate facts and reproduce them in the form of readable matter. I was one of the majority. True, I had been in our Berlin office and had seen quite a bit of the world for my age. But I was no more than a spectator. Because a journalist writes about exciting things it does not mean he leads an exciting life. I suppose my life had been more interesting than it would have been in, say, my father's insurance business. Nevertheless, though I had led the free and easy life of Central London with a flat of my own and no responsibilities, it had really been quiet and respectable. Certainly I had never been in any serious scrapes.

I was, therefore, no more equipped by my civilian

life to get out of the fix I was in than the next man. And I certainly wasn't any less scared. I sat there literally petrified. Behind the closed door of that lavatory I had the temporary illusion of security. Outside, I faced the uncertainties of a situation that was rapidly getting beyond me.

I tried to steady myself. Somehow I had got to go back into that hut as though nothing had happened. I settled down to consider how the document had got into my Army pay-book. The more I thought about it, the more I realised that it must have been placed there after my interview with Ogilvie the previous night. Obviously no such definite action would have been taken until it was known first that Ogilvie was not willing to have me transferred, and secondly, that I was continuing to make a nuisance of myself. My Army pay-book had been in the breast pocket of my battle top all the time. The paper could have been placed in it whilst I was asleep. But that meant there was one of Vayle's agents actually in the detachment, and at the same time it would have been risky, to say the least of it, in a crowded hut. No, the most obvious time was during the morning's short alarm. I had taken post in my shirt sleeves owing to the heat. I had left my empty battle blouse on my bed, and the hut had been empty.

It was then that I realised I had discovered something. The hut had not been completely empty. The whole detachment had been on the gun, but there were still the two workmen. And I remembered seeing the younger one pedal off on his bicycle. The older man had been alone in the hut. As soon as I remembered this I had no doubt as to how the paper had been planted on me. For no apparent reason the workmen had chosen that particular morning to turn up to do a job that we had never expected to get done at all. Now I knew why they had come. But what amazed me more than anything was that they were taking all this trouble over me. I could not believe that I was really dangerous to them. It could only mean one thing—that they felt themselves vulnerable if the attention of the authorities was persistently drawn to this idea of a plan. And since they were evidently leaving nothing to chance, it meant that the scheme, whatever it was, was vitally important. It also meant that at any moment I should be faced with further developments in the plan to put me out of the way. Somehow they had to arrange for the document they had planted on me to be found. It was a nasty thought.

But at least I had the consolation of knowing that I was really on to something. It strengthened my resolve to go through with it—to break into Vayle's rooms, to badger the authorities, to do anything to expose the plan.

I opened the door and went back into the hut. Hardly any one looked up as I came in. Most of them were lying on their beds, smoking, or already asleep. I was glad. It gave me a chance to recover my confidence.

Kan, who was sitting at the table, smoking, suggested a game of chess. Anything to take my mind off my position. We settled down amongst a litter of unwashed crockery.

I had just driven his king into a corner and checked him with a knight, when the door opened.

"Party, party, 'shun!"

It was Ogilvie with Wing-Commander Winton. They were accompanied by a man who looked like a workman.

"Where's Sergeant Langdon?" Ogilvie asked. His voice sounded gruff and tense. I had a sudden premonition of trouble.

"He's in his room, sir," said Bombardier Hood. "I'll fetch him."

The sergeant had a separate room at the end of the hut. A moment later John Langdon appeared, looking very boyish with his hair all tousled and his eyes still full of sleep.

"Identification parade, Sergeant Langdon," snapped Ogilvie. "I want every one lined up down the centre of the hut."

"Very good, sir." He turned about. "Bombardier Hood,

right marker!" Hood took up his place at the far end of the room. "On Bombardier Hood in one rank fall in!"

Automatically we jostled into a line and stood at ease. "Detachment, detachment, 'shun!"

"Thank you, Sergeant. Now"—Ogilvie turned to the workman—"see if you can spot your man." And as the fellow walked slowly down the rank, he said to Langdon, "A man in the uniform of a gunner has been reported asking rather obviously leading questions of the post-office men laying the operations lines."

I stood very stiff, my eyes fixed on the wall opposite and my muscles tensed. I knew what was going to happen. I sensed rather than saw the man pause opposite me. Then his slow face said, "I think this is the man."

"Who is it? Hanson? Ah!" Out of the corner of my eyes I saw Ogilvie glance significantly at the C.O. "Well, Hanson, what have you got to say?"

My knee joints felt weak. The blood hammered in my head. "I think there's some mistake, sir," I heard myself saying. "I have never seen this man before, and I have never spoken to any of the men laying the lines."

"But you know they're being laid?"

"Certainly, sir. Every one in the camp must know that by now."

"What were you doing between seven-thirty and eight last night?"

"In the Naafi, drinking, sir. Sergeant Langdon will bear me out. He was there too."

"Is that right, sergeant?"

"Yes, sir."

"Do you still think this is the man?" Ogilvie asked the workman.

"I think so." His voice sounded sullen. "I can't be sure. His face was in the shadow. Also I'm not certain about the exact time. I didn't think of that until afterwards."

"Did you go to the civilian bar at all last night, Hanson?" Ogilvie asked.

"The supper canteen? Yes, sir. I went there shortly after eight with Chetwood and Fuller."

"I see. But you did not speak to this man?"

"No, sir. I was with the others the whole time."

"This man says a gunner engaged him in conversation in the canteen and that later he saw him jotting down notes. He has now identified that gunner as you. And you admit that you were in the canteen at about the time he states." Ogilvie turned to Chetwood. "Do you agree that Hanson was in your company the whole time, Chetwood?"

"As far as I can remember, sir." I experienced again that sense of undeveloped hostility about me. Chetwood could easily have committed himself to a direct "yes." But he had hedged.

Ogilvie looked at me uncertainly. I could see that he did not know what to do. "You realise that this is a very serious charge, Hanson?"

I said, "Yes, sir. But it is quite untrue." My voice trembled despite all efforts at control. "This is the first time I have ever seen this man."

Ogilvie turned to the workman. "I don't feel justified in pursuing the matter unless you can say definitely that this is the man."

There was a pause whilst the fellow thought this over. He looked searchingly at me once or twice as though trying to make up his mind. At last he said, "I can't be absolutely certain. But he looks very like him." He hesitated, and then said, "Perhaps if he would submit to a search. As I told you, I saw him jotting something down on a piece of paper afterwards. If he is the right man he probably still has the paper on him."

"How do you know he was taking notes of his conversation with you?" Ogilvie was annoyed and I think he was inclining to take my side.

"I don't. That's why I suggest a search. That would satisfy me."

Ogilvie glanced at the C.O. Winton gave an almost

imperceptible nod. " All right." Ogilvie turned to me.
" Do you object to a search?"

" No, sir," I said. " But I strongly object to being
suspected on such flimsy grounds."

" I understand. The whole thing is most distasteful
to me." He turned to Langdon. " Will you go through
Hanson's kit, Sergeant? All papers to be examined
thoroughly and take care that you leave no hiding-place
unsearched. Now Hanson, come with me into the
sergeant's room and we'll go through everything you
have on you."

It was a most degrading business. Ogilvie left nothing
to chance. I understood his thoroughness. He was
determined to prove definitely to his own satisfaction that
I was all right.

When it was all over and they had found nothing
incriminating, he merely said, " That's all, Sergeant
Langdon," and marched out of the hut. He was furious at
the ignominious position in which he had been placed.
I had some satisfaction out of the episode, for I surprised
a look of something like frustration in the eyes of the little
workman.

I felt excited now that the ordeal was over. It had
achieved something. I now knew two of Vayle's satellites.
There was the workman who had planted the diagram
in my Army pay-book that morning. And there was this
little man with his fresh round face and watery blue eyes
that had a quick darting alertness.

As soon as the door closed behind him I became
conscious of the unnatural silence in the room. I knew that
every one was just dying to discuss what had happened
and that my presence embarrassed them. Rather than
face the barrage of speculation and comment at my
expense, I went outside. As I closed the door I heard
Micky say, " Bloody sauce, coming in like that and holding
an identification parade!"

I lit a pipe and went over to the pit to talk to the air
sentry, a little Welshman called Thomas who was old
83

enough to have been through two years of the last war. He asked me what Ogilvie had wanted. I told him what had happened. He thought it over for a moment. Then he said, " These civilians, they get panicky. They get so as they think every one but themselves is a spy. Indeed and I remember a case in 'eighteen. The poor devil was shot for something that he never did at all. And all because of a civilian who laid a charge before he had paused to consider." And he launched into a long story about a soldier who had been shot at Arras just before the big offensive.

It was very hot out there in the glare of the sun. I took my battle-dress top off and lay down on the top of the parapet. Thomas chattered on. He was a great talker. I closed my eyes. The light on my eyeballs was red as it shone through my closed lids. I felt a sense of satisfaction. Things were moving, though as yet I had taken no positive action. It seemed to augur well. And yet at the back of my mind I felt uneasy. I had so narrowly escaped an extremely awkward situation. It was only chance that I was not now under arrest pending a court-martial. The next time I might not be so lucky. And that there would be a next time I was quite certain. They had shown their hand too openly to me not to make sure that during the next few critical days I should be out of the way.

But uneasy though I was, it did not prevent me from falling fast asleep on top of the sandbags. Mental strain, in addition to the nervous and physical strain from which every one was suffering, had made me incredibly tired.

I slept for nearly three-quarters of an hour. Yet when I went back into the hut some of them were still talking about what had happened.

" Just because a bloke's picked out in an identification parade, it don't mean he's a Nazi," Micky was saying. " Anyway," he added pointedly, " he ain't going to 'is grandmuvver's funeral to-morrow."

There was an awkward silence as I came in. Instinctively I knew that it was Chetwood who had caused Micky's quixotic outburst. But strange to say, I did not feel afraid of their hostility for the moment. I felt confident and at ease. "Well," I said, "I hope you boys have made up your minds whether I'm a Nazi agent or not."

I had caught them on the raw. Chetwood, Helson, Fuller and Bombardier Hood all seemed trying to appear unconcerned. But at the same time they were watchful. And I knew that Chetwood and Hood, at any rate, were suspicious. I should have to be careful. From now on everything I said and everything I did would be marked. I lay down on my bed, pulled a blanket over me and pretended to sleep.

The afternoon seemed to pass slowly, unaccustomed as we were to such a long period free of alarms. Some slept, others played chess or cards. The hut was quiet save for stampings and hammerings on the roof. Micky, with the aid of Fuller, was endeavouring to camouflage the hut with branches of hazel cut from the woods at the foot of the slope. I understood his frame of mind, and only wished that I could have found something to do that would have kept me occupied. In a way, I was as scared as he was, though, strangely enough, it wasn't the prospect of being bombed that scared me. That was something tangible. I am a great believer in fate. If a bomb is going to get you, then it's going to get you, and there's damn-all you can do about it. It might just as well be the wheels of a bus in peace-time. But I was deliberately walking into danger. There was a difference.

The second Take Post of the day came at about five, just as tea had arrived. It did not develop and all that came of it was that the baked beans on toast were cold. Micky had practically finished the hut by the evening, so that it looked like Malcolm's army before Dunsinane.

I spent the evening trying to read, of all things, Liddell-Hart's *Foch*. I was in a deck-chair out in the open patch of grass between the hut and one of the newly constructed pill-boxes. It was quiet and still— a beautiful summer evening that made one think of the river. The peace of it was incredible. The sun sank slowly in a golden glow. An Anson and an old Harrow, cumbersome yet very light off the ground, came in and took off after a short stay. That was the only activity. There might have been no war on. God! how I wished there weren't! I was too conscious of how changed the scene might be in the short space of twenty-four hours. And all the time I was progressing slowly through Liddell-Hart's account of the follies of the last war, epitomised in the slaughter of Passchendaele.

I was sitting facing the roadway and shortly after seven-thirty my eyes strayed more and more from my book. Despite an assumption of calm, there was an unpleasant fluttering in my stomach. I found myself hoping that Marion would not come.

But she did, and my heart sank. I saw her when she was down near the hangars. Even at that distance I could see the fair straight hair beneath her cap catching the slanting sunlight. I watched to see whether she would turn in at Ops. But no, she came straight on, strolling leisurely towards the pit. When she was about fifty yards away I rose to my feet and went into the hut, to show her that I had seen her. I got my pipe, and by the time I came out again she had turned and was walking back towards Ops.

Well, the die was cast. I couldn't turn back. I felt much easier now that everything was settled. I sat and read on until the light began to fail, shortly after nine. When I went into the hut I found it empty. The detachment on Stand-to were already in the pit. The others had all drifted off to the Naafi. I had a momentary sense of lostness. But it did not last, for I had too much on hand.

I made my bed and collected my washing things. Langdon was on Stand-to that night, having changed with Bombardier Hood because there was a party at the sergeants' mess the following night. He raised no objection to my request for a bath. It was the only excuse I had for leaving the gun site at that time. The showers were in the big permanent blocks to the west of the hangars.

I made straight for the educational block. There was no

moon yet and it was beginning to get really dark with clouds coming up from the west. It looked like rain.

The trouble was that I had not studied my terrain. I had found out roughly how to reach Vayle's rooms. But I naturally presumed that if he was out he would have locked the door. Some alternative method of entry had to be found. At the most I had about forty minutes in which to carry out the whole scheme. A bath couldn't possibly take longer and I did not want to upset Langdon. I decided to risk everything on a roof climb.

But first I had to make certain that Vayle hadn't changed his plans and stayed in. I went straight into the educational block and up the stairs. The ground floor was composed of two big lecture rooms, one with desks and the other full of a litter of band instruments and sports kit. Upstairs were two large recreation rooms with a billiard table and table tennis. These rooms, like the two downstairs, were separated by sliding partitions. At the far end was the library, which was very well supplied with technical books. It was above the library that Vayle's rooms were situated.

I tossed my washing things on to a chair in the farther recreation room, and then, making certain that the players were all engrossed in their snooker game, I crossed the passage and climbed the short flight of stairs that led to Vayle's green-painted front door.

I rang the bell. It sounded faintly in the rooms beyond. Then I turned the handle of the door. As I had expected, it was locked. Worse still, it was a Yale lock. I had two Yale keys amongst my collection. I tried them, but they would not even fit into the keyway. To break in was out of the question. The door looked solid and any noise would bring the snooker players out. The roof was the only chance.

I went back down the stairs and out into the fast-gathering dark. A quick glance at the front of the building, still dimly visible, told me that there was no way up there. Anyway, I should have been seen. I went round to the back, through a narrow alleyway between the

Educational and the bulk of Station Headquarters. It was quieter here and there was a screen of faded laurel bushes.

I gazed up at the side of the building. There was a drainpipe. But I was in no doubt about my ability to climb drainpipes. The Educational was not a tall building, compared with the big blocks of the living-quarters and Station Hearquarters which surrounded it. Moreover, it had a sloping roof and gables. It had, I think, at one time been a house. The aerodrome had grown up round it, and it had been added to as the needs of education and recreation increased. It was in the older, gabled part that Vayle's rooms were.

I had hoped to find a skylight. But as far as I could see there was none. My eyes drifted over the windows. They were casement type, and one was slightly open. It looked like a bathroom window, for it was smaller than the rest and appeared to be of frosted glass. Below it were pipes. And below them and a little to the right was what originally, I suppose, had been the kitchens, but they had been converted into a cloakroom.

It seemed the only chance. I was wearing canvas shoes. I might just be able to make it. I slipped through the archway of the laurel hedge and climbed on to the sill of the outhouse window. A press-up on the guttering, which fortunately held, and I had made the roof. From now on I was above the shelter of the hedge and risked being seen. I pressed forward as quickly as possible.

The roof was steep, but I made the ridge of it with an effort. By standing upright on it against the wall of the main building, the bathroom pipes were about level with my chin and the sill of the window I was making for was only just out of reach.

I glanced round. I could now see beyond the laurel hedge and the grass space behind it to the barrack blocks. A door opened and two figures emerged. I waited until they were out of sight round the angle of Station Head-quarters. There was now no one in sight that I could see. I turned back to the wall and measured the distance to the sill above my head. My muscles felt weak yet tensed. If I failed to grip it or if I had not the strength to pull myself up, I had only the sharp edge of the roof to land back on.

I hesitated. Twice I nerved myself for the spring, and twice my nerve failed me at the last moment. And then suddenly I had jumped, pressing up with my right hand to the wastepipe. My fingers grazed the edge of the sill and closed on it. I hung for a second, my muscles slack, taking the weight of my body on my left hand. Then with a wriggle I forced myself upwards, exerting all the energy of both arms and scrabbling against the brickwork with my feet.

I thought I should never make it. But a final effort and my knee was on the wastepipe beside my right hand. After that it was easy. I got both hands on the sill and pressed up until I was standing on the wastepipe. I pulled the window wide open and wriggled through. Before closing it again I looked out towards the barrack blocks. One man was just going in the door. But he showed no sign of having just witnessed anything unusual. Otherwise, there was not a soul in sight.

So far so good. I closed the window and lit a match, shielding the flame with my hand. It was a bathroom and lavatory combined. I opened the door and found myself in a narrow passage. The last flicker of my match showed me the front door at the other end—only this time I was looking at the inside of it. I went on tiptoe down the passage. There were two doors leading off to the right. I opened the first slightly. There was no sound and it was very dark, for the blackout curtains were drawn. I switched on the light. It was a bedroom. There was no one there. It was a cold, bare-looking room with cream-distempered walls and an over-modern gas fire. The other room, which also proved to be empty, was more cheerful. There was a heavily banked-up fire in the grate—a clear indication that Vayle had gone out for the evening. The walls were covered with a pleasant biscuit-coloured paper which gave an illusion of sunlight. The curtains were a dark green, and there were one or two tasteful little water-colours on the walls. To the right of the fireplace was a bookcase, to the left a radiogram. But what interested me most was the big, old-fashioned roll-top desk under the window.

I decided to start on this, as the most likely repository for the clue for which I was seeking. My luck seemed definitely in—the desk was open. I pushed back the roll-top to find myself confronted by an untidy litter of papers, books, note-books and pocket-worn letters. I glanced at my watch. It was twenty to ten. I had thirty-five minutes in which to carry out my search and get back to the site. It didn't seem long when I had no idea what it was that I was looking for. I began methodically to go through the litter. But as I proceeded I discarded caution in favour of speed. What did it matter if he found out that someone had searched his rooms. In fact, it might help. It might scare him into the open. In any case, it was quite clear that he had already decided to get me out of the camp one way or the other.

It took the better part of quarter of an hour to go through that desk with all its drawers and pigeon-holes. In the end I reached such a frantic state that I was just throwing the stuff on to the floor as soon as I had glanced at it. There were books on tactics and military history, books on dynamics and ballistics and higher mathematics, mixed up with red paper-covered books filled with notes in a clear, rather ornamental hand. There were bills, masses of them, demand notes, letters from friends. These last I paid particular attention to. But they seemed harmless enough. In fact, when I had been through the contents of the desk and emptied the last drawer on the carpet, I knew nothing more about Vayle's activities than I had done before, except that he was a reluctant payer of bills, a first-class mathematician, something of an expert on military history and tactics, and a man who had a large circle of friends.

I turned in disgust from the desk and gazed anxiously round the room, softly lit by the standard lamp in the corner next to the radiogram. I was feeling nervous.

Time was passing. The regular and inevitable tick of the clock on the mantelpiece filled the tiny room. I had to find something. I had to. I felt desperate. My skin pricked with sweat. This was the only positive action I could take. If I found nothing, I should never be able to convince the authorities of the danger of the position. And if I couldn't convince them of that, then——

My eyes searched the room and came to rest on a little tallboy standing behind the door. More drawers to search. I flung myself into the task of searching them. More papers, books full of notes, receipts, some pages of the MS. of a book on military tactics with innumerable illustrations of imaginary battles to amplify the arguments, a jumble of cigarettes, cards, old pipes, and the other odds and ends that inevitably sprinkle the drawers in a bachelor's rooms.

At length I stood up. The floor about me was littered with papers and books, tossed on to it in my frenzy to do the impossible and examine everything in a few minutes. I gazed around, hot and frustrated. Where else might I find anything? The bookcase! One by one I pulled the books out and tossed them on to the floor, after first holding them up by their covers so that anything slipped between their pages would fall out. By this method I gleaned a few letters and odd pieces of paper with notes on them or the solution of mathematical problems.

When the bookcase was empty I straightened my aching back. Nothing! What about the bedroom? Perhaps the suits in the wardrobe would yield something. It was a forlorn hope. I had started across the room when I suddenly saw the wallet. It was lying on the mantelpiece, perfectly obvious, even at a casual glance. It seemed incredible that I could have spent nearly twenty minutes in that room and not have noticed it. I pounced on it eagerly. Two pound notes, stamps, several visiting-cards and a photograph. Idly I glanced at the last. It was faded and torn at the edges through constant friction against the leather of the wallet. It showed a short, well-built man with a long head, full lips and rather prominent nose. It was an intelligent face, the prominent jaw and alert-seeming eyes suggesting a powerful personality. It was not a face that was easy to forget. I felt a slight tremor inside me. This was Vayle. On his arm was a dark, vivacious-looking girl, her features and figure tending to plumpness. She seemed vaguely familiar. I turned the snap over. A faded rubber stamp on the back showed unmistakable German lettering. I made out the word " Berlin ".

I was just on the point of returning it to the wallet when something in my brain clicked. Quickly I turned it over and gazed once more at the photograph itself. And then I knew I was right. The girl was Elaine. She was a little thinner now, a little less round in the face. It was a younger, more naturally carefree Elaine—or else it was very like her. I turned it over again and looked at the stamp. The letters " 1934 " were just visible above the Berlin. In 1934 Vayle was in Berlin with Elaine. It was an important link.

And at that moment I heard the jingle of a key in the front door. I looked wildly round. There was no possible place to hide. The door opened and shut and footsteps sounded in the passage whilst I stood there petrified. Then in frantic haste I slipped the photo into my trouser pocket, The next moment the door had opened and Vayle stood there gazing at me and at the wreckage of his sitting-room.

I must have looked a fool, standing there with my mouth agape in the midst of that litter. A sudden cloud of anger showed in his face, flushing his cheeks. But his eyes, grey eyes that matched his iron-grey hair, remained detached and alert. The storm of anger passed. He came forward into the room. " It appears I have a visitor," he said. " Perhaps you would introduce yourself." He went over to the mantelpiece and took a cigarette from a glass cigarette box. He lit it with a lighter.

My confusion subsided. But my fear mounted. His manner was so easy and pleasant, and his eyes, that watched me all the time, were so hard. I knew I was not equal to dealing with a man of this calibre. " I think you have heard of me," I said. " My name is Hanson."

I tried desperately to match his ease of manner, but I was conscious of the tremor in my voice as I spoke.

"Ah, yes," he said. "I remember now. A gunner." But there was no flicker of interest or recognition in his eyes. They remained unchanged—cold and watchful. Instinctively I felt that he had known who I was the moment he had opened the door. He drew slowly at his cigarette. He said nothing, but he watched me closely. I couldn't help it—I lowered my eyes before his gaze. And as soon as I had done so I shifted my feet and did not know where to look or what to do with my hands. I felt such a fool caught there in the act of burgling his flat. I was worried, too, about what action he was going to take. Here was his chance to get me away from the 'drome. My only hope was that he would consider this too great a risk. If he had me arrested it would mean a court-martial. And at a court-marial I would be able to press home my reasons for entering his flat. They would have no grounds for disbelieving me, since I could show that I was not short of money, and my editor would back me. And there was that business of framing me with the diagram and arranging for me to be searched. That could be used too. Pity I had burned the diagram. But Vayle didn't know that.

I plucked up courage at the realisation that the position was not entirely to my disadvantage. Moreover, it seemed to offer the last final proof—for there was still a little bug of doubt lurking in the far corner of my mind. If Vayle had me arrested, that doubt would be very gravely strengthened. But if he didn't, I should know for certain. It would mean that he dared not take the risk.

I looked at him. He was still watching me, leaning on his elbow against the mantelpiece. "Well?" I said.

"Well?" he countered. And then added: "Suppose you explain what this is all about?" A slight movement of the eyes indicated the litter of books and papers that covered the floor.

"I said: "I think you know the explanation."

He appeared to hesitate. Then he nodded slowly. "Yes,

perhaps I do. I heard about the telegram you tried to send to your newspaper. I wanted to talk it over with you there and then. But Wing-Commander Winton wouldn't hear of it. He said the matter must be left to your own officer. I see I should have insisted. It would have saved this—" he paused to choose his word—" this sacking of my rooms."

"You didn't by any chance ask for me to be transferred immediately to another unit?" I suggested.

"No," he said, and he sounded sincere. He indicated one of the big easy-chairs by the fire. "Sit down and we'll talk this thing over." His voice was quiet, yet there was a firmness about it. It was a voice to be obeyed.

But I stood my ground. "I prefer to stand," I said. I was desperately in need of all the confidence I could muster, and I knew how small it would make me feel to sit here with his standing and talking down to me.

He shrugged his shoulders. "As you please," he said. "First, perhaps, it would be as well for me to mention that it is in my power to have you arrested with very unpleasant results to yourself."

"I don't think you will do that," I said. "You have too much at stake to take a risk of that sort."

"Oh!" His thick eyebrows went up. For a second I sensed that I had him at a disadvantage. He wasn't sure of something. "That brings us to the point I want to discuss with you. Perhaps you would explain just why you suspect me of being a Nazi agent?"

"How did you know I suspected you of being a Nazi agent?" The question came pat from my lips almost before I knew I had spoken. "In my wire I only asked for information about you."

"My dear boy, the C.O. told me all about the whole wretched business." His voice sounded patient.

"Then you know why I suspect you."

"I know what you told Wing-Commander Winton. I want you to tell me, so that we can discuss the points at issue. It seems to me," he added, "that it is much better to thrash this matter out. Having met you and knowing something of your background, I am not fool enough to doubt the integrity of your actions. It wouldn't give me any satisfaction to have you arrested, knowing the reason you have broken into my rooms." He sank down in to the armchair behind him and waved me to the one on the other side of the heath. " Now," he said, as I sat down, " What exactly is the trouble?"

I hesitated. I couldn't very well sit there dumb and say, " I won't tell you." It would be too childish. Besides, the man had a right to know why I suspected him and I couldn't see that it would do him any harm. So I told him about the way in which the Jerry pilot had dried up and about the plan to immobilise the fighter 'dromes of which he had spoken. " If there is a plan," I said, " and it's my belief the fellow spoke the truth, it could only succeed with inside help. That help would presumably have been planted some time back, and would have achieved a sufficiently strong position to be a decisive factor." I stopped. There seemed nothing more to say.

" And you think I am at Thorby for that purpose?" he said.

I nodded, uncomfortably aware of the persistence of his gaze.

He heaved himself up a little in his chair and threw his cigarette end into the fire. " The point for me to make is that you are suspecting me on what appear to be the most trivial grounds. I won't press that point, however, because obviously you believe those grounds to be sufficient. No doubt your suspicions are supported in your own view by the fact that—and I presume you know this—I spent many years in Germany teaching at the Berlin University and that I came to this country in 1934."

He paused, and since he seemed to expect it of me, I nodded.

" I think the best thing for me to do is to give you a short résumé of my life and leave you to think it over. Perhaps you don't believe it at the moment, but we're both aiming at the same thing. I, with my knowledge of tactics, am trying to help the staff here to carry out their duties in defending this country whilst at the same time doing what I can to help the men in their studies. My object is the same as yours in standing to your gun. And because we're both working to one end, I'd prefer to settle this matter amicably. But, understand this," he added, " I think my work here, which is partly in the nature of research, is important. And I don't intend to have it nullified because of the sudden panic-prejudice against any one with any connections with Germany. If I had you arrested now, I don't doubt you would press your accusations. You would probably be severely dealt with, but at the same time the authorities might consider it advisable at the present time to relieve me of my duties. I am too interested in my work not to fight like hell to prevent any risk of that happening."

His gaze was fixed intently on me. Faintly in the quiet of the room I heard the sirens go. He took no notice. " As a newspaper man, I am presuming that you are intelligent," he said. " I hope you understand my position. Now for the background. I was born in this country. My father was a naturalised German, my mother was half Irish, half Scotch. I was educated at Repton and Cambridge, and when I left the university my father, who was a business man of many interests connected with the foreign fruit trade, sent me abroad to learn the business from his various branches. Oh, I should say that in the last war he continued his business. I was still at school then. I just missed it, though I tried to volunteer. In 1927 I settled in Germany. I had found I wasn't interested in business as such, and when a job at the Berlin University came my way I took it. I remained there over the difficult period of the slump and the Nazi landslide. I stuck it for a time, but when the pogroms started, I decided it was time to get out." He shifted in his chair and lit another cigarette. As an afterthought, it seemed, he said, " Perhaps I should mention that my father was a Jew. Originally the name was Veilstein. But when he

96

became naturalised he changed it to Vayle." He blew a cloud of smoke ceilingwards. "Now, is there anything you would like to ask me? I think you'll find little difficulty in checking-up on what I've just told you when you have the opportunity."

"There's just one point," I said. "Did you know a girl called Elaine when you were in Berlin?"

He seemed a little surprised at my question. Then suddenly his brow cleared. "Ah, Elaine Stuart, you mean? She is a Waaf." I saw his eyes, in a quick glance, had taken in the wallet lying on the mantelpiece. "No doubt you saw a photograph of the two of us in that wallet. She was a student in Berlin in 1934. A lovely girl. I was very fond of her. Now she is here, and we were able to see something of each other again. It is one of those coincidences——" He spread his hands in a gesture that was essentially foreign.

Then suddenly a look of concern showed on his face. "You haven't taken that photograph, have you?"

I felt a guilty flush creep into my cheeks. I wanted to say "No." I wanted to keep that photograph, just in case. But instead I found myself saying, "I'm afraid I did. It looked as though it might be important at the time. I'm so sorry." And I handed it back to him.

"Thank you very much." His politeness seemed so unnecessary when it was his own property. "Is there anything else you want to know?" he asked.

At the moment my mind was a blank. I could think of nothing.

He rose to his feet. "Then perhaps you would think this matter over very carefully before doing anything further. And if you do think of any points after you've left here, do come and talk them over before you jump to conclusions —especially if it is likely to involve searching my rooms again in an attempt to find something that will help you." He smiled a little ruefully and for the moment he seemed very human. "I was hoping to get some work done before going to bed, but now I must clear up after you."

. I had risen to my feet also, and he led me out to the front door. "I think you will find this an easier way out," he said and, smiling, held out his hand.

I shook it, and the next second I found myself on the narrow stairs leading to the recreation rooms. And above me was the little green-painted front door, shut as I had seen it before. I went down and retrieved my washing things from the chair on which I had left them, and went out. It was very dark now, though searchlights illumined the sky to the south-east, and it was as though the whole fantastic escapade had never been. It seemed so unreal there in the reality of the dimly seen, familiar shapes of the aerodrome.

I looked at the luminous dial of my watch. I was surprised to find it was only just ten. So much seemed to have been crammed into that one hour. I broke into a run. Our detachment was due to take over at ten. I reached the gun-pit just in time. I expected to be questioned as to why I had been so long having a bath. But no one seemed to realise I had been longer than usual. They were all busy discussing the news in orders that we were now officially allowed to fire up to 20,000 feet, a thing we had constantly been doing ever since the Blitz started.

Chapter Six

THE ATTACK

We got little sleep that night. They seemed to come over in an endless stream. Sometimes we could see them in the searchlights. But we got no chance to fire. No 'planes went up from Thorby. It was unpleasantly cold with a chill mist rising from the valley. We were able to sleep from one to four, whilst the other detachment was on duty. But when we came on again at four an occasional machine was still drifting home and the All Clear did not go until just before Stand-to.

I had plenty to occupy my mind during those long cold hours. Vayle's attitude, after all, had not been unreasonable, and I was only too conscious of the fact that my suspicions, which had at one time seemed so certain, were founded on little more than conjecture. What had impressed me, I think, more than anything was the frank and easy way in which he had explained the photograph. After all, one does suddenly meet old acquaintances in strange places. There were Marion Sheldon and John Nightingale to prove that coincidences of that kind are not uncommon. Yet I refused to believe that I wasn't on the right track. Vayle was a clever man with a hypnotic personality. And after all, he had not had me arrested. My own explanation of this was, I felt, as good as his—though I had to admit that his was reasonable enough.

It was lucky that I did have something to think about, for during our later period of duty I found myself alone on one side of the gun pit whilst the rest were congregated round Bombardier Hood on the other, talking in low tones. I did not notice this at first. When I did I wandered over to the group, thinking they were discussing something of general interest. As I came up to them I heard Hood saying, " Well, anyway, that's what Langdon told me "

" I'd like to know——" Chetwood began, and then he saw me and stopped. There was an awkward silence. The group gradually broke up. I was uncomfortably aware that I was the cause.

I lit a cigarette and went out of the pit and got a deck-chair. I remembered once being sent to Coventry at my prep. school. The sensation was much the same. But lying in my deck-chair with my eyes half closed, it seemed so transient and unimportant.

Time and again I went over my encounter with Vayle and all the papers I had been through in his rooms. But I got no further forward. I felt stale. And I had a sort of feeling that things were developing. Every now and again I noticed the little group near the telephone, which had re-formed. I was conscious, too, of the fact that I was at any rate partly the subject of conversation, for occasionally they glanced over in my direction.

I wished Langdon were in charge. He would have stopped it. Instead Bombardier Hood and Chetwood were leading the discussion. Gradually the sense of being an outcast intruded on my thoughts. I began to feel uneasy, though common sense told me that it wasn't important. It was getting on my nerves. I found myself glancing more and more often in their direction. And every time one of them seemed to be watching me with a stealthy, almost furtive glance. I had a sudden sense of being trapped—caged like a prisoner. My superiors were against me. And now, it seemed, I was becoming cut off from my own companions. Even Kan, whom I had got on with so well, was there, glancing surreptitiously in my direction when he thought I wasn't looking.

At last I could stand it no longer. I rose to my feet and went across to them. They watched me in silence as I approached. There were Hood and Chetwood and Kan standing a little apart from the rest, Micky and a small man called Blah whose nose and dark, wavy hair betrayed his nationality. He had replaced Fuller, who was billet orderly. The undercurrent of hostility was almost defiant. Their antagonism was that of uneasy consciences. I sensed with pleasure that they were almost afraid of the fact that I was going to take the initiative.

The knowledge of this gave me confidence. "Don't you think that you've discussed me amongst yourselves long enough without making any comments you wish to make about me to my face." I tried to appear off-hand, but the tremor in my voice betrayed my emotion.

"I don't follow you." This from Bombardier Hood, and there was the inevitable truculence in his tone.

"I can't put it very much plainer." I turned to Kan. "Perhaps you'd tell me exactly what the trouble is."

He glanced uneasily at Hood. "It's nothing, really, dear boy. I mean it's not important, what."

"That's right. Not important at all," Chetwood put in.

Then out of the blue Micky put in : " Not important ! Cor, stone me. You blokes make me sick. You take a man's bloody character away, crowing over it like a lot of old women, yet you daren't say a word to 'is face."

" Thanks, Micky," I said. I turned to the others. I felt suddenly angry with them. " Now then, let's have this out. What was it that Langdon told you, Bombardier Hood?" I asked.

He hesitated a second. Then, with a slight shrug of the shoulders, he said : " Well, if you want to know, Sergeant Langdon was told in the sergeants' mess that the Jerry pilot we brought down mentioned something about a plan to capture British fighter stations when he was questioned by the Intelligence officer. What we're wondering is just exactly what it was that you and the Jerry found to talk about."

" We noticed you pretty soon shut up when Winton and Vayle came along," put in Chetwood.

" All right," I said. " Here's the whole conversation as I remember it." When I had told them all the German had said, I added : " Next time you want to accuse any one of being a Nazi, have the guts to discuss the matter with him direct."

As I turned away I felt that the little sermon might just as well be applied to myself and my suspicions of Vayle. When I next glanced round at the group it had broken up somewhat. Hood was standing by himself. Of one thing I was certain. I had made an enemy of Hood. He was not the man whom you could put in an ignominious position with impunity. He was too much on his dignity. But I didn't care. It was too trivial to worry about.

Then somebody—Kan, I think it was—remembered that it was now Friday. For a time I was forgotten in an animated discussion of what, if anything, might be expected to happen. It produced a queer change in the mood of the pit. Micky began muttering to himself. He looked old and rather pinched. Any sort of strain seemed to cause the flesh to sag on his skull. I imagine he had had a hard life.

I glanced round the pit. Dawn was beginning to break, and in that pale light it was incredible how white, almost ill, every one looked. God! how tired we were at that time!

We got to bed again at six thirty—all except an air sentry. It was worth missing breakfast for the sake of that extra sleep. When I woke up again, it was half-past nine and the Tannoy was going. "Mussolini's act in declaring war at that precise time was a dagger in the back of stricken France. This dictator has thoroughly played the part of a jackal to his——" It was a Tannoy test with extracts from the previous day's papers.

I ate some chocolate whilst getting into my clothes, and then went down to the barrack block to get a wash. I was just crossing the square when the Tannoy blared out, "Attention, please! Attention, please! Tiger Squadron to readiness immediately." Even though I was alone I could not help laughing. The announcer had a marked lisp, all his R's were pronounced as W's. The roar of aircraft engines being revved up awoke on the flying field. Almost immediately the Tannoy ordered: "Tiger Squadron scramble. Tiger Squadron scramble immediately. Scramble." The lisp was very marked in the word "scramble", which became "scwamble". Then: "Swallow-tail Squadron stand by."

I hesitated. Was there time for a shave? I was half-way across the square, within fifty yards of the wash-house. I might just manage it. But I did hate the idea of being caught by a flap with my face covered in lather. I decided to risk it. But I had not reached the edge of the square before the Tannoy called Swallow-tail Squadron —that was the new one—to readiness immediately. That decided me to turn back. With both squadrons going up a flap must be imminent. As I recrossed the square, Tiger Squadron roared overhead in four flights of three.

"Good-morning."

It was a girl's voice. I turned. Marion Sheldon was standing there, looking very slim and boyish.

"Don't we know each other any more?" she said, smiling.

"What do you mean?" I asked a little vaguely. The truth is, I was wondering what this activity portended and trying rather unsuccessfully to quieten the fluttering of my stomach.

"Why, you walked right past me and cut me dead." She laughed. "What were you thinking about so intensely?"

"Oh, nothing," I replied. "How's things? Finished those fatigues yet?"

"Not quite. Two more days." She came forward so that she was quite close to me. I remember thinking how beautifully clear the whites of her eyes were and how ridiculously tip-tilted and saucy her nose looked. "What happened last night?" she asked. "I was so worried about you."

I told her briefly. When I had finished she said: "I'm glad it wasn't altogether wasted. Did you by any chance find out his Christian name?"

I thought for a moment, trying to recall it from the letters I had glanced through. "Joshua, I think," I said. "Yes, Joshua."

Lightly her feet moved in a little war-dance. "It all fits in," she said. "Elaine was talking in her sleep last night. I've got the next bed to hers. I woke up to hear her saying, 'I won't stay, Joshua, I won't stay. You must get me out.' Then there was a lot of gibberish I couldn't make any sense out of. Then: 'You must get me away, Joshua. You must. They'll hit the hangars.' What's that suggest to you? I should add that she got up this morning looking positively haggard and was as jumpy as anything."

The chill in my stomach told me what it suggested to me. But I didn't see any point in frightening her unnecessarily. "Did she say anything else?"

"Oh, quite a lot, but just a jumble of words. She kept on talking about her birthday and Cold Harbour Farm—that's the name of a book, isn't it?"

"No, Cold Comfort Farm," I told her, and we laughed.

"Of course it is," she said. "Anyway, there was nothing else of interest, only what I've told you."

At that moment the sirens began to go in the distance. I glanced round the square. A soldier on a bike with tin hat on and gas mask at the alert came pedalling down the roadway from our orderly room. "Here it is!" I said. "Take post! I thought we shouldn't have long to wait." It was Mason on the bike. I waved to him to acknowledge that I had received the summons. "You're not on Ops. to-day, are you?" I asked Marion.

"No, I've just come off," she said. "Why?"

"Thank God!" I exclaimed. "See that you get into a shelter when there are alarms on. I must go now. Cheerio." I waved my hand to her. As I broke into a run, the Tannoy announced Preliminary Air-Raid Warning. "All personnel not servicing aircraft or on ground defence to take cover." Every one began running—the guards to their posts, the rest to the dug-out shelters.

Just as I reached the edge of the flying field itself, Micky came up with me, riding Langdon's bicycle. "All go, ain't it, mate," he said. But his cheerfulness was very forced. His eyes looked wildly bright in the pallor of his face. As he rode on I thought that probably there were bombees, just as there were murderees. And if ever there was a bombee, I thought Micky must be one.

Most of the detachment were already in the pit by the time I got there. "There's a big raid crossing the coast," I heard someone say. I put my tin hat on and my gas mask at the alert. "You'd better look after that 'phone," Langdon told me. There was the usual scramble for cotton-wool. That was before every one was issued with proper ear-plugs. On a three-inch it is absolutely essential to have something in your ears. The trouble is that the gun is an old naval weapon converted for anti-aircraft work, and in order to get the necessary degree of elevation the recoil had been reduced from two feet to eleven inches with a consequent big increase in the noise of the charge.

" Attention, please! Attention, please! Swallow-tail Squadron scramble! Scramble!"

A car swept by carrying pilot officers from the mess to the dispersal points Severa. mcre of them came running down the roadway. They were in full kit. Among them I recognised John Nightingale He was running with that easy, shambling gait of his. As he passed our pit he waved his hand to me. I acknowledged the salute.

" That's Nightingale, isn't it?" asked Kan.

" Yes, we were at school together," I said. I couldn't help it. I glanced first at Hood, then at Chetwood. In view of their recent attitude, I felt it was almost a claim to respectability to know the ace leader of the new squadron.

Nightingale had disappeared into the dispersal point just past our pit. The sound of engines revving was shatteringly loud. A moment later his 'plane came out of it. He had the hood of the cockpit thrown back, and I saw him wave to his crew. The 'plane's number was TZo5. He slid the hood over his head and the 'plane taxied at a tremendous rate over to the start of the runway. Where aircraft from the dispersal poins were already gathering.

The 'phone went as the squadron began to take off. I picked up the receiver. " Four," I said as our number was called out. " Hold on a minute," came the voice of Gun Ops. " There's a plot coming through." I waited. Then: " There's a formation of about two hundred 'planes twenty-five miles away to the south-east flying north-west. Height, twenty thousand feet."

I passed on the information to Langdon. The pit received the news in silence. We were accustomed by now to big formations. But I knew what every one was thinking. I was thinking it too. Was Thorby their objective?

" Attention, please. Attention, please!" The Tannoy again. " Attack alarm! Attack alarm! All personnel to take cover immediately. Take cover immediately. Attack alarm! Off."

We waited, tense, watching the sky. It was very blue, except for little wisps of cloud high up. Swallow-tail Squadron disappeared, tiny specks, climbing south-eastwards. Langdon had the glasses. Every now and then he searched the sky in an arc south and east. Though it was only a little after ten, it was very hot in the pit. The glare of the sun was terrific, so that one's eyes felt hot and tired trying to see little specks that would only show when the sun glinted on them high up in the azure bowl of the sky.

"They'll be coming right out of the sun," said Helson.

"Yes, it's just right for them," added Blah. "We won't be able to see a thing." He was nicknamed Blah because he had a rather exaggeratedly aristocratic voice and was fond of words.

"Cor, you're just the kiddy for 'em if they land," said Micky. "You better lose that identity disk of yours, I tell you—that is, if you've got your religion down as Yiddish."

We laughed. It was a relief to laugh at something. Blah laughed too. "I've already lost it," he said. "The trouble is I can't lose my nose."

"You could cut it off," suggested somebody.

"Spoil my beauty! Kan wouldn't give me a part after the war if I did."

"Listen!" said Bombardier Hood.

Faintly came the sound of distant engines, flying high.

"Sounds like them," Chetwood said.

"Christ! And not a single fighter of our own in sight," said Kan.

The throb grew louder. "Did that Jerry really say we were to be bombed to-day?" Micky asked me.

I nodded.

There was silence

"Cor, I'd like to git at 'em wiv a baynet. Come down, you bastards! Come down!" Micky's face was strained as he muttered his challenge to the sky. He turned to Langdon. "Wot d'you think, John. Is it our turn to-day?"

" Oh, give it a rest," said Bombardier Hood.

" Look! Up there!" Chetwood was pointing high up to the north-west. " It glinted in the sun just for a second."

We strained our eyes. But none of us could see anything, though we could hear the throb of the engines very plainly now. The sound seemed to come from the direction in which he was pointing.

" There it is again," Chetwood said. " I can see them all now." He began to count. " Twenty-one, I make it."

" Yes, I see them," said Fuller.

Langdon was searching with his glasses. I strained my eyes, but could see nothing. A 'plane may be quite easily visible, yet if you haven't focused your eyes for the correct distance you can't see it.

" Here, you take a look," said Langdon, handing Chetwood the glasses. " If there are only twenty-one I don't expect it's Jerry. But a squadron may have got over London without being spotted."

Chetwood took the glasses. After a moment he said, " It's all right. They're Hurricanes."

The 'phone rang.

A queer chill feeling spread inside me as I listened to the voice from Gun Ops. I put the receiver back and turned to Langdon.

" Come on, mate, tell us wot it is," Micky said before I could open my mouth.

" That first raid has been broken up," I said. " But there's another raid just crossing the coast. There are fifty bombers escorted by two very large formations of fighters. The bombers are at twenty thousand and the fighters at twenty-five and thirty thousand."

Nobody spoke. Unconsciously we all began watching the sky again. Micky was muttering to himself. I glanced round at the upturned faces. We were a scruffy-looking lot. Hardly any of us had managed to get a shave that morning. And though we were all burnt brown with the sun, our skin looked pale and tired under the tan.

Up above, the two squadrons of Hurricanes were

circling over the 'drome. Every now and then the tail-arse Charlie of each squadron—that is, the 'plane that weaves from side to side across the formation to guard its rear—sparkled like a pin-point of silver tinsel in the sun.

I don't know how long we waited, watching the sky. It seemed an age. Nothing happened. Only those two squadrons circling and circling. It was the first time we had ever had two squadrons patrolling the base. Time seemed to pass without our knowing it. There was very little conversation. Even Micky, always full of wisecracks, was silent. The strain of waiting was telling on every one.

Suddenly the Tannoy blared forth again. "Attention, please! In a few moments aircraft will be landing for refuelling and rearming. All crews to stand by. The 'planes are to be got into the air again as quickly as possible. All crews stand by. Off."

"Must be some fighting somewhere," said Chetwood.

"Wish they'd fight nearer here," said Micky. "I'd like to see the Jerries tumbling down and the old gun going bang, bang, bang! Wouldn't half put the wind up 'em, I tell you. Eh, John?"

"You may regret that wish yet, Micky," Langdon said.

I glanced at my watch. It was ten-past eleven. Those raids must surely have been turned back. I looked up at the sound of a 'plane much nearer than any we had yet heard. It came in fast and low from the east. "What is it?" someone asked.

"Hurricane," Langdon told him.

It was one of Tiger Squadron. It circled the 'drome only once and then landed very bumpily. The crew were ready with the petrol lorry. Other aircraft began to straggle in—one with his tail badly shattered by a cannon shell, another with a wing riddled. Mostly they landed shakily in their haste. Some did not even bother to circle the 'drome once, but landed on the grass regardless of the slight wind.

The crews worked like fiends, filling their tanks and reloading their guns. Most of them were off again in little over ten minutes. Others began to come in. Several of Swallow-tail Squadron, Nightingale amongst them. And one or two Spitfires from another 'drome. I saw Nightingale go off again, and wondered if it felt much different than to stay down here waiting to be bombed.

A quarter to twelve. The pit seemed easier now—less strained. It looked as though the raid had petered out, though obviously fighting was still going on. Twice we had rung Gun Ops., but they knew nothing more.

Then suddenly someone said, "Listen!"

Faintly came a low, solid-sounding hum. It was very far away. We looked up at the two squadrons overhead. They were still circling. Then the Tannoy went again. "Attention, please! Attention, please! Mass formation attack alarm! Mass formation attack alarm! All aircraft that can be got off the ground to take off immediately. All aircraft scramble!"

Uncontrollable, my heart was suddenly in my mouth. It was the first time we had had a mass formation attack alarm.

The sound grew steadily louder. There was no throb about it. Only a deep hum. The aerodrome was alive with revving engines and figures buzzing like flies round every dispersal point as the 'planes were got into the air. And then, as suddenly, the place became dead. The 'planes had gone, black dots in the sky, rapidly dwindling as they scattered, some unfuelled, some unarmed, some almost unserviceable, and one or two Miles Magister trainers. Not a soul was to be seen over the whole landing field, and not a 'plane, save those few incapable of taking the air. Only the heat blazed on the tarmac, making the air dance above it.

"There they are. Look!"

I turned and, shading my eyes, gazed up in the direction Bombardier Hood was pointing. He began counting. And then gave it up. "God! There are more up above

See them?" For the moment I could see nothing. There was not a cloud in the sky now— even the little wisps had been burnt out of it. I strained my eyes until I was seeing a myriad tiny specks of light in the heat. I closed them and shook my head. All the time the noise of engines was getting louder. It was coming up from the south-east. Langdon was gazing intently up through his glasses. I could see our fighters. I watched them as they ceased circling and streaked off into the sun. Then suddenly I saw the approaching formation. It was quite clearly visible as our fighters raced to meet it. It seemed unbelieveable that I had not been able to see it before.

The Jerries were massed in solid formation at about twenty thousand feet—dark dots against the blue sky. And above them more, just specks of tin that caught the sun. The gun barrel moved slowly up as the layers followed the approach of the formation. Langdon still watched it through his glasses. At length he lowered them. " I think it's us," he said very calmly. " Fuse twenty-five. Load!"

Bombardier Hood set the fuse of the shell he had ready beside him on the parapet and handed it to Fuller, who rushed it to the gun, Micky rammed it home with his gloved hand and the breach-block rose with a clang. The layers reported On.

Langdon waited. I felt chill, though the glare of the sun was terrific. The heavy drone grew louder every second. Even without glasses I could make out the shape of them.

" Junkers 88," pronounced Langdon.

" Must be about fifty of 'em," said Hood.

" Them's fighters up above, ain't they?" asked Micky.

Langdon nodded. " Swarms of them."

It was impossible to see the shape of the fighters with the naked eye. But I could see that they were spread out in a great fan formation above and behind the bombers.

Suddenly, out of the glare of the sun, came more 'planes in a wide sweep. " There go our fighters," cried someone. We all watched, breathless. Twenty-one against more than two hundred. It seemed so hopeless—such futile heroism. My fists were clenched and my eyes were tired as I strained upwards. I wanted to look away. But the sight of those few 'planes—British 'planes—sweeping in to the attack of that huge formation fascinated me. I felt a surge of pride at being of the same race and fighting side by side for the same things as those reckless fools.

The bomber formation came on steadily, almost slowly. There was the inevitability of a steam-roller about it. I thought of the Armada and Drake's frigates. But in this case the enemy had a superabundance of frigates themselves. Down they came upon those two defending squadrons in steep, fierce dives. The squadrons broke before they had reached the bombers. But I saw one or two get through to that steady attacking formation. The solid hum of aircraft rose to a furious snarl as we began to get the noise of those steep dives with engines flat out. And then above the noise of revved engines came the sound of machine-gun fire. It was a noise that set one's teeth on edge. It was like tearing calico.

One bomber fell away from the formation, smoke pouring from it. I heard myself shouting excitedly. I was too worked up to have a very clear impression of what was happening. Every one in the pit was muttering or shouting with excitement. Another bomber fell, but it pulled out of its dive and made for home. The air was full of the roar of engines and the distant chatter of machine-gun fire. It was impossible to make out our own fighters from the Messerschmitt 109's. All were inextricably mixed in a milling, dog-fighting mass. But the bomber formation came inexorably on. And high above it the topmost tier of defending fighters kept formation. In ones and twos our machines came racing to join in the fight, some almost certainly short of fuel and ammunition after fighting over the coast.

And above the din of the engines and the fight came the Tannoy: " Ground defences take great care before opening fire. Our fighters are attacking the formation."

But Langdon, who was watching through glasses, said : "Take the leading flight of bombers. Any one see any of our fighters there?"

No one could. The layers reported On. Langdon waited a moment, gauging the range. The formation seemed to be passing to the east of the 'drome now; it was well strung out in flights of three.

"Fire!"

The gun crashed. I saw the breech-ring recoil and flame and smoke pour from it. I heard the whistle of the shell as it left the barrel. Another ammunition number ran up with a second shell. Micky rammed it home and the gun fired again. The noise was shatteringly loud. Hood had several shells already fused. The ammunition numbers were holding them ready. I braced myself for the next shot.

Not till we had fired five rounds did I glance upwards. Four puffs of white smoke showed well amongst the leading flight. As I watched, another puff of smoke appeared just behind the leader. The 'plane seemed to buck and then dived away in a streamer of smoke. And as it fell it suddenly exploded. A flash and only a little cloud of smoke showed where a second before a German bomber had been.

"Fuse twenty-two!" Langdon yelled.

Hood worked furiously with the fuse key—a circle of metal which fitted over the nose-cap of the shell so that it could be turned and set to the correct fuse.

Steadily the gun went on firing. And in the intervals between our own shots I could hear the other three-inch cracking away furiously. Little cotton-wool balls of smoke marked the passage of the formation.

"Fuse twenty!"

They were almost east of the 'drome now. In a moment they would be past us, heading for London. I glanced away at the dog-fight between the fighters. And even in that glance I saw two 'planes spin out of the mêlée in a long spiral of smoke. The fight had moved almost over our heads. Suddenly the scream of a diving 'plane sounded above the din of the action. I looked quickly round.

For a second I was at a loss to know where it came from. Then I saw it. Just north of the 'drome it was, falling absolutely perpendicularly, its engines flat out. I saw it plan view as it dived out of control behind some trees. I saw the spout of earth and smoke it shot up. I felt slightly sick at the sight. I could imagine some poor devil fighting at the controls and then desperately trying to pull back a hood that had jammed. It had dived into the ground at quite 500 m.p.h. And all the time these thoughts were running in a flash through my mind I could still hear the growing crescendo of the engine. It was as though I had been shown in a dream what was going to happen. And then came the sickening crash, terrifyingly loud, to relieve my suspense.

I looked up again at the formation of Junkers. The leaders were turning slowly westwards, towards Thorby, puffs of smoke all round them. The gun kept up a constant fire. I was getting used to the noise now. My ears were singing, but I no longer braced myself involuntarily before each shot.

And as I watched the German 'planes bank I knew what was going to happen. And sure enough as they banked they began to drop into a dive. I had seen the same thing happen to Mitchet. Now it was our turn. Strangely enough, I felt no fear. I seemed outside myself and comfortingly detached. With a critical eye I seemed to watch the completely automatic actions of my body as it ducked down, head thrown back, watching those silvery eggs fall from beneath each 'plane.

It seemed an age that I waited, tense and expectant. The only sounds were the three-inches, the screaming engines of the dive-bombers and the more distant sound of machine-gun fire.

And then suddenly all hell seemed to be let loose on the 'drome. As the Jerries pulled out of their dives at about seven thousand feet, the Bofors and Hispano and Lewis guns all let loose. The red tracer shells of the Bofors, like little flaming oranges, could be seen streaming lazily up to meet the bombers.

Then a fountain of earth shot into the air just behind the dispersal point to the north of us and shook the pit. Pandemonium broke loose as bomb after bomb fell. All over the aerodrome great gouts of earth hung for a second in the air, and as they fell, others rose.

And all the time Langdon stood there easily, just behind the gun, controlling the fire. Many of the team were crouching against the parapet for shelter. But the layers were still on their seats and Micky was engrossed completely in the business of firing. There was a momentary pause when no shell was brought up to the gun, though Hood was still there fusing them. Without thinking, I ran across to the pit, grabbed a round and held it for Micky to punch home.

For the next few minutes I knew nothing of what was happening as my whole attention was concentrated on the task of keeping the gun supplied. All I knew was that outside that concentration of effort absolute pandemonium was going on. Shrapnel was flying all over the place, bits of metal whining as they flew through the air just above the pit.

Others began to join Fuller and myself in taking shells to the gun. We were beginning to get used to the continual crump of bombs which shook the pit as though there was an earthquake. I remember once hearing the whine of a bomb—it was particularly loud—and looking up to see the thing coming straight for us. Instinctively I fell flat on my face. It fell, a second later, barely twenty yards from the pit. The noise was deafening. Part of the sandbag parapet crumbled inwards and great clods of earth and stones fell all round us. One fellow—Helson, it was—was knocked right out. But a second later the old gun was going again. We got one 'plane, I know. We got it in the midst of its dive, and it continued straight on, crashing into one of the hangars and blowing up in a great burst of flame.

And in the midst of all this racket the telephone rang. It was just luck that I heard it. I dived for it. I picked up the receiver to find the message already coming through.

"——low to the south. Another raid coming in low to the south—— Very low. Another raid coming——" The voice from Gun Ops. sounded frightened and jerky.

"How near?" I cut in.

"Very near," came the answer.

I caught Langdon's arm and yelled the message into his ear. "Stop," he shouted. "Lay just over the hangars. Shrapnel, fuse two. Load!" The gun swung round.

Chapter Seven

AFTERMATH

It seemed such waste to cease fire and stay, waiting, with the gun pointing over the hangars, instead of firing at the dive bombers which were still coming down on us. To the south the sky was empty. It flashed across my mind that some fifth columnist might have tapped the line. But it didn't really matter, for we should have had to cease firing anyway. The weight of the attack was falling off as our own 'planes, reinforced by stragglers from other fighter stations and by reserve squadrons which had been thrown in, were worrying at the bombers, upsetting the precision of their dives and foiling their attempts to reform *en masse* as they pulled out of their attack.

The other three-inch had also ceased firing. There was only the roar of battle overhead and the dull thuds of the bombs falling on clay soil. For the first time since the action started I realised that my shirt was wet with sweat, yet I did not feel warm. In fact, I did not feel anything. I could have had my arm blown off and I wouldn't have noticed it. I understood then why men continue to fight at the height of battle though mortally wounded. I could have done the same then. It wouldn't have been heroism. I am not an heroic person. It was just that I had no feelings, recorded no impressions. I saw the hangar blazing where the Jerry had crashed, with the foam squad and other fire-fighters working to put it out. I saw half the officers' mess was blown in and one of the barrack blocks by the square was just a shell. I noticed that there were few bombs on the flying field, but that the surrounds had been well plastered. I just noticed these things. I did not think about them. I made no move to help Helson, who was still lying on the cinder floor of the pit, blood oozing from a cut on his forehead. No one moved to help him.

These observations took but a second. And then we heard the ominous sound—the whine of fast-flying aircraft low to the south. It grew in an instant to a roar that drowned the sounds above us. And then they were there, like magic, over the hangars. Strung out in a single line, they came fast and low—so low that I saw one of them lift his port wing to overtop the wireless mast by the main gates. They were not more than thirty feet above the barrack blocks as they laid their eggs. Wing tip to wing tip they seemed to be. I saw the bombs cascade from beneath their fuselages.

Sharply came Langdon's order : " Fire !"

The gun cracked. And at the same moment the whole camp seemed to lift in a pall of smoke and high-thrown masonry and earth. The remains of the half-demolished barrack block appeared to rise into the air, blasted into a thousand pieces. At the same time there was a roar like thunder. And against these black spouts of smoke and buildings that had risen like a solid wall across the camp the 'planes showed silver as they roared towards us through the hot sunlight. They seemed huge. Dorniers they were—Dornier 215's. I recognised the hammer head. They seemed to fill the whole sky. And amongst them a great puff of black smoke. Two of them rocked violently as our shrapnel smashed into them. But still they came on.

The gun cracked again and then again. The other three-inch was firing too. But it had no effect. They were already too near for the fuse we were using. They had split up now. Breaking into two formations in line astern, they swept up each side of the landing field. Suddenly

I was frightened. It was the first time I had felt frightened. For I knew in that instant, suddenly, what had been clear to my subconscious for some time : they were going for the ground defences. Not only the ground defences, but the personnel of the aerodrome as a whole. The bulk of the hangars stood clear and solid and undamaged against the pall of smoke and flame that was rolling over what had been the barrack blocks, the Naafi and the canteen. Yet I still stood there, fascinated, as the 'planes swept down on us.

A bomb fell close to Gun Ops. and another by an Hispano pit. A brick and concrete pill-box only fifty yards from us was hit. One second it was standing there, just as it had been a fortnight back, and the next it had disintegrated into a pile of rubble spewed callously into the air. And then the first 'plane was upon us. At point-blank range Langdon gave the order to fire, in the desperate hope that we should score a direct hit. I suppose we missed. At any rate it swept unfalteringly over us, its great wing span casting a shadow over the pit that seemed to me like the shadow of death. I could see the pilot, sitting woodenly in his cockpit. I saw his teeth bared and thought how it must take nerve to do what he was doing.

And as it swept past a little line of jumping sand ran along the top of the parapet. The rear gunner was firing at us. I ducked. But just before I ducked I saw the Bofors on our side of the 'drome open fire on the 'plane. It's little flaming oranges streamed towards it. And then one hit and another, bursting along the fuselage. The great 'plane staggered and then crumpled up and plunged towards the earth. I didn't see it crash. By this time the next plane was over us and the rear gunner was pumping a stream of bullets into the pit. Something struck the back of my tin hat, jerking my head forward so that for a second I felt my neck must have been broken. I heard it whine into the air. Then I was crouching down against the parapet for protection. Bullets sprayed along the cinder floor and punctured the sandbags in perfect symmetrical lines. Above the din I could hear the clang and whine as they hit the gun and ricocheted off.

And all the time Langdon stood erect and the layers remained on their seats and Micky continued to fire. It was fuse one now, and the noise of the charge seemed to be followed almost immediately by the burst of the shell. Hood was fusing the shells, crouched close to the ground, and the ammunition numbers ran up to the gun with them, bent almost double.

Incredible it seems, looking back, but only one man was hit—it was a lad called Strang, and he only had his hand torn by a ricochet. Yet as each 'plane swept over us, little darts of flame that were tracer bullets streaked into the pit. None, thank God, struck any of the open ammunition lockers.

Once Langdon shouted. A second later a piece of metal fell into the pit. One of our shells had burst very close to a 'plane. I sensed the stagger of the machine as its shadow crossed the pit.

From my crouched position I caught a glimpse of a Hurricane diving practically vertically on to the hangars. I thought it was going to crash. But it flattened out and came down on the tail of the sixth Dornier. The sound of its eight guns could be heard for a second above the din. The stabs of fire from their muzzles were visible even in the glare of the sun. It looked like one of those little war toys made in Japan that have a flint spark. I glimpsed the lettering on the fuselage—TZ05. Nightingale's plane! And my heart warmed to that daring piece of flying.

Automatically I had counted the 'planes as they came over. It was the fifth that we had damaged. And close on its tail as it went over us came the sound of the next one. And then something hit the parapet opposite me, covering me with loose sand and spilling the shells from a locker on to the floor of the pit. And as the parapet collapsed the 'plane passed directly over us, so low that if I had jumped up I felt certain I could have touched its wings.

And as the noise of it died away to the north, firing

ceased and everything was strangely quiet. I looked up at the cloudless blue of the sky. The dive attack was over, and all that remained of it was a ragged formation of 'planes heading south-eastwards, nose-down for home. And then in the unnatural quiet we heard a new sound—the crackle of flames.

I got to my feet and gazed round. Thorby looked a shambles. The whole camp to the south of the landing field was enveloped in smoke. Through it I could see the hangars, still largely intact. But the other buildings were broken and battered shells from which great tongues of flame leapt up clear against the background of black smoke. And between the camp and our pit stretched a profusion of bomb craters, like old mole hills.

There was no doubt about it: they had gone for personnel, not for the field itself or even the aircraft, of which, as it happened, there were quite a number in the hangars waiting to be serviced.

Heaven knows how many planes that German squadron had lost. We heard later that it was one of their crack squadrons. It had to be. It was a crazy, beautiful piece of flying. They must have known that Thorby was well defended before they undertook the flight. It would need nerve to take on such a job in cold blood. There was one down at the north end of the flying field, a crumpled wreck. And another had plunged into the scrub near the remains of the one we had brought down the other night; it was burning furiously. Others, too, must have been hit. And then the rest had to get home in the face of our fighters without height.

All the time I stood taking in the chaos that was Thorby, Langdon was yelling at me. But I was too dazed to take it in. "Go on! Get out of the pit! All of you. Can't you understand you're standing by a bomb? Get out!"

Suddenly I grasped it. I glanced at him wonderingly. Where was the bomb? I couldn't see one. I looked round the pit. Hood and Fuller were carrying Helson out. Chetwood was helping Strang. Others were standing about, dazed, or following Hood sheep-like out of the pit. Micky was cowering in a corner, sobbing, white-faced and panic-stricken. He had remained at his post throughout the action, calm and unperturbed by the hail of metal that had sung about him. Yet now that it was over, the reaction made a coward of him. Kan's face was chalk-white and he staggered slightly as he left the pit. Blah just stood there, dazed and pale.

"Get out or you'll be blown up." I realised that Langdon was yelling at me. He was pointing at the parapet in front of me. Only then did my brain function. The parapet had collapsed because a bomb had hit it—a delayed-action bomb. I turned again to find Langdon struggling with Micky. Between us we got him out of the pit, stumbling over the litter of shell cases. He was shaking like a leaf. Kan and Blah came with us, alive at last to the danger.

We took him into the hut. From there I looked back. Protruding from the broken parapet were the fins of a bomb. The nose was buried in the sand. Dropped from only thirty feet or so, it had not had the impetus to bury itself deeply. A cold chill ran down my spine as I realised what would have happened if it had been a percussion type instead of a delayed action. God! how lucky we had been!

"We've got to get it away from there," Langdon said. "Must get the gun into action as soon as possible."

"There's rope in the store hangar," I said. "Can I borrow your bike?"

"Yes, of course."

I took it and pedalled off down the roadway, weaving my way in and out between the craters. Anything for action. I was feeling very shaken. The smell of cordite was strong, especially round the craters, and as I neared the hangars the acrid smell of smoke filled my lungs. I passed what was left of the officers' mess and made for the square. As I did so I heard a single Tannoy loudspeaker ordering all men not servicing aircraft to report to the square for fire-fighting.

The chaos of that square was quite indescribable. It was bounded on three sides by blazing buildings. They had dropped incendiaries as well as H.E. The fire-fighting equipment was quite inadequate for the task. The smoke was blinding. It filled my eyes to choking point and made them run. Men and girls were running everywhere. Some were screaming. The place reeked with pain and nervous exhaustion. I passed a dug-out shelter which had been hit. They were getting the dead and wounded out. I felt slightly sick and was convinced I could smell the blood.

There was broken glass everywhere and my back tyre was soon flat. Ambulance and A.R.P. fire-pumps were beginning to come in from districts around. I reached the Educational without being knocked down. There was nothing left of it. The station hospital had gone, too. It was just a pile of rubble with one wall standing and the front door, upright in solitary splendour. A girl in a torn Waaf uniform staggered through the ruins and came out by the front door. She closed it carefully behind her. Her face and hair were coated with a thick dust of powdered masonry and her hands were bleeding.

I thought suddenly and sickeningly of Marion. Where had she been during the raid? Had she gone to a shelter? Of course she must have done. Was she in the one that had been hit? Questions passed through my mind unanswered. I knew that she meant something to me. What, my confused mind could not realise. All I knew then was that the memory of her face, those clear eyes, that tilted nose, that straight fair hair, hurt. It was like green grass and the river, like a mountain at sunset, against that chaos of broken brick. It was the glimpse of beauty in the midst of ugliness that hurt—the need for beauty that was out of reach. It was symbol of the best that was in me, chained to the horrors of man-made catastrophe that was the moment's reality.

I turned up the road leading to the rearmost hangar. Almost immediately I had to get off my bicycle. The road was full of rubble. This was where the bomber we had brought down had crashed. A whole hangar had collapsed like a pack of cards. The tail of the machine with the swastika on it was sticking up out of the ruins of the collapsed roof. It was a miracle it hadn't caught fire for the roof had been built of wood.

The hangar I wanted adjoined it on the other side. The road in front of me was blocked by the remains of the Naafi Institute. I left my bike and clambered through the ruins. The north wall was still standing and by keeping close to this the going was quite easy. At the farther end, where it adjoined the next hangar, part of the roof was still intact.

Smothered by the dust and smoke and intent on reaching the store hangar, where I knew I should find the rope I wanted, I did not see Vayle until I was right on top of him.

I looked up, startled. He was hardly recognisable. His clothes were torn and covered with dust and his usually well-groomed hair was dishevelled. There was something about his face that frightened me. Pain and bitterness seemed to mingle in the set of his mouth. And his eyes had lost their cold alertness and were fever bright. He looked at me without recognition.

I was just hastening on when I glanced down and saw the thing at his feet. It was the crumpled body of a girl. The face was drained of all colour, and the blood from the gaping wound in her head was congealing with the dust on her face and clothes. I hesitated. And then I realised that it was Elaine Stuart, and I hurried on. The memory of Vayle's wild dry eyes lingered with me as I passed into the store hangar.

She was dead, of course. No doubt of that. And she had meant a great deal to him. That wild dry-eyed look! I remembered the photograph. Why had he kept that all these years? And then a thought occurred to me. Suppose she had been his wife?

And in a flash I saw it all. The raiders had gone for personnel, not for the hangars. Vayle had known this. Elaine and he had gone to the hangars and not to the shelters. She, with a woman's premonition, had been afraid of this and had cried out in her sleep against it. But in the morning he had soothed her fears and now, because we had downed a bomber with a lucky shot, she lay dead at his feet.

I picked up a big coil of light rope lying beside a pile of flares. I could not help feeling sorry for the man. He had thought the hangars the safest place in the 'drome. I could imagine how he felt.

I had to go back the same way. The end of the other road I knew was blocked. And because of the piled-up ruin of the roof I had to pass quite close to Vayle. He looked at me. And this time into his dazed eyes came recognition. With it came a look of surprise that I did not quite understand. He seemed somehow shocked at the sight of me. I thought he was going to speak to me and I hurried by him. What was there I could say? The stricken look had never left his face though the expression had changed when he recognised me. For the moment at least the girl meant more to him than all his plans.

I retrieved my bike and rode back to the square, the rope slung over my shoulder. It was heavy and I found it difficult to negotiate the scattered debris. Even in the short time I had been getting the rope, things had changed in the square. There were men everywhere, running to shouts of command. Three proper fire-engines had arrived, and more ambulances and A.F.S. fire-pumps. There were civilian cars too, doctors' cars mostly. And the dead and wounded were being laid out on the grass at the edge of the square. Hoses were being run out and great jets of water were being poured into the blazing blocks.

Clear of the square I passed an Army car with its engine running. There was no one in it. I realised suddenly that we should need something to tow the bomb away. I left Langdon's bike and commandeered the car.

It took me but a moment to get back to the gun site in it, bumping over the grass of the flying field because the roadway was too full of craters. Langdon grabbed the rope as soon as I pulled up. He did not hesitate, but ran straight to the bomb, paying the rope out as he ran. We watched, half expecting the thing to go off as he tied the end of the rope round the fins. He did it quickly, but he showed no trace of nerves. It was not the sort of thing you want to think about beforehand. Yet Langdon had known that he, as detachment commander, was going to do it, all the time I had been away getting the rope.

As he ran back I tied the other end of the rope to the rear bumpers of the car. The rope was about fifty yards long, but even so I did not feel very happy about it as I climbed back into the driving seat. I took the strain slowly in bottom. And as I moved forward with the full weight, I could feel the bump and slither of the bomb at the end of the rope as it followed me like some terrible hobgoblin.

But it was soon over. I left the thing well out on the flying field and, untying the rope, drove back to the site.

"That's marvellous of you, Barry," Langdon said as I got out of the car.

I felt myself blushing. Blushing had been an awful bugbear to me in my youth, but I thought I had grown out of it. "It's nothing to what you did," I said to hide my embarrassment.

"You'd better return the car now. And at the same time you can take Strang to the first-aid post. His hand is giving him a good deal of pain."

Strang protested. But he was as white as a sheet and, in spite of a rough-and-ready bandage, blood was dripping quite freely from his hand. They got him into the seat beside me and I drove the big car back along the edge of the field.

As I came into the square the one undamaged Tannoy that I had heard before announced : "Preliminary air-raid warning. All personnel not engaged in urgent work take cover. Preliminary air-raid warning."

The crowd in the square seemed to thin out like magic and vanish. I drove through the scatter to the nearest ambulance. I attracted the attention of a nurse who was trying to stop the blood of a poor fellow whose leg had been shattered. She seemed incredibly cool and impersonal. She glanced at Strang's hand whilst continuing to work on the man's leg, " You'll be all right for the moment," she told Strang. " Just stay around till we've patched up some of the worst cases. We'll soon fix that for you." She belonged to a Canadian ambulance unit.

I wanted Strang to get immediate attention. But a glance round told me that the staff of every ambulance in sight was equally busy. There was nothing for it but to let him stay and take his turn. An alarm was on and I had to get back to my site. With Thorby in its present disorganised state anything might happen. The great thing was that the guns should be fully manned.

I sat him down on the grass. " They'll fix you up in no time," I said. He did not answer. He was dazed with pain and loss of blood. I went back to the car.

I was just on the point of climbing into the driving seat when I noticed a civilian lying on the grass near by. Something about the white leathery skin of his face made me pause. Streaks of blood from a cut on his forehead showed scarlet on the white sweat of his face. His pale-blue eyes were wide and staring and his lips moved as he muttered to himself. His left shoulder and arm appeared to have been badly crushed. His clothes had been cut away from the shoulder and his hurt roughly dressed. It was his boots that brought recognition to my mind. They were clumsy hob-nailed boots—a workman's boots.

I went over to where he lay, groaning and muttering to himself. And as I stared down at him, I knew I was right. He was the workman who must have planted that incriminating diagram in my pay-book. " Well, serve him right," I thought. And I was just turning away when I heard his lips mumble : " It won't hurt you if you splash water over it."

Some childhood memory of playing boats. But because it was spoken in German and not with the slight Scottish accent I had last heard him using, it drew my interest. And I bent down to listen, remembering how Elaine's sleep babbling could have told me something. But it was partly gibberish, partly childhood memories that he mumbled. It was all in German and occasionally he got a word wrong or mispronounced it. If he were a German, and that seemed probable as he would surely babble his own language in his delirium, it seemed reasonable to suppose that it was a long time since he had been in Germany.

I bent closer. " I'm sorry you won't be with us for the day." I spoke in German. It seemed funny to be speaking of *der Tag* in another way. He showed no sign of having heard. I shook him and repeated my statement.

His eyes remained wide, unseeing and expressionless. But apparently my voice made contact with his subconscious, for he murmured : " I'm all right. I shall be there. I'm to drive one of the lorries." He tried to raise himself, his eyes sightless. " It'll be all right, won't it? Say it will be all right."

" But you won't remember what day it is," I suggested, still speaking German.

" Yes, I will." He mumbled so that I could scarcely hear him.

" I don't think so," I said. " You don't remember the day now."

" Yes, I do. Yes, I do. It's—it's——" He struggled desperately with his memory. " It's—— I pick the stuff up at Cold Harbour on——"

His moment of lucidity seemed suddenly to vanish. The sweat poured down his ashen face with the effort he had made. He relapsed into the uncouth babblings of his delirium. But I scarcely noticed it. My mind had grasped avidly at the vital point. Cold Harbour! Elaine had talked of a Cold Harbour Farm in her sleep. Cold Harbour was not a very common name.

I was excited. I began trying to draw him again. And when that failed I tried direct questions. But I could get no sense out of him though I shook the poor devil till the sweat turned the blood to water on his face with the pain of it.

In the end I had to give it up. I got back into the car

and drove it across to where I had first found it. Langdon's bike was still there. I was just mounting it when a lance-corporal dashed up and caught me by the arm. "What the devil were you doing with that car?"

I had just started to explain when a brass hat with red tabs all over him came panting up. I saluted. "What's all this?" he demanded. "My car. You took my car. Why?"

I told him.

"That's no excuse. Monstrous behaviour! Name and unit? Make a note of it, Corporal." And with a snort he disappeared inside the car. He was in a hurry to get off.

I rode back to the site. They were all in the pit. Nobody spoke. They were all watching the sky. They looked strained, terribly strained. I realised that my shirt was sticking to me. The air throbbed with the heat. I took my helmet off to wipe the sweat from inside it with my handkerchief. "Where's Micky?" I asked. Kan was at the firing position.

"He's not feeling very bright," Langdon said charitably. "He's gone to the shelter at the dispersal point over there."

"Not very bright!" said Bombardier Hood. "He's scared out of his wits. Can't take it."

"Well, we're none of us feeling very brave," said Langdon.

Mason suddenly arrived on a bike. He was the only link with Gun Ops., the telephone having been hit. But I didn't hear the plot he gave Langdon. I was staring at my steel helmet. There was a scarred dent on the back of it. On the back of it! And I was remembering just where I had been standing and which way I had been facing when that bullet had ricocheted off my helmet. And a cold shiver tingled up my spine as I remembered that I had been facing the field and all the planes had passed in front of me or over the pit. None had passed behind me. Yet the dent was on the back of my tin hat. I hadn't taken it off until this moment, so that I knew I had not had it on back to front. Besides, I remembered how my head had been jerked forward.

Somebody had fired at me from behind! And into my mind came a picture of the surprised look on Vayle's face as I had passed him in the hangar.

Chapter Eight

EVERYMAN'S HAND

I was scared. More scared than I had ever been in my life. I could stand up to bombing. I knew that now. There was something impersonal about being bombed—about war altogether. It was not a direct attack. The bomber was not trying for me personally. My life was in the hands of fate—always such a comforting thought. One took one's chance, and there was nothing one could do about it.

But this! This was totally different. There was nothing impersonal about an attempt to shoot one in the back. It wasn't just a random shot into the pit by some fanatical fifth colmnist, I knew that. I had been the specific target. This was murder, not war. I could face machine-gun bullets—again an impersonal attack. But a deliberate attempt on my life made my scalp crawl with fear. I did not take my chance with others. There was no comfortable feeling that my life rested in the hands of a kindly fate. I had to face this alone. I was under sentence of death at Vayle's orders. And I knew now why surprise had for a moment ousted the grief from his face when, standing beside Elaine's body, he had looked up to see me in the hangar.

I suppose I must have looked pretty scared, for John Langdon put his hand on my shoulder. "It was nice of you to tow that bomb for me," he said. "I couldn't have done it. I had expended what little nerve I had on tying the rope to the bloody thing."

His remark had the desired effect and, momentarily detached, I watched my ego warm to that kindly praise. It amused me, too, to think that my own fear was a particular and personal one. Every one else in the pit was scared of one thing—a further attack on the 'drome. And I didn't give a damn about that. I was scared because I was singled out for a murderous personal attack. And because their fear seemed trivial by comparison with mine, I experienced a sudden access of confidence. Their hostility seemed unimportant now, and I felt quite equal to any questioning.

But there was no hostility and no questioning. I had known what was going to happen, but I had stayed on the site. That and the business with the bomb put me right in their eyes. But Westley—poor little man, who had eventually obtained compassionate leave to attend his grandmother's funeral and had left early in the morning, came in for a good deal of discussion.

The 'planes came back in ones and twos to land as best they could on the pitted 'drome. The glare of the day wore slowly on. Time lagged in the heat. Exposed though we were, there wasn't a breath of wind and the drought-baked earth was hot to the touch. Anxiety and impatience combined with fear to nag at my tired mind. Would this interminable alarm never end? I wanted to find out what had happened to Marion—to see that she was all right. And John Nightingale hadn't come in. The All Clear had gone on the Tannoy soon after the alarm. But we had been kept at our posts. They were no doubt windy, as Langdon said.

Ogilvie came round in his car with chocolate, cigarettes and beer scrounged from the ruins of the Naafi. For once quite human, he stayed and chatted, apologising for keeping us standing-to.

Gradually the atmosphere in the pit changed, apprehension giving way to annoyance. Every one seemed to become morose. Kan scarcely raised a smile when, in reply to a question from Oggie, he described the raid as "Too, too utterly shattering, what, sir." The only bright spot was that his inexhaustible flow of personal supplies from Fortnum and Mason's saved us from experiencing any serious inconvenience at the loss of our lunch. For a time the sight of Micky slinking back from the shelter of the neighbouring dispersal point gave the pit a topic of conversation.

During the afternoon I got permission from Langdon to go over to the dispersal point and find out what had happened to Nightingale. But they knew no more than I did. He was missing—that was all.

Finally, at three-forty-nine we were allowed to stand-down. By that time I had forgotten my own fears in my anxiety to find out what had happened to Marion. And then, of course, Langdon had to pick on me to do the first air sentry. It was my turn, it was true. But I could have burst into tears with impatience.

I wasn't alone for long in the pit, for as soon as they had boiled some water on the primus, Langdon and Blah came out to clean the barrel and do a cursory examination of equipment. Half an hour of my hour's guard passed very quickly. But after that it began to drag. I had been almost continuously on the pit for six hours. Reaction from the excitement of the action had left me tired and dispirited. Fortunately this had one advantage in that it dulled my sense of fear. I was too weary to think, and so imagination, the source of all fear, was numbed. The glaring heat of the sun seemed undiminished. A mug of tea and some cigarettes were brought out to me.

I didn't seem hungry, but the tea was very welcome. And when I had finished it, I stood there in the sultry heat and stared at the wreck of Thorby, not consciously recording what my eyes saw. The fires were under control now and only an occasional wisp of smoke drifted up from the ruins. From where I stood there was little to show the fearful nature of the attack. The bulk of the hangars still stood intact, screening the desolation I had seen from the square. People came and went between the camp and the dispersal points, the cars weaving their way in and out among the craters that dotted the edge of the field. Lorry loads of Royal Engineers were brought out to fill up craters on the runways and to deal with D.A. bombs.

A car drew up just beyond the pit. It was an R.A.F. car and someone got out. I took no notice. I was watching a Hurricane, whose tail appeared to be badly damaged and whose undercarriage had failed to work, coming slowly in to a pancake landing.

"Excuse me, could you tell me what hospital Gunner Hanson has been taken to?"

It was a girl's voice. I turned, still watching the 'plane out of the tail of my eye. "What did you say?"

"Barry!"

I forgot about the plane. It was her voice. But my eyes were full of colours through staring into the sun. I did not recognise her at first. Her face was in shadow. But I knew the cut of her hair. "You're all right, then." My voice sounded cold as I tried to hide my emotion. It was such a dull remark.

But she didn't seem to notice it. "It really is you, isn't it?" There was a momentary break in her voice.

"As far as I know," I said, and we laughed and the spell of awkwardness was gone.

"I didn't recognise you in your tin hat," she said. "You see I—I wasn't expecting to find you here at all. I was told by a Waaf from the sick bay that a soldier with the name Hanson on his identity disc had been found in the square, badly wounded. I thought it must be you. But she didn't know what hospital he had been taken to.

"Well, thank God, there is apparently another Hanson in the camp," I said. "Where were you?"

"In a shelter at our quarters outside the 'drome. It might have been worse, I suppose. A bomb fell on the wing of the house and it collapsed on the end of our shelter, but no one was injured. Things are pretty bad down in the camp. All the barrack blocks are gutted, the Naafi, Station Headquarters and three shelters were hit. Have you seen the hut where the Guards and R.E.s were billeted?" I shook my head. "Absolute shambles. They're blown all over the place. Looks like one of those film shots of an American hurricane. And there's no gas, water or electricity." She hesitated. "I suppose you regard this as just a prelude?"

It was no use telling her "No." She wouldn't have believed it. I said: "The attack was against personnel and not against the 'drome itself. The runways are fairly clear of bombs." I left her to figure out the significance of that.

"You mean, they want to use it themselves—to land troops?"

We were silent for a moment, and I said: "It's lovely now, isn't it?"

It was not a very bright remark. But she understood what I meant. The peace and stillness of a late August day. It was so beautiful after the havoc. And again I found myself thinking of the river. It was such a perfect day for lazing in a boat. Marion in sailing rig—how well she would fit into the picture! How well she would fit into any picture that I could conceive!

I lowered my gaze hurriedly as she looked up at me. Strange that this should be such a perfect moment of beauty when all about us were the weapons and havoc of war. In that moment I achieved a wonderful sense of peace. The realisation that whatever the horrors and disasters a man has to face he can still find beauty came to me suddenly, together with knowledge that only man-made things could be destroyed by war. Whatever happened there was always the sun and the stars and the beauty of nature to be shared. My mind, alert now, grasped at that—they had to be shared. That was the secret of the enjoyment of beauty. Alone, beauty had always seemed so painful in its transience. Time never stood still so that you could hold a moment and keep it. But shared, the beauty of a moment seemed complete. Instead of being purposeless, except for the delight of one's gaze, it fulfilled itself by welding two personalities together. And in that brief moment that Marion stood there in silence I felt that we were very near. And I was content that it should be so.

The spell was broken by footsteps approaching the pit. It was my relief. "Are you going to Ops. now?" I asked her.

"No. I ought to go back to billets and help with the clearing up. They got the wing in which I sleep, so I've lost most of my things."

"I'm sorry," I said. "I'll walk down with you as far as the main gates."

I handed over to my relief and then clambered over the parapet and joined her. We didn't say much at first and this time the silence was an embarrassed one. But suddenly she asked me if I'd seen anything of Vayle. "As far as I was able to discover, he remained in the camp," she said.

I told her of Elaine Stuart's death and of how I had found Vayle standing over her in the deserted and half-ruined hangar. I went on, of course, to tell her of the workman who had spoken in German in his delirium and who had mentioned Cold Harbour Farm.

Then my brain suddenly clicked.

"What was it Elaine said in her sleep about her birthday?" I asked.

"I don't really think it had any bearing on what you're after," she said slowly. "She just said, 'It's my birthday,' I think she said that twice. It was mixed up with a whole lot of babbling, which I couldn't understand at all. It's all so hazy now. I was half asleep myself. In fact, I'm not at all certain I didn't dream it. I suppose she really did say something about Cold Harbour Farm. Funny that the workman should have mentioned it too."

"I must try and trace that fellow," I said. "In the meantime, can you find out when her birthday would have been?"

"I expect so. Somebody is bound to know it. But do you really think——" She stopped with a slight shrug of

133

her shoulders. " I mean, as a deadline it doesn't seem very satisfactory."

I was only too conscious of this. " But I've nothing else to go on."

" What are you going to do then?"

" I don't know. I was thinking of that dent on the back of my tin helmet. Find out where Cold Harbour Farm is. And if Elaine's birthday was, in fact, on one of the next few days, I should assume there was some connection."

" Yes, but what can you do about it?"

" God knows!" I said. " Time will tell, I suppose."

She suddenly took my arm. " Don't do anything foolish, Barry. It's a matter for the authorities."

" Yes," I said. " But I've nothing concrete to tell them. You can't expect them to act on a mixture of conjecture and doubtful coincidence."

We were nearing the shell of the officers' mess, and I suddenly saw a familiar figure coming towards us from the direction of the hangars. " Oh, good!" I said. " John Nightingale is all right. He was missing."

" I'm glad," she said. " I don't know him personally, but he's got a wonderful reputation in his squadron."

He recognised me as I saluted him. " Glad to see you're still alive in this shambles," he said.

" And you," I said. " All I could find out from the lads at your dispersal point was that you were missing. What happened?"

" Oh, nothing much, except that I was ignominiously brought back by car."

" Well, the last I saw of you was diving on top of one of those low flying 'planes. That was you, wasn't it? It was a very steep dive to within a few hundred feet."

" Yes," he admitted. " I bagged a couple of 'em, but the second one put a burst right across me. Got the petrol tank and smashed up the landing gear. Made a bit of a mess of the cockpit too. I just managed to pancake the old girl at Mitchet." He shook his head with a grin. " Lovely bit of flying," he said. " They were hedge-hopping all the way from Tunbridge Wells. They were so low as they topped the hill into Thorby that they ploughed through the tops of the trees."

" Their losses are going to be pretty heavy to-day, aren't they?" asked Marion.

" Well over the hundred, I should think," he said. " My squadron has bagged over thirty for the loss of four machines. You couldn't miss. We met them just after they had crossed the coast. We came at them out of the sun and swooped straight down on to the bombers. They were massed so thick they seemed to fill the sky in front of us. I got two before the first tier of fighters came down on our tails. Everything was a mix-up after that."

Understatement. Understatement. Understatement. Yet the scene was vivid in my mind. The huge mass formation of bombers, flying steady and unbroken even when attacked, the ugly black crosses plain on their silver wings. And above, the tiers of fighters waiting to pounce on any attackers. And the attackers when they came no more than a squadron or two at the most.

" What brought you down on the tail of our low-flying attack?" I asked.

" We got a radio message through. I could only spare one. We were badly outnumbered. By the way," he said, " I was in Town last night and I got in touch with your friend. He said he had already received a message from you."

I told him how Marion had managed to get a message through. Then I said : " Have any other fighter stations been attacked to-day?"

The reply was " Yes," and he named two of the biggest, both near the coast.

" What did they go for?" I asked. " The runways and hangars or the billets and ground defences?"

" Well, from what I hear, they've done much the same as they've done here—concentrated on the billets.

Much the best way of putting a station out of action. They did it at Mitchet just the same and they're having an awful job to feed and house the men. If this were winter the stations would be practically untenable."

"Look," I said, "can you do something for me? I want to get hold of Ordinance Survey maps for south-east England. And I want them in a hurry." It was rather an abrupt opening, but I could not think of any way of leading up to it.

"I've got R.A.F. maps. What do you want them for?"

Marion touched my arm. "I must get back," she said. "I'll try and find out what you want and I'll come down and see you in the morning." She was gone before I could remonstrate, walking quickly and purposefully towards the square.

"What do you want them for?" John repeated.

And then I told him the whole story of Vayle and the plan to immobilise the fighter 'dromes. And this time I left out nothing. Someone might as well know everything that had happened.

When I had finished I said: "I expect you think I'm a fool—imagining things and jumping to conclusions. It's what any sane person would think. But I'm perfectly serious. I know all the weaknesses. And, God knows, the whole structure of my suspicions is flimsy enough. But I can't convince myself that I'm wrong. And this attempt to shoot me, daft though it seems, is real enough to me. I had to risk your ridicule so that somebody would understand if something happened to me."

He was silent where I had expected some probing questions about my conjectures. But he made no direct comment. All he said when he broke the silence was: "R.A.F. maps won't be any use to you, they're mainly physical. I'll have to try and get Ordinance Survey maps. There's a Cold Harbour Farm down on Romney Marshes, and I've heard of another one somewhere. You may find several. How will you know which to choose, and what are you going to do when you've made up your mind which it is?"

"It'll be the most central one for the south-eastern fighter stations. But what I'm going to do about it, God only knows."

"If you could persuade the authorities to raid it, they might raid it when there was nothing incriminating there."

"I know the difficulties," I said rather wearily. "At the moment I'm just taking the fences as I come to them."

"All right," he said. "I'll find you those maps by to-morrow evening, all being well. In the meantime, good luck!"

When I got back to the site Ogilvie was just leaving. Men were wanted to erect huts and marquees. "Six men, then, Sergeant Langdon," he said. "Parade outside what was Troop Headquarters at seven-thirty. That will give them a chance to get a rest first."

I stood aside for him to pass out. As the door closed behind him Micky, who had been pretending to sleep, said: "Cor, give me an 'arp an' let me fly away."

"Why the hell can't the R.A.F. do it?" demanded Chetwood. "Damn it, they've spent most of the day in the shelters doing nothing."

"Well, I'd rather be above ground in this heat," said Langdon. "Anyway, it's a case of everybody doing what they can."

The grumbling did not stop, however, until Hood came back. He had been over to the other site. "Well, how did they get on?" asked Langdon.

"Oh, they claim our bombers, of course. Actually they had a pretty bad time. The pit is simply surrounded by bomb craters. No casualties at all, though—except young Layton. He's been taken off to hospital suffering from shell-shock. Simply went to pieces. Just couldn't take it."

"Well, he's not the only one," said Chetwood.

"Yes, but the others aren't hospital cases," said Hood. And there was no sympathy in his voice. "They just know where they're best off."

"Oh, I don't know," put in Kan. "'Imagination doth make cowards of us all,'" he quoted, quite unconsciously giving us the benefit of his profile in the approved Gielgud style. " That's the trouble with Micky. He's ignorant, and he's cursed with imagination."

" Who's igorant?" demanded Micky, sitting up in bed. " Why don't you talk about a bloke to his face, instead of waiting till he's asleep. You ain't goin' to talk about me like that," he told Kan. " I'm as good as you, mate, any day. I bin a foreman wif men under me, see? Just because you got money you think you can say wot you like. I didn't go to Heton." There was a wealth of scorn in the way he said Eton. " I had to work for my living. You can grin, but I bloody well did, mate. And I ain't so igorant. Uncle of mine built Alexandra palace."

" And Burne Jones was your stepfather—we know," said Chetwood. Micky, for purposes of aggrandisement, regarded all eminent Joneses as close relatives.

" Why you pick on me when I was trying to stick up for you, I don't know," said Kan in an aggrieved tone.

Micky's sudden outburst seemed to have exhausted him. He lay back again. " Can't you let a bloke sleep," he complained.

" Well, you can always go back to your funk hole," said Hood bluntly.

" If we was in the bleedin' infantry I'd show you how to fight. An' it wouldn't be you wot was wearin' the stripes. It'd be me, mate. This ain't fightin'."

Langdon changed the conversation by asking Hood whether the hut on the other site was damaged at all. Apparently it was much the same as ours, which had quite a lot of shrapnel through the roof and the north side. I found my blankets littered with glass when I came to make my bed. There were only one or two windows unbroken. And it wasn't difficult to find souvenirs in the form of jagged pieces of shell casing. They were all over the hut. One fellow found a piece in his kit-bag, and another bit had broken a milk bottle on the table and lay in the bottom of it.

I was one of the six detailed to help pitch tents. We were outside the orderly room by seven-thirty. The whole Station Headquarters was a complete wreck. The burnt-out remains of the troop lorry were strewn across the road. Behind us was the square, littered with broken glass and rubble. And all around it was a shambles of blasted and gutted buildings. But at the far side the flag-pole, its white paint now blackened, still stood, and from the top of it the R.A.F. flag drooped in the still evening air.

The tents were being pitched on the edge of the flying field nearest the camp. Hundreds of men—R.A.F. and Army—were on the job. The ground was hard as iron and the tents stiff with camouflage wash. We worked like niggers till ten o'clock. And in the fading evening light I wandered back to the camp with Kan. Once again, I looked behind me. And suddenly the fear I had felt when I realised that somebody must have deliberately fired at me returned. I don't know why, except that there was somebody behind me when I looked round. He was a vague shadow in the half light flitting in and out among the bomb craters. It wasn't that I thought I was being followed. It was just the fact that someone was behind me, I suppose.

We went straight to bed. But it seemed I had barely got to sleep before the sound of running feet woke me. It was a Take Post all right. Before the five of us had got into our clothes the sirens were going. It was just twelve. The alarm was short, however, and by twelve-thirty I was alone in the pit, it being my turn for guard.

I didn't enjoy the half-hour before the next detachment took over. Strange how dependent one's nerves are on one's mood. Up till then night guards hadn't worried me at all. The site was not an isolated one. It was in a well-guarded camp, and any one I had seen moving about I had regarded automatically as friendly. Now, because of that dent in the back of my tin hat, I found myself listening, tensed, to every sound. And it was strange how many sounds there were I had never noticed before. And when any one moved by the Guards' pill-box or came down the road I found myself gripping my rifle hard.

But nothing happened. It was just that I was tired

and my nerves were frayed. The sirens were giving the All Clear as my relief came out.

The next day, Saturday, dawned with a promise of more heat. The air was sultry with it. Shortly after eight-thirty a lorry from Battery brought us dry rations and a big tank of water. We managed to shave, but there was no water for washing. Water is a thing that in England one takes very much for granted. There is something very unpleasant about being so short of it that you can't wash. I can think of few things so shattering to morale.

Two alarms took up most of the morning. Marion did not show up, and after lunch I wandered down to the square in the hope of seeing a Waaf I knew from whom I could find out what had happened to her. The raid had made my confinement to the site seem such a small matter that I knew Langdon would not object.

But I was out of luck. I saw no Waaf I knew. The camp seemed full of workmen, demolishing the wreckage and piling the rubble into lorries. I could not help thinking that if every station was bringing in civilian labour to clear up the mess after a raid, they must be full of fifth columnists. It was so simple. And I went back to my site feeling very uneasy.

And then occurred something that thoroughly scared me. It may have been just an accident. It had happened before on the 'drome. But that it should happen so that it nearly caused my death seemed significant.

I was just passing the first dispersal point, about two hundred yards short of the site. There were Hurricanes in it. I remember noticing that because one had its tail badly shot up. I had just taken a cigarette out of my case and I stopped suddenly to light it.

And as I did so there was a rat-a-tat-tat of machine-gun fire and a stream of tracer bullets flashed past me. They were so close that I am certain that if I had put out my hand it would have been shot away.

The noise ceased abruptly as it had begun and I found myself staring at nothing in a dazed kind of way. I was brought to my senses by the match burning my fingers. I dropped it and looked quickly at the dispersal point. Everything was as it had been. There were the two Hurricanes, wing tip to wing tip, and the air shimmering in the heat from the tarmac. Nothing had moved.

Yet that stream of tracer bullets had come from the dispersal point. And suddenly a cold sweat broke over me as I realised that if I had not stopped abruptly to light that cigarette I should be lying in the roadway riddled with bullets.

I had an intense desire to run then. At any moment the chatter of the gun might start again and this time I was a static target. Unwillingly I forced myself to walk into the dispersal point. There was no one there. There was no one in either of the 'planes. I was puzzled. Guns don't usually go off by themselves, however hot it is.

An A.C.2 suddenly appeared in the exit at the back of the dispersal point. He was rubbing his eyes stupidly. "I thought I heard a noise," he said vaguely.

I told them what had happened. "You ought to report and examined the leading edge of the wings of the nearest machine warily. "Here we are," he said, and showed me the blackened port-hole of one of the guns. "Can't understand what made it go off, though. There's nobody here at the moment but myself and these were all left at safe."

I never did discover what made that gun go off. But there was no doubt in my own mind that it was deliberate and that it had been meant to kill me.

I was feeling very shaken by the time I got back to the site. "What's the matter with you?" asked Chetwood. "Seen a ghost?"

"No. Why?" I asked.

"Cor, tell 'im, somebody," said Micky.

"You're as white as a sheet," said Kan.

I told them what had happened. "You ought to report it, mate," said Micky. "It's only bloody carelessness. Same thing happened to a bloke called Tennyson in May. Only just missed him."

"Hallo," said Hood. "Jones is with us again." Micky had been back at his post on the gun that morning, but he had been silent and morose, which was definitely out of character.

"I want no vulgartisms from you or anybody," said Micky. He hated being called by his surname.

"Vulgartisms!" echoed his faithful stooge, Fuller, with a hoarse cackle, and every one laughed.

"Take post!"

We scrambled out of the hut just as Tiger squadron, which had been revving up for the last five minutes, left their dispersal points for the runway.

We were on the gun for nearly two hours that time, and though we saw a dog-fight over towards Maidstone, nothing came our way. Swallow-tail Squadron followed Tiger Squadron into the air, and I caught a glimpse of John Nightingale as he flashed by in his little green sports car. I wondered anxiously whether he had remembered to see about those maps. It was the third time he had been up to-day. It hardly seemed likely that he could have found either the time or the energy to go routing out maps for crazy-seeming gunners.

But this did not worry me for long, because fear returned to oust all other thoughts from my head. The preliminary air-raid warning had not then been given. Three workmen were engaged in repairing the telephone line between our pit and the dispersal point to the north of us. I became conscious after a time of the fact that one of them, a small, sharp-featured little man with steel-rimmed glasses, kept on pausing in his work to gaze at us. At first I just wondered why he found us so interesting. And then I found myself watching them, waiting for him to look up. Once it seemed that our eyes met, though it was quite impossible for me to tell at that distance. But after that he did not look in our direction again. He seemed consciously to avoid doing so, and it was then that I began to feel uneasy.

I tried to argue that my nerves were frayed with all that had happened during the last few days and that I was badly in need of sleep. But it was no good. I could not argue myself out of that sense of unease, which was so like the feeling I had experienced on guard the previous night when I had jumped at all the common sounds that I had never been conscious of before. I remembered only too clearly the sharp jerk of my neck as that bullet struck the back of my tin hat, and the stream of tracer bullets that had flashed past me only an hour ago.

When the preliminary warning went on the Tannoy, now in full working order again, the three men laid down their tools and hurried along the tarmac past our pit on their way to the station shelters. I watched the man closely as he passed us. He had pale eyes set too close together above a thin nose, and it seemed to me there was something furtive about him. Not once did he glance in our direction. He had a smooth loping walk and he did not talk to either of his mates.

I tried to forget about him. And for a while I succeeded as I watched the dog-fight high in the blue bowl of the heavens to the south-east of us.

And then suddenly I caught sight of him standing by the dispersal point between us and the camp—the one from which I had been nearly killed. I don't know why, but my heart leaped into my mouth as I saw him standing there. He was gazing in our direction. It seems amazing that I should recognise him at that distance. But I did. I confirmed his identity by borrowing Langdon's glasses, ostensibly to look at an imaginary 'plane.

I never did discover whether he was a fifth columnist. I never saw him again. But whether or not he was watching me, he certainly had me scared. And when I looked up and found he was no longer standing by the dispersal point—was, in fact, nowhere in sight—my sense of uneasiness increased. I found myself watching furtively all the vantage points from which a shot could be fired into the pit. It is an unpleasant feeling to be waiting for the impact of a bullet that may come from anywhere at any moment. I felt chilly despite the glare and the palms of my hands were wet with the sweat of my fear.

The alarm seemed interminable. We watched 'plane after 'plane come in, looking at them eagerly through the glasses to see if the canvas coverings of their gun ports had been shot away—sure sign that they had been in action.

A pilot officer whom Langdon knew came and chatted with us for a few minutes. He had been in the dog-fight over Maidstone and had shot down two Me. 109's. He was with Swallow-tail Squadron and told us that he had seen Nightingale bale out after diving his machine, which was on fire, into a German fighter. But the news that upset me most was that Crayton Aerodrome had been the target, and that two more fighter stations had been attacked in the morning. It all seemed to fit so easily into the German plan as I had envisaged it.

It was then that I realised that I had to get out of Thorby. I tried to kid myself that I had come to this conclusion because more fighter stations had been attacked and I was the only person who realised the significance of these raids. But all the time I knew that it was because I was afraid. I wonder how many people have been really afraid in their lives. The sensation is a horrible one. I was cold yet the sweat poured off me. My knees felt weak and I dared not look any one in the face for fear they should see what I knew was mirrored in my eyes. I had lost all confidence in myself. The sense of being caged in Thorby was more acute than ever. I could just see the barbed-wire boundary half-way down the slope between our hut and the trees at the bottom of the valley. It seemed such a slender line to mark the boundary between death and safety. Yet I knew that I should not be safe until I was on the other side of it. There had been two attempts on my life, and by the grace of God I was still alive. The next time—the third time—I might not be so fortunate. I had to get out of Thorby. I just had to get out of the place. The urgency of my fear drummed the phrase through my head to the beat of the blood in my ears.

"Come on, wake up!" I came suddenly out of my absorption to find Blah offering me a cigarette.

"Sorry," I said and took one.

He produced his lighter which had been given to him on his birthday earlier in the week. It was a heavy silver one and he was still rather proud of possessing it. He snapped it open. There was a spark, but nothing happened. He tried again and again whilst the detachment watched with sly amusement. But it wouldn't light. At last, exasperated, he exclaimed, "You Anti-Semitic swine," and put the thing in his pocket.

It was a little thing, but it changed my whole mood for the moment. I couldn't help laughing at the way he said it. And after I had laughed, Thorby seemed somehow less hostile. And when I looked about me again it was at any aerodrome baking peacefully in the sunshine and not at a prison with barbed-wire bars.

It was nearly five before we were allowed to stand-down. As soon as we had finished tea I got Kan to play a game of chess with me. Anything to keep my mind occupied. But I couldn't concentrate. We hadn't been playing more than ten minutes before he had taken my Queen. In a fit of annoyance I swept the board and gave him the game. "It's no use," I said. "I'm sorry. I can't concentrate."

Chetwood took my place. I went over to my bed and began to make it. The loss of my Queen seemed so symbolic. Everything seemed to be going wrong. Marion hadn't turned up. Nightingale had baled out— God knows when he would be able to produce the maps I wanted. And I had to get out of the place. I just had to, before I was murdered. I felt very near to tears as I unfolded my blankets. How was I to get out? The main gate was out of the question. And there were Guards all round the barbed-wire boundaries, patrolling night and day. The only way was to slip through the wire at night and take a chance that I shouldn't be seen. But it was a big risk. Almost as big a risk as staying. And there were Guards in the woods at the bottom. Automatically I was considering the wire below the hut as the best place to get through. But I couldn't leave until I knew where Cold Harbour Farm was and when the plan was due to break. "But I must get away. I must get away." I found suddenly that I was muttering this to myself over and over again, my eyes filling with tears because of my tiredness and my frustration. My mind was uncontrolled, incoherent—full of nameless terrors that would not exist if I could only think the matter out calmly.

"Hanson! Waaf outside wants to see you."

I looked up. Fuller, who was acting as air sentry, was standing in the door. "Eh?" I said stupidly as my mind tried to grasp what I had heard quite clearly.

"Waaf wants to speak to you. She's over by the pit."

A sudden flow of new energy coursed through my body. "All right," I said, and dropped the blanket I had just picked up and went outside.

It was Marion all right. And when I came up to her I could think of nothing to say except, "Have you found out when her birthday was to have been?"

I was horribly conscious of the fact that I had spoken very abruptly to hide my nervousness.

"Yes," she said. It may have been my imagination, but it seemed to me that she gave me a rather puzzled look. "It would have been on Sunday."

"You mean to-morrow?"

She nodded.

The imminence of what I was expecting steadied me. I did not say anything. To-morrow meant to-morrow morning, surely. To immobilise the fighter 'dromes must mean a landing from the air and that would almost certainly be carried out at dawn. There was so little time— less than twelve hours.

"What's the matter?" Marion asked.

"Nothing," I said. "Just that there isn't much time if I'm to do anything, and I don't know what to do."

"No, I don't mean that. I knew that would worry you. But you seemed so strange when you came out."

"I'm sorry," I said. I felt suddenly scared of losing

my one ally. Almost unnoticed an intimacy, deeper than just the words we spoke to each other, had grown up between us. It seemed so easy to break the thread that made that intimacy—it was so indefinable, so slight. " It's just that I'm tired and worried."

" Hadn't you better tell Winton or someone in authority all you know?" she pleaded.

" Yes, but what do I know? Nothing. I've told John Nightingale. He didn't laugh at me, thank God! That's the best I can do. The rest is up to me."

" But what can you possibly do?"

" I don't know. I shall have to get to this Cold Harbour Farm to-night."

" But how? You won't be able to get leave, will you?"

" No. I'll just have to take a chance on breaking camp."

" But you can't possibly do that." The anxiety in her voice gave me a perverted thrill. " You might get shot."

I laughed a little wildly. " That wouldn't be anything new," I declared. " They've already had two attempts at shooting me."

" Barry!" Her hand gripped my arm. " You don't mean that. You're not serious, surely."

I told her about the bullet that had hit the back of my tin hat during the previous day's raid and about the burst of tracers that had streamed past me from the dispersal point that morning.

" But why don't you tell your officer?"

" Because I can't prove anything," I said, exasperated.

" Oh, if you want to be obstinate, be obstinate," she said, her eyes wide and two angry spots of colour showing in her cheeks.

" But don't you understand," I said, " in each case they might easily have been accidents? Ogilvie would just think the raid had upset me and I should be sent off to Battery for a rest. It's no good. I've just got to get to Cold Harbour Farm to-night. That reminds me," I added suddenly. " John Nightingale promised to get me Ordinance Survey maps for south-east England. But he can't. He bailed out in a dog-fight this afternoon.

God knows where he is. And I must have those maps, otherwise I can't tell where the wretched place is. Have you got any in Ops.?"

"Yes, but I can't take them away."

"No, but you could search through them. It would take some time, I know, but——"

"I certainly will not," she cut in. "I'll do nothing to help you embark on this crazy expedition."

My troubles seemed suddenly to roll away as I gazed down at her defiant, anxious little face. "That's kind of you, Marion. But please—you must help me. It's just as dangerous if I stay here. And if I didn't go and what I am afraid of happened, you'd never forgive yourself, I know."

She hesitated.

"Please," I said. "It's the only chance."

"But you can't be certain that what I heard Elaine say in her sleep had any deep significance."

"Yes, but what about the injured workman?"

"I can understand your regarding the coincidence of their both speaking of Cold Harbour Farm as significant, but Elaine's birthday probably has no bearing on the business."

"Three more fighter 'dromes were attacked to-day," I said. "During the last three or four days practically every fighter station of any size in south-east England has had a bad pasting. It just happens that the date of her birthday is about the time I think they will strike if they're going to. Your arguments are just the sort of arguments that I know would be raised by the authorities if I went to them. I've made up my mind that I'm on the right track. The only question now is, will you help me or not, Marion?"

She didn't say anything, and for a moment I thought she was going to refuse.

"Well?" I asked her, and again I was speaking abruptly, for I was afraid that I had lost her as an ally.

"Of course I will," she said simply. But she spoke slowly, as though considering something. Then suddenly she became businesslike, almost brusque. "I'll go and look through those maps right away. I'll come back and tell you the result of my labours as soon as possible."

"You'll find it somewhere in the centre of a ring drawn round the fighter 'dromes, I expect," I said as she turned to go.

"I understand," she said.

I watched her walk briskly away, thinking how strange it was that people should have different sides to their personalities. I had just seen Marion for the first time as the efficient secretary. My God! I thought, and she would be efficient too. What a wife for a journalist! The thought was in my mind before I realised it. And suddenly I knew that she was the one girl for me. And then I kicked myself mentally as I realised that I had been thinking only of the things she could give me, and had not given a thought to what I could give her. And what could I give her? "Hell!" I said aloud. And then went back into the hut as I saw Fuller looking at me curiously.

The next few hours dragged terribly. I was not afraid, thank Heavens! I had something concrete to do now and there was no room in my thoughts for fear. But as the evening wore slowly on I experienced the sinking sensation that one gets just before a big match. I passed part of the time reconnoitring my line of escape. The barbed wire, I knew, would not be difficult to negotiate. It was dannert, that coiled wire which is stretched so that it stands in hoops. By parting two of the hoops it was fairly easy to step through it. It was the sentries I was worried about. I went over and had a chat with the Guards' corporal at the neighbouring pill-box. By fairly persistent, but not too obvious questioning, I discovered that there was roughly one sentry to each five hundred yards of wire. There were also some sentries in the wood along the valley. But they were very few—one at each end. They were supposed to meet in the middle once every hour. There was a path running through the middle of the wood. These shouldn't worry me, but because they were the unknown factor they worried me a good deal more than the sentries along the wire.

Marion did not turn up until nearly ten. I was on stand-to then. I went out of the pit to meet her. " I think I've got it," she said as I reached her. " I found two. One down in Romney Marshes. That isn't any good, is it?"

" No," I said. " Nightingale told me of that one."

" The other isn't quite in the centre of the south-eastern fighter area, but it's not far off. It's just off the Eastbourne road in Ashdown Forest."

" That sounds hopeful," I said. " There were no others?"

She shook her head. " I don't think so. I went very methodically through the maps for Kent and Sussex. I don't think I missed anything."

" I'm sorry," I said. " It must have been a frightful job."

" No, it was rather fun in a way—all the peculiar place-names one had never heard of before, and some that one had. You know the Eastbourne road, don't you? You go through East Grinstead and Forest Row and up to Wych Cross, where the Lewes road forks off. You keep left here on the Eastbourne road and about half a mile farther on there are one or two cottages on the left. Another half-mile and there is a lane turning off to the right. Take this, fork right along what appears to be a track, and you'll come to Cold Harbour Farm."

" Marvellous," I said.

" When do you start?"

" As soon as it's dark—about eleven. The moon doesn't rise till late now. My detachment doesn't go on until one, so I shall have two hours before they miss me."

" Do you think you can get out all right, though?"

" Unless I have bad luck, it should be easy."

"Well, good luck, then," she said, and squeezed my hand. " I must get back. Your boys are already beginning to talk about us."

She had half turned to go when she stopped. " By

the way, Vayle went off in his car just before eight this evening. He won't be back to-night."

" How do you know?" I asked.

" A boy I know in Ops. told me. He's studying to become a navigator. He saw Vayle getting into his car and asked him whether he could come and have a word with him later in the evening about some problem he was stuck on. Vayle is apparently good about helping people. But he told him that he couldn't as he wouldn't be back to-night."

" That looks hopeful," I said.

She nodded. " That's what I thought. And if you're not back before dawn I shall see Winton myself."

" Bless you," I said.

For a second she hesitated and her eyes held mine. I often wonder whether she was trying to memorise my features for fear she should never see me again. We were very near to each other in that moment. And then she turned quickly on her heels and left me.

When I got back to the pit I came in for a good bit of chaff, but it passed me by. I was thinking of other things. "You and Micky are a pair," said Chetwood. " Both of you look worried and secretive."

" Don't talk so bloody daft," said Micky violently.

The violence of his reply should have told me something. But it didn't. I was engrossed in my own thoughts and barely noticed it. Zero hour was very close now.

Chapter Nine

COLD HARBOUR

At ten we were relieved. Usually the whole detachment went straight to bed in order to get as much sleep as possible. But, of course, Kan and Chetwood had to choose this evening of all evenings to start a discussion about the stage, Chetwood holding forth about the full-blooded qualities of the ham actor, and Kan naturally standing by the more sophisticated modern school. They sat up arguing over a hurricane lamp till a quarter to eleven while I lay in bed and fumed.

At last quiet descended upon the hut. I waited till eleven-fifteen to make certain that every one should be sound asleep. The place was full of the soft, sibilant sound of steady breathing. I slipped out of bed and put on my battle blouse. Except for this, I had gone to bed fully clothed. For the sake of quietness, and if necessary speed, I put on canvas shoes. Before leaving I thrust my kit-bag and overcoat under my blankets, so that when the guard came in to wake his relief he would think I was still sleeping.

None of the recumbent figures stirred as I opened the back door of the hut. It was dark outside save along the western sky where the last light of day still lingered, throwing the pit into silhouette with the muzzle of the gun and the sentry's tin hat quite visible. I closed the door of the hut softly and paused to listen. Not a sound from inside. I went a little down the slope towards the wire and there sat down to watch and accustom myself to the light. The nearest I had ever got before to my present escapade was stalking in Scotland, and I knew enough not to hurry even though time pressed.

Gradually I was able to see more and more until at last I could make out the thin coils of dannert stretched tenuously out along the slope of the hill, and behind loomed vaguely the black bulk of trees at the bottom. But still I waited. I had to know the position of the sentry.

At last I heard him. He was pacing slowly along the inside edge of the wire and every now and then his bayonet clanked in its rifle socket. I waited till he had passed. I was just rising to my feet when I heard a sound behind me. It was a click. I thought for a moment that it must be the latch of the hut door. But there was no further sound, and at length I rose to my feet and moved swiftly towards the wire. And at that moment the sirens went. I hesitated, cursing. And then I hurried

on, realising that their wail would cover any slight noise
I might make getting through the wire.

In a second I had reached the sentry-beaten path
inside the wire. I glanced quickly along it in each
direction. There was no sign of the sentry. I had brought
a pair of leather gloves I had had in my case, and with
these on my hands I parted two of the coils and stepped
into the gap. I then parted the farther side of the two
coils and, raising myself on tiptoe, swung my right foot
over into this gap. But to bring my left foot over as well
seemed an impossibility. The wire barbs were digging
into me painfully. I set my teeth and lifted my left leg
back and round. I thought I had done it, but a barb just
caught my canvas shoes. I lost my balance and fell
headlong. I caught my head on the ground—it was as hard
as concrete—and there was a searing pain in my left leg.

But when I staggered to my feet I found I was clear
of the wire. I listened. The still night air was silent. No
one seemed to have heard my fall. Crouching low and
taking advantage of what little cover there was on that
bare slope, I hurried down to the shelter of the wood.
Looking back, I could see no movement. At the top
of the slope there was the vague silhouette of the hut
and the gun, and away to the right was the bulk of the
dispersal point.

I went cautiously forward into the wood. It was
pitch dark here and I had to feel my way, working round
trees and bushes by hand. Every yard of progress seemed
to take an age, but though my one desire was to get through
the wood as quickly as possible to the road beyond, I
steadfastly refused to be hurried by nerves.

It is a very unnerving sensation to pass from open
country into a wooded place when you are going in fear
of your life. For ten days I had been living on the bare
hill-top of the 'drome. I knew all the sounds of that open
stretch of ruined downland. During that time I had never
heard the rustle of a tree in a current of air, the scamper
of a squirrel through light branches, or the movement of
dried leaves and twigs caused by the night life of a wood.

It was all new to me, and each sound, terrifying at first, had to be sorted out and understood before I dared move forward again.

Once, behind me, I heard the snap of a twig where something heavier than usual had pressed on it. That sound alone held me poised with one foot forward for fully a minute.

At last I made the path that ran through the centre of the wood. There was no sound apart from the faint stirring of the branches high above my head. I crossed the ten feet of open ground without a challenge. This gave me confidence and I pressed forward faster. My lack of caution brought its own reward, for I tripped over a mound of earth and only just saved myself from falling into a deep trench. There was more barbed wire beyond it, but it was just a few strands, not dannert, and quite easily negotiated.

It took time, however, and as I slipped over the last strand a twig snapped only a few yards behind me. The sound of it seemed loud in the stillness. I froze. My senses warned me that it was not one of the usual noises of the wood. A second later came the unmistakable sound of somebody stumbling and the thud of a body as it pitched into the trench I had just crossed. A muttered curse and I heard the man pick himself up cautiously.

Silence for a moment. Then he began to negotiate the barbed wire. I slid quietly behind a tree, my heart pounding against my ribs. My immediate reaction was that one of the Guards was trailing me. But reason told me that if it was one of the Guards he would have known the position of the trench and would not have fallen into it. Moreover, I had heard no clatter of a rifle as he fell. And that muttered curse! Surely he would not have uttered it if he had been trailing me.

The man, whoever he was, was very near me now. I could hear the pant of his breathing. Then the sound was lost in the whir of a car coming up the road. The wood about me suddenly took shape as the blacked-out headlights swept past only a few yards beyond where

I stood. It only lit the wood up for a second before it drew level and was gone, but in that second I saw the man who was coming towards me and recognised him.

"Good God, Micky!" I said. "What the devil are you doing here?"

I sensed the shock of my voice as the car swept on and the blackness, more impenetrable than ever, settled once more on the wood.

"Who's that?" His voice sounded hoarse and frightened.

I hesitated. The road was close, much closer than I had expected. Once on it I could give him the slip and he would never know who it was. "Is anybody there?"

And because I felt his fear, I said: "It's Hanson."

"Hanson?" he whispered. "Cor lumme, you didn't 'alf give me a fright."

"What the devil are you doing?" I asked.

"Doing a bunk, same as you. Though I didn't think you was that scared."

"Good God!" I said. "You mean you're deserting?"

"Who says I'm deserting? I ain't deserting. I'm transferring. I'm going to volunteer in the Buffs."

"But why?" I asked.

"Cos I ain't gonna stay in that bleeding aerodrome to provide target practice for Jerries. That ain't fighting. It's bloody murder. I want to be in something where I can fight the Jerry proper. I want to get at 'em wiv a rifle and baynet."

"But if you're caught you'll be regarded as a deserter."

"Admitted. So will you. But I ain't aiming to get caught."

"The odds are against you, Micky," I said. "Why not go back now while you've got the chance."

"And be bombed again without being able to do nothing to stop it. Not bloody likely. Wot about you, anyway?"

"Well," I said. "I'm not exactly deserting."

"I suppose you're resigning. You got a nerve telling me to go back, whilst you're running like hell yourself.

Wot d'you think I am? Are you going to volunteer in some other unit?"

"No," I said.

"Well, I am—see? I want ter fight for me country. I ain't deserting. Come on, let's get out o' here while the going's good."

It was no use arguing with him. Time was too precious and at any moment we might be overheard. I followed him down a gentle slope and over a wooden stile on to the road. "There's a garage just down the road," I said. "We'll get a car from there."

But we were in luck. We hadn't gone more than a hundred yards when we heard a car coming towards us. "Stand by to board," I said to Micky. And as the dull headlights came round the bend ahead of us, I stepped out into the middle of the road and signalled it to stop. It pulled up with a shriek of brakes. It wasn't a car at all but a Bedford truck.

"Can I see your identity card?" I asked as the driver leaned out of the window of the cab. I glanced at it and then flashed the torch I had brought with me in his face. "I'm afraid you'll have to get down while we search your cabin," I said.

"What the hell's the matter?" he grumbled.

He showed no signs of moving. "Come on, look sharp!" I barked. "I haven't got all night to waste."

"All right, mate, all right," he muttered as he climbed out. "What's the trouble, anyway?"

"Looking for a Bedford truck full of H.E.," I told him.

"Well, you've only got to look at the bloody thing to see it's empty," he said.

"The driver may have dumped it," I explained. Then to Micky I said: "You search the other side. Come on, look sharp. The fellow doesn't want to waste all night. He's probably late back already."

"You're right there, sir," I think he thought by my voice and the way I had spoken to Micky that I was an

156

officer in battle dress. " Shan't be in bed till one and due to clock out again at eight in the morning."

I had climbed up into the driver's seat and made a pretence of searching with my torch, whilst in reality I was noting the position of the gears and foot controls. " That's too bad," I said. At the same time I slammed home the gears, revved the engine and let the clutch in with a bang.

I heard the beginning of his shout, but lost it in the noise of the engine as I raced through the gears. In a second it seems I had swept past the turning that led to the main gates of the aerodrome. And in less than ten minutes I had swung left on to the main Eastbourne road and was making for East Grinstead. Fortune had favoured us. A Bedford truck, empty, has a pretty turn of speed. The moon was just rising and the added light enabled me to push her. On the straight stretches I was showing nearly sixty on the clock.

In less than half an hour from the time I had expropriated the lorry I had passed through East Grinstead and Forest Row and was climbing the long winding hill that leads up to Ashdown Forest.

Just past the Roebuck at Wych Cross I forked left, and about a mile farther on I came upon the turning off to the right of which Marion had spoken. I switched my lights off. The moonlight was quite strong now. " Well, Micky," I said. " This is where I leave you."

" Wot's the game?" he demanded suspiciously.

" How do you mean?" I asked.

" Ain't I good enough for you, then."

" Don't be silly," I said.

" Well, wot's the idea, then? You got a hideout you don't want me to share—that's it, is it?"

I hesitated. It didn't seem to matter much if I told him the truth. " I haven't got a hideout at all," I said. " You see, I'm really not deserting. In a few hours' time I shall be back at the aerodrome."

" If you do it's the Glasshouse for you and a brick

wall, I tell you, mate. Anyway, if you're going back, wot's the good of getting out."

"Because I had to get to a certain farm to-night," I said. "I'm playing a lone hand against a gang of fifth columnists. They've got a plan that will enable the Germans to capture our fighter aerodromes. I aim to stop them."

He looked at me. In the faint light from the dashboard I noted the sidelong, furtive glance. "You ain't kidding?"

I shook my head. "No," I said.

"Sure?"

"Cross my heart."

A sudden gleam came into his small close-set eyes. "Cor lumme!" he said. "Wot a break! Like a book I bin reading all about gangsters in America. Will they have guns?" he asked.

"Probably," I said. And I couldn't help grinning though I felt queasy inside because it was so near to zero hour.

"Cor lumme!" he repeated. "That's the way I like to fight—'and to 'and. I wouldn't 'alf like to give a Jerry a sock in the kisser—just one and I'd be 'appy. Come on! Let's get at 'em."

I glanced at him. It was incredible. A coward in the face of bombs, yet here was the spirit that made British Tommies go in fearlessly with rifle and bayonet against an enemy armed with light automatics. Again I hesitated. He looked as though he might be useful in a rough-house—small and tough, probably a dirty fighter. I had no illusions about my own abilities in a fight. He might be very useful.

"All right," I said, and slipped the lorry into gear again. "But there may be no scrap and no gang of Nazis. I may be wrong."

I changed quickly up into top and kept the engine ticking over, so that we made little noise as we ran over that flat open heath. The road was nothing more than a rough gravel track. And in the dim moonlight the country ahead and on either side looked desolate.

There were no trees, and the only relief from the interminable heather was the gnarled and twisted skeleton of gorse bushes, black and flowerless from a recent fire. My uneasiness grew with my surroundings.

"Cor, don't 'alf seem creepy," Micky muttered, voicing my own thoughts. I couldn't help remembering *Childe Rolande to the Dark Tower Came*. There was a very slight mist and the place reeked of desolation. When last I had seen Ashdown Forest it had been in sunlight, and it had seemed warm and friendly, with autumn tints glowing in the heather. I had been motoring down to Eastbourne to spend a week-end with some friends. Now it was no longer friendly, and I thought of the Ancient Britons who had fought and died here in their hopeless attempt to stem the tide of Cæsar's advancing legions. So many of the more desolate parts of Britain seem to house the ghostly memory of that tragic race.

The track forked. Evidently I was on the right road. I swung right. The road was now definitely no more than a cart track, grass-grown in the middle and full of pot-holes. At the end of it should be Cold Harbour Farm.

I passed an even smaller track leading off to the right. Then a patch of gorse bushes seemed to jump up at me out of the pale mist. I braked and swung the lorry off the track. It was time, I felt, to carry out some sort of reconnaissance. I stopped so that the lorry was screened as far as possible from the track and climbed out.

Micky followed. "Where do we go now?" he asked in a hoarse whisper.

"Up this track," I said. "It should lead us to a place called Cold Harbour Farm."

"Cor, stone me, wot a name!"

We went on in silence, two shadows slinking through the pale ethereal light, our canvas shoes making no sound on the baked surface of the path. About a quarter of a mile farther on we passed through a gate. It was open and its rotting timbers hung drunkenly from rust-eaten hinges. Painted roughly on it was the name—Cold Harbour Farm.

The track swung away to the left, and a little farther on we had our first glimpse of Cold Harbour Farm, a low, rambling building with a jumble of outhouses and a big barn at the farther end.

"Sort o' spooky, ain't it?" whispered Micky. It was one of those buildings that look dilapidated even at a first glance—an untidy place, with gables. There was still no sign of a tree, only the stunted gorse bushes. Neglect had allowed them to encroach to the very door.

We moved stealthily now, leaving the path and crossing what seemed once to have been a garden, for there were vestiges of rhododendrons and even roses amongst the choking growth of heather and gorse. We took the building in the flank and came out upon what had once been a gravel terrace. The gabled wing of the house looked dark and deserted. The roof tiles were green with moss and broken in places, and the woodwork of gables and windows was rotting. Everything was deathly still in the damp air. We crept round to the front. It was a long building and must at one time have been owned by quite a prosperous family. The sweeping outline of a drive was still visible amidst the chaos of the advancing heath. I gazed along the whole length of the decaying building. No chink of light showed in any of the windows. No sound disturbed the stillness of the night. Ivy had taken a stranglehold everywhere. Undisturbed, it billowed up even to the roof.

My heart sank as I looked at the place. I just couldn't see Vayle making it his headquarters. London seemed a much more likely place for him to meet other agents. Out here in this God-forsaken spot every visitor would be bound to be noticed and commented upon by whatever local inhabitants still existed in the neighbourhood.

In any case, the house, being quite a big one, would in itself be a subject for gossip.

I went up to the front door. It was clearly not the original door, for it was of cheap deal with a brass handle. The brown paint was cracked and peeling. I tried it, and to my surprise it gave to my pressure, creaking slightly as I pushed it open.

We went in and I closed it behind us. All was silent in the darkness of the house. No, not quite. Faintly came the ticking of a clock. It sounded somehow homely, suggesting that the place was inhabited. I switched on my torch. We were in a big low-ceilinged hall. In front of us was a flight of narrow stairs covered with a threadbare carpet. The hall itself was flagged with here and there a tattered rug. There was a fine old refectory table with straight-backed chairs. The rest of the furniture was Victorian. The place looked dirty and neglected. The huge open fireplace was littered with fallen plaster, and the ceiling, which showed in strips between the heavy oak beams, was blackened and in places had crumbled so that the laths were visible.

I opened the door to our left and flashed my torch round. It was a big room with Victorian furniture of the ugliest and most uncomfortable type, the walls covered with photographs and texts and every flat surface a jumble of knick-knacks. French windows led on to the terrace by which we had just approached the house. The heavy plush curtains were undrawn. There was no black-out and several panes were missing. The air felt damp and stale. The room was obviously not lived in.

" Puts me in mind of one of them smash-up-the-'appy-'ome tents at the fair," whispered Micky. " I couldn't 'alf do something to all them little bits of china wiv a couple of cricket balls."

I closed the door and we crossed the hall to the door at the far end. This led to a smaller and more homely room. The Victorian furniture had been blended with additions from Drages, and in the far corner a rather fine grandfather clock ticked away impassively, the brass of the pendulum flicking back and forth across the glass porthole of its case. The time was twelve-fifteen. There were the burnt-out cinders of a recent fire in the grate.

Back in the hall I tried the only door we had not yet looked through. This was to the left of the hearth and led to a cold brick-floored passage. I went down it full of a wretched feeling of depression. Either there had been nothing in the coincidence of Elaine Stuart and the injured workman both talking of Cold Harbour Farm whilst unconscious or else I had picked on the wrong one. I felt suddenly hot and chaotic with anxiety. If I had picked on the wrong one and something did happen this morning, it would be horrible. Looking back, my efforts to defeat Vayle seemed so puny and haphazardly organised—much too haphazardly organised.

I stopped before a door. Micky followed me, bumped into me. I suppose he must have put out his hand to keep his balance, for out of the corner of my eye I caught sight of something white falling, and the silence of the house was splintered by what seemed to be the most appalling crash. I turned the beam of my torch downwards. On the red brick floor lay the shattered remains of a white vegetable dish patterned with blue flowers. We stood motionless, listening. Not a sound disturbed the stillness of the house save the gentle ticking of the clock in the small room. In the quiet it had seemed shatteringly loud. If there were any one in the house it must surely have woken them.

I opened the door and we passed through into a typical farmhouse kitchen, big and rambling, with sculleries, a boiler house and a lavatory. There was no sign of dirty crockery. We wandered through into the scullery. Beyond was what had once been the dairy. Most of the whitewash had powdered off the walls, but in a corner there was still the old butter churn. I don't know why I had pursued my search of the house to the kitchen. I had no idea what I was searching for. I went on automatically. But I knew I should find nothing. The furniture, the dilapidation— it was all in keeping. This was no centre of a fifth columnist organisation. I felt sick with anxiety. It was a mistake to have left the 'drome. I had laid myself open to a charge of desertion and gained nothing by it. I forgot in that moment that I had gone in fear of my life at the 'drome.

We had just gone back into the kitchen when a pale light showed in the open doorway leading to the passage. I snapped my torch off. The light grew steadily brighter. There was a shuffling sound along the brick floor of the passage. I heard Micky's sharp intake of breath close beside me. I stood there, fascinated by the light that showed the framework of the door and made dark shadows of every piece of peeling plaster. I made no attempt to hide.

Suddenly a guttering candle came into view. And the bony hand that held it shook slightly. And then appeared an apparition that seemed to have walked straight out of Dickens. It was an old gentleman dressed in a nightgown with a faded dressing-gown over it. He wore a red wooly night-cap and in his hand he held a poker. My first inclination was to laugh. It really was an incredible sight. But despite his costume he had a certain dignity. He stopped at the sight of us and blinked at us through his steel-rimmed glasses. " Soldiers, eh?" he said.

I nodded. I suddenly felt a most frightful fool. Much more of a fool than when Vayle had caught me in his rooms. " I—I'm sorry," I said. " We thought the house was deserted. We were hitch-hiking home and lost our way trying to make a short-cut to the Eastbourne road. We thought we might find shelter for the night. The front door was open," I finished lamely.

" Tut-tut," he said, and fingered his drooping white moustache. " Don't say I forgot to lock the door again. I'm getting very forgetful. And the house is a little in need of repair. You want shelter for the night, you say?"

I nodded. I could think of nothing to say.

" Well, well, I expect that could be arranged. It won't be very comfortable, I fear. I'm a bit of a recluse these days—at least that's what the neighbours think. Let me see now. There's a room next to mine. There's a double bed there and I expect we could find you some blankets. You're quiet fellows, I hope?" He peered at us closely. "I sleep very light now. Getting on, you know."

"Really, sir," I said, "it's awfully kind of you. But we wouldn't dream of bothering you."

His eyes stopped blinking and looked straight into mine. They were very blue eyes, I remember. "You said you wanted shelter for the night, didn't you?"

"Yes, sir, but we——"

"Well, then," he interrupted me, "don't haver, man. It's the least we can do for our gallant lads. Now you'll be wanting something to eat, I expect. I see you had found your way to the kitchen all right." He chuckled as he shuffled over to the pantry.

It was an impossible situation. I looked at Micky. "Do we stay?" I asked.

"'Course we stay," he whispered.

There was nothing else for it. I hadn't the heart to walk out on the dear old boy. Besides, there was no point in doing so. We might just as well sleep here as anywhere else. If anything was going to happen that morning there was nothing I could do about it now. This was the wrong Cold Harbour Farm. That's all there was to it. Probably there had never been a right one. God, what a fool!

The old boy fussed over us like a mother. We had cold ham—heaven knows where he got that ham from, for it was a big one—and bread and butter, and milk to drink. It wasn't till I smelt that ham that I realised I was very hungry. I enjoyed that meal. He talked mostly of the Boer War. And afterwards he took us upstairs to a room under one of the gables. He gave us blankets and lit a candle for us. "Good-night," he said, bobbing his funny little red cap at us. "I trust you sleep well." He closed the door on us and a second later the key ground in the lock.

That startled me a bit, I must say. My first reaction was to glance at the window. The room had evidently been a nursery at one time, for it had small iron bars across it. My instinct was to beat upon the door and demand that it be unlocked. But when I looked at Micky and then at myself in the black-marked mirror over the mantelpiece, I couldn't altogether blame him. We looked a pretty disreputable pair, with dark rings of sleeplessness under our eyes and torn, dirty clothes.

Micky, who had as usual made a very heavy meal, threw himself on to the bed just as he was. "The old boy's a bit of orl right, ain't he?" he said. A grunt of satisfaction and he closed his eyes, not bothering about the blankets. Eating and sleeping were Micky's sole recreations in the Army. There was nothing for it but to follow his example. I took off my battle blouse and shoes and lay down beside him, pulling a blanket up over me.

But sleep did not come easily. I was worried about what might happen. And I was worried, too, about how my escapade would be regarded. Would Ogilvie believe my explanation when I reported for duty again, or should I find myself under close arrest for desertion.

I suppose I must have dosed off, but I don't remember waking. I just found myself suddenly in a state of complete consciousness and felt that I must have been awake all the time. Then I realised that my mind was alert yet not concentrated on the troubles that had been worrying me. For a moment I did not understand why this was. Then I heard it. Faintly came the sound of what I thought at first must be a car grinding along in bottom. I was just turning over to go to sleep again, thinking it must be on the main road, when I remembered that the road was some distance away—too far for the sound to travel unless the wind carried it and the night was still. Moreover, there was no reason for a car to be travelling along that road in bottom.

The sound gradually drew nearer. Suddenly I realised that it wasn't a car at all. It was much heavier. And it was much nearer than the road. I jumped out of bed and went to the window. The moon was well up now, and though there was still a slight mist I could see something moving behind a clump of gorse bushes about five hundred yards away. When it came out into the open I saw it was a lorry. Another followed close behind and then a third. I watched them as they disappeared, merging into the mist. The sound of their engines gradually dwindled. I waited and was at last rewarded by the sight of a glimmer of light on the main road. Two other lights followed. They were moving south.

I glanced at my wrist-watch. It was just after one. Three hours to go to the first light of dawn. I hesitated. Those might have been Army lorries. But I remembered that the injured workman had spoken of driving to Cold Harbour. What I was looking for might not be at the farm itself. The farm might be quite harmless, and yet something—an arms dump, for instance—might be located in the vicinity and referred to as Cold Harbour for convenience.

But I still hesitated. I had lost all confidence in my own judgment. I was afraid of making a bigger fool of myself than I feared I had done already. And whilst I was standing there trying to figure it out there came again that faint sound of engines grinding in low gear. I watched the clump of gorse bushes behind which I had first seen the three lorries. There were four this time. I waited till I could see their lights on the main road. They, too, had turned south.

I swung round from the window, my mind suddenly made up.

"Micky!" I called softly, shaking him by the shoulder. "Micky! Wake up!"

"Uh?" He rolled over and blinked his eyes at me sleepily. "Wasamatter?"

"We've got to get out of here," I told him.

"I don't see why. We're very comfortable, ain't we?"

"Yes, but there's something funny going on."

"You just tell me when to laugh," he mumbled, "and I'll laugh."

"Don't be a fool," I said, and shook him violently.

"Orl right, orl right," he grumbled and climbed off the bed. "Wot's the trouble?"

I told him what I had seen. "I want to try and find

out where the lorries are coming from and what they're carrying. And we haven't much time," I added. I had got into my battle top and was putting on my shoes.

"Probably the poor bleedin' infantry doing night ops.," he said unhelpfully. He was still half asleep.

I went over to the window. It was a drop of about twenty feet and it wasn't a soft landing. However, the ivy looked pretty tough. The only difficulty was the bars. They were much stronger than most nursery window bars. Moreover, when I looked at them closely I found that they were not the type that screw into the window frame, but had been cemented into deep sockets.

I looked more closely at the cement, scraping the coat of paint away with my clasp knife. It wasn't new, but I was certain that it was very much newer than the window frame in which it was set.

It was then that the scales suddenly fell from my eyes. These bars were not here because the room had once been a nursery. And the door had not been locked just because we looked pretty desperate characters. The old man was a fake.

I tugged with all my strength at the bars. They did not move. Micky came and considered my efforts. "You'll never loosen those, mate," he said. "Better try the door."

"That's locked," I said as we went over to it.

"Well, it can be unlocked, can't it?"

"Yes," I said, amazed at his denseness, "but the key happens to be on the other side."

"Gimme your clasp knife. I flogged mine one night when I was tight."

I unhooked the knife from my lanyard. He opened the spike and inserted it in the lock. A few minutes later I heard the key drop on the other side of the door. "It's easy if you've got the right tool," Micky muttered as he gently worked the spike in the lock. "This thing is too thick by 'alf."

There was nothing I could do to help. I stood by and waited in a fever of anxiety for fear he wouldn't be able to do it. But at last there was a click and he straightened up.

"Cor lumme," he said, "I ain't lost me touch, 'ave I? Come in useful when I get demobbed, won't it?" and he gave me a wink.

"Grand!" I said. "Let's go."

Quietly I turned the handle of the door and opened it. The passage outside was dark after our room, which had been flooded with moonlight. I put my head out of the door and glanced up and down. There appeared to be no one there. I flashed my torch. The passage was empty. As I stepped out into it there was a slight sound at the far end of the stairs. I stopped dead, poised on one foot. The house was deathly still. Nothing stirred. And faintly came the tick of the grandfather clock.

It might have been a mouse, or even a rat—the place was probably infested with both. I started forward again. Micky shut the door of our room behind us. We made the stairs and still the house was silent about us.

But as we descended I began to find it an oppressive silence. I had an unpleasant feeling of panic—a desire to run out of the place before those silent walls closed about us for ever. It was one of those houses that have atmosphere. I had not noticed it when I first entered it, flushed with a sense of adventure. But now that I knew the place to be hostile I was frightened of the atmosphere, an atmosphere of sly violence that made its Victorian apparel appear no more than a smug veneer.

But we made the front door without disturbing that silence. I drew the bolts and undid the chain. The lock was, for a wonder, well oiled and the key turned with scarcely a sound. I opened it and the moonlight flooded the hall in a great swathe, lighting the refectory table and the great fireplace with a ghostly pallor. I was thankful when Micky had closed the door behind us.

We moved along the house to the left and made open country in the shadow of the barn. As soon as we were in the heather I broke into a trot. I could just see the clump of gorse bushes behind which the lorries had passed. It took us only a few minutes to reach it, and about a hundred yards farther on we came upon a grass track half grown over with heather. Though the ground was hard it was possible to see the tracks of the lorries faintly marked where the wheels had beaten down heather and grass. It looked like the path that had forked off from the Cold Harbour Farm track.

We set off down it in the direction from which the lorries had come. We hadn't gone far before we had to go to cover in order to let three more lorries rumble past. " Here, wot's the idea?" Micky demanded as we scrambled out of the heather and regained the track. " Them was R.A.F. lorries."

" That's what we've got to find out," I said.

· I was quite convinced now that I was on to something. Obviously if Vayle wanted to get something, such as arms or explosives, with which to assist an air landing, into our fighter 'dromes, he had to use R.A.F. lorries and men in R.A.F. uniform driving them. Provided they had the necessary passes, they would be admitted to the aerodromes. No questions would be asked and the lorries would not be searched.

Almost unconsciously I had increased the pace until at last the track bore away to the right and dipped into a big gravel pit. We left the path here and, crouching low, struck farther right, keeping to the level ground until at last we came out on the edge of the pit. We wormed our way forward until we could look over the edge.

Micky gasped as he crawled up beside me. Parked in the pit below us were more than thirty big R.A.F. lorries. At the time I wondered how they had managed to obtain so many Air Force vehicles. Later I learnt that the organisation included men in the motor transport section of most of the fighter stations. The place seemed alive with men in R.A.F. uniforms. Some were sergeants, but mostly they were just aircraftmen. I saw no officers. The lorries were being loaded with what appeared to be large compressed-air cylinders. They looked very much like the hydrogen cylinders used for inflating barrage balloons. They were being brought from a hole in the far side of the pit. There were big piles of gravel on either side of the entrance, suggesting that the cache had been hidden by a heap of this gravel.

The lorries nearest the entrance to the pit appeared to have been loaded up. The drivers of the first three stood in a group chatting, obviously waiting for the order to move off. Many of the aircraftmen engaged in loading the lorries farther down the line had belts with revolvers in holsters. There were guards armed with rifles at the entrance to the pit where the ground rose to the level of the surrounding heath, and there were also several patrolling the edge of the pit. This caused me some uneasiness and I kept an eye on our rear and flank. But there seemed to be no guard near where we lay.

Then from behind one of the lorries walked a figure I knew. It was Vayle. I recognised his quick, purposeful walk despite the officer's uniform he wore. He went straight up the line of lorries to the drivers of the first three. Some twenty men followed him. I would have given anything to hear what he said to those men. The conversation did not last more than a minute. Then he glanced at his watch and a second later they had climbed into the lorries and the engines came to life. The men who had followed him piled into the backs of the lorries, about seven in each. The gears of the first grated and it swung out of the line towards the entrance. The other two followed. A moment later they disappeared and the sound of their engines gradually faded on the still night air.

Vayle came back along the line of lorries. His step was light and buoyant. There was pride and confidence in that step. I didn't like it. He came over to our side of the pit. I thrust my head a little farther forward so that I could see directly below me. Four men were standing there, silent, their hands and feet restless. Vayle walked straight up to them. "Any questions?" he asked. His voice, crisp and commanding, was just audible to me. "Good. The time is exactly one forty-six." He had waited for the precise minute, looking all the time at what appeared to be a stop-watch. They checked their watches by his. The timing was apparently an important factor. "You're quite clear about everything?" They nodded. "Make certain that the smoke containers are well covered. Argue rather than shoot. And see that the runway is clearly indicated. Fifty feet is the height. All right?" Again they nodded. "You'd better start, then. Good luck to you." They saluted. It was an Air Force salute, but somehow it was not quite an English salute—the body was too tense, the heels pressed too tightly together. They moved off to the next four lorries. Men began to pile into the back of them, again seven to each lorry.

"Don't move!"

The order came from behind us. My heart was in my mouth as I turned my head. Standing over us were three men. Two were guards. They had us covered with their rifles. The third was a civilian, and he had a revolver. It was he who had spoken. "Stand up!" he ordered.

We clambered to our feet. "What are you doing here?" he demanded.

"Just watching," I said, wondering what attitude to adopt. "What's going on?"

"That's none of your business," was the reply. "This is R.A.F. property. I shall have to hold you until we prove your identity."

"What is this—secret?" I asked.

He did not answer my question. "See if they're armed," he told one of the guards. "Put up your hands." The man stepped forward and ran his fingers quickly over us. "Unarmed," he reported.

"All right. Take them away and see that they don't escape. We'll deal with them later."

"Wot's the idea?" Micky demanded. "We ain't doing no 'arm. If this is private property, why don't you put a fence round it?"

"Take 'em away," the man commanded, and the two guards closed in on either side of us.

To attempt escape was out of the question. They would pick us off before we had gone a dozen yards.

And to wait for a chance that would probably never occur was equally hopeless, since minutes had become vital. The lorries were moving off, batch by batch, to a definite schedule. I knew something now of what the plan was—smoke to hamper ground defences as parachutists and troop carriers were landed on our most vital aerodromes. Something had to be done, and done quickly. "I want to speak to Mr. Vayle," I said. The man's quick glance of surprise did not escape me. "It's important," I added.

"I don't get you." The man's voice was wooden. He was giving nothing away.

"You understand perfectly," I replied.

"Who is Mr. Vayle?"

"Will you stop arguing," I said angrily. "In case you are not aware of it, your officer's name is Vayle, and he is librarian at Thorby aerodrome. Now will you kindly take me to him at once. There's no time to waste."

"What do you want to see him for?"

"That is a matter between him and myself," I replied. He hesitated. Then he said, "All right."

We were escorted along the edge of the pit, the two guards on either side and our civilian captor bringing up the rear. We entered the pit by way of the track. As we walked down the line of lorries, the men standing about fell silent. There were signs of nervousness in their interest. I was not surprised. It was a perilous game they were playing. It meant death if they were caught, and death was a possibility even if their plan succeeded.

Vayle turned as we came up to him. He was watching the loading of the last few lorries. He showed no surprise at the sight of us—only anger. "What the hell have you brought these men here for, Perret?"

"They got away from the house, as you expected, sir," replied our guard. "I arrested them at the edge of the pit over there."

"Yes, yes. But why the devil must you bother me with them?" You know the orders. Take 'em away!"

"Yes, sir. But this man"—he indicated me—"knew your name and insisted that he must see you. He said it was important."

Vayle swung round on me. "Well, what is it, Hanson?" he demanded sharply.

He was impatient at our intrusion. This was his big moment. He had worked for this for the past six years. He had made provision for everything—even for me. I could understand his irritation.

"I thought you might be interested to know that the game is up. The authorities at Thorby know the whole plot." It was thin, but it was the best I could do on the spur of the moment.

The lift of his thick eyebrows proclaimed his disbelief. He had planned carefully and his confidence was unshakable. I felt myself getting rattled. "You tried to kill me," I went on. "But you didn't suceeed." Then I suddenly remembered. "I told Winton everything. He didn't believe me at first. But when I showed him the diagram that was planted on me, he was sufficiently convinced to take precautions."

As soon as I mentioned that diagram I saw a sudden doubt mirrored in his eyes. He hesitated. Then he laughed. It was an easy, natural laugh. "It's no good, Hanson. If Winton really had taken precautions, why should you bother to warn me? Why should you have come out here at all?" He glanced at his watch. "Excuse me a moment." He left us and went down the line to give his blessing to the next group of lorries.

As soon as they had left, he came back to where we stood waiting. He was smiling and his eyes, which rested for a moment on mine, were cold. "Well, Hanson," he said, "this is the parting of the ways, I think. I go on—I hope—to a great victory, a victory that will make even the collapse of France look small. In a sense it will be my victory, for this is my scheme, and without the fighter 'dromes we could not invade Britain."

He paused, and for a moment he was no longer with us. His eyes had a far-away look. He was gazing at the castle of victory that his imagination had built for him. And then suddenly his eyes snapped out of their trance and became alive again. "And you," he said, "you go on——" He spread his hands in a singularly foreign gesture. "I am sorry," he went on. "I admire your nerve and brains. You saw something that others could not. And when you tried to tell them they wouldn't listen. It's a pity that you weren't content to sleep peacefully at Cold Harbour in the belief that you were mistaken. I knew Ryan would fool you. He's a dear old man. And so right in that setting. Did he talk to you about the Boer War?"

I nodded.

"I thought so. But I expect he omitted to mention the fact that he fought for the Boers, not the English. When he rang through to me, he told me that all your suspicions of the place had been allayed. What revived them? Was it the lorries?"

Again I nodded.

"Yes, I was afraid of that. It was my reason for having Perret watch you." Once again he glanced at his watch. "Well," he said, "your activities have added a certain zest to the game. I am glad to have known you. Goodbye." He bowed quite naturally and quite seriously. Then he addressed the man called Perret. "Get 'em into their lorry and drive it back past the Roebuck on to the hill down into Forest Row. There's quite a steep drop on the first bend; tip it over there and set fire to it. You understand?"

"I understand, sir."

The tone of the man's voice was significant. Vayle turned away. The matter was settled. It was not even a tense moment. There was nothing to grip one's imagination. There was nothing emotional or stirring about his words. The order had been given quietly, matter-of-factly. It might have been an ordinary every-day matter. Yet, in fact, it was cold-blooded murder. And the strange thing was there was nothing sinister about Vayle, no animosity in the way he spoke. I could not hate him.

I even found it difficult to blame him. Micky and I were just pawns that threatened his queen, pieces of grit that could mar the smooth-working machinery of his scheme. It was necessary that we should die. In the interests of his country he had given the necessary orders. He had shown no morbid interest in our reaction to his death sentence. He had made no attempt to gloat over our wretchedness. It made murder seem so natural. Two slugs had got in his cabbage patch and he had trodden on them.

That was my first reaction—surprise at murder done without feeling. But fear followed as we stumbled between our guards across the heath. Perret led us straight back to our lorry. It was quite evident that he knew exactly where it was. At first I could barely realise that those quiet, simple words of Vayle's meant that we should be dead in a few minutes' time. But after we had been trussed with ropes and bundled into the back of the lorry with a tarpaulin over us, I began to grasp the full significance of those orders. " —— and set fire to it." Should we still be alive when they did that? Was death by fire quick? I began to shiver. What was it like to die? I had never thought about it much. It all seemed so incredible. If only I had fallen asleep like Micky and had never heard the lorries grinding across the heath. Yet if Vayle's plans succeeded, all our gun team would probably be dead, too, in an hour's time.

I rolled over in the darkness. " Micky!" I spoke softly, for I knew one of the guards had come in the back of the lorry with us. " Micky!"

" Wot is it?" His voice sounded hoarse and strained.

" I'm sorry, Micky," I said. " I didn't think it would end like this."

He did not answer. I felt he must be angry. He had every right to be. " Micky," I said again. " I'm sorry. That's all I can say. It's just one of those things. A bit of luck and we'd have pulled off something big. He was too clever for us."

I heard him say something, but his words were lost in

the jolting of the lorry as it gathered speed on the rough lane leading down to the main road. "What did you say?" I asked.

I suddenly found his face close to mine. "Stop shooting yer mouth off, can't you?" he said quietly. "I'm lying on your jack-knife. It must 'ave fallen out of your pocket when they pitched us in 'ere. I'm trying to open it."

I lay still, not daring to hope, wondering what chance we had even if we did manage to cut ourselves out of the rope that bound our arms and legs. It was pitch dark under the tarpaulin, and it smelt strongly of malt. The jolting of the lorry hurt my shoulder. I wriggled over on to my other side. As I did so the lorry swung sharp left, flinging me on to my back and banging my head against the floor boards. After that the going was smoother. We had turned on to the main road. I leaned over towards Micky. "We've only got about four minutes," I said.

"Orl right, orl right," he grumbled. "Don't fuss. I've got the bloody thing open."

I could feel his body against mine. It was rigid as he struggled to cut through the ropes. Then suddenly it relaxed and he brought his feet up. His right arm moved stealthily—but freely.

"Yes, but what do we do when we've cut ourselves free?" I whispered. I felt helpless and rather a fool. The initiative should have been mine. I had got the lad into this scrape and felt it was up to me to get him out of it. Yet the leadership had passed from me.

His arm moved and his hand took hold of my arm, feeling for the rope. "You see," he whispered as he sawed at my bonds. A strand gave and then the knife slipped and cut into my hand. But my arms were free. A second later my feet were free too.

He stretched away from me a moment and then put his mouth close to my ear. "I can feel the end of the tarpaulin," he said. "You gotta take a chance. Move slowly to the other side of the truck as though you was still bound, and start 'ollering like you suffered from

176

clausterphoby—ain't it? I want 'is attention on you, see? Leave the rest to me."

"O.K.," I said.

He wriggled back against his side of the lorry. He took my jack-knife with him. His foot tapped my leg. I slid along the floor as far as I could without disturbing the tarpaulin. As soon as I felt it pressing against my back, I put my arms against my side and braced my legs together, so that I moved forward exactly as though I were still bound. At the same time I began to yell, " Let me out! Let me out! I can't stand it. Everything is black."

I heard the guard's feet move towards me. I tensed, nerving myself for the blow. And at the same time I kept yelling to be let out. His boot caught me in the ribs, rolling me on to the floor and knocking the breath out of me. But I began to scream.

" Shut up, you bastard, or I'll club you with my rifle."

I put my arm up to protect my head and continued to scream. I heard the sling swivels of his rifle rattle. I did not hear him raise it but I sensed it.

The blow never fell, however. There was a faint choking sound, and then the rifle clattered on the floor of the lorry. A second later his body thudded on the boards. I struggled clear of the tarpaulin to see Micky retrieve my jack-knife from the man's throat. I felt slightly sick. Blood was bubbling up in great gouts where the knife had been. Against the red of his neck his face looked horribly pallid in the moonlight.

The driver of the lorry suddenly braked. I glanced at the glass window at the back of the cabin. It had been slid back and the barrel of a revolver suddenly appeared. It was pointing to Micky. " Duck!" I yelled.

He dropped in the instant, and as he dropped, the revolver cracked and the bullet sang through the air in the direction in which he had been standing. I dived for the body. Subconsciously, I suppose, I had noticed the man's revolver when I first saw him lying on the boards, though the only thing I had consciously recorded was his throat. I slipped it from its holster and dived back to the shelter of the cabin, where Micky had already taken cover. The revolver turned, nosing blindly in our direction. It was the civilian, Perret, who had fired. But now he could not see us without leaning right across the driver. The lorry was drawing up. There was only one thing to do. and I did it.

I fired through the back of the cabin at the point where I thought his head would be. I hadn't fired a service revolver since my schooldays when I was at Bisley. My arm must have been too slack, for the kick was much greater than I had expected. This, coupled with the fact that the lorry swerved badly, caused me to lose my balance, and I fell headlong into the middle of the tarpaulin. For a moment I thought I had hit the driver by mistake. But by the time I had picked myself up he had got the lorry back on to the road again.

The brakes were no longer being applied. At the same time he was not accelerating. It was clear that he was undecided what to do. I peered cautiously through the little window of the cabin. Perret was huddled in a heap over the gears. I couldn't tell if he was dead or not, but he had a nasty wound across the side of his head.

I poked my gun through the window. "Draw up," I ordered the driver.

He glanced at me out of the corner of his eyes. He saw the gun and braked.

"Get that rifle," I told Micky. "I'll cover him from here. As soon as the lorry stops, jump out and cover him from the roadway."

He nodded. "Orl right," he said, and picked up the rifle. An instant later the lorry jerked to a stop. He was over the side before the wheels had stopped moving. "Put your hands up," I told the driver. "Now get down." There was no fight in him. He climbed down into the roadway, his hands above his head. He was a big, thick-set man and his bewilderment and fear were almost comical. I suppose he thought he was going to die. I got down from the back of the lorry and took his revolver from its holster. "Turn round," I ordered. As soon as he had done so I passed the revolver to Micky, barrel foremost. "Do you know how to knock a man out without killing him?" I asked in a whisper.

"You just watch me," he said.

He spat on his right hand and a second later he hit the man. The thud of it seemed to go right through me. Yet I saw him crumple up on the ground with a complete sense of detachment.

We pulled him to the side of the road and bound him with the rope that had been used for us. I stuffed his handkerchief into his mouth and put a length of rope round his head to keep the gag in. Then we got the other two bodies out of the lorry. Both of them were dead—the bullet I had fired at Perret had cracked the man's skull. We dragged them into the wood that bordered the road and hid them in some rhododendron bushes.

Then we went back to the lorry and drove on. I had driven fast on my way out to Cold Harbour, but on the return journey I pushed the Bedford to the limit of its speed. We had all too little time to spare. As we swept by the Roebuck and down the long hill with the bend on which we were to have been murdered, I saw that it was past three. And though I drove as fast as I dared, we did not run into Thorby village until twenty past.

"I'm going into the camp by the way I came out," I told Micky. "Are you still deserting or are you coming in with me?"

"I weren't deserting," he shouted angrily. "I were just transferring. You know that."

"Well, are you still going to transfer yourself, or are you staying with me?"

"I never deserted a pal yet."

"You mean, you're returning to camp with me?"

"I suppose so. But why d'you have to make it more difficult for us by going back the same way? Any one would think it was a bloody obstacle race. Why not drive up to the main gate and ask to see old man Winton?"

"Because time is precious," I said. And as I spoke we passed the turning that led to the main gates of the aerodrome. "Besides," I added, slowing down, "Winton probably wouldn't believe me. We've got to get hold of those lorries before we tackle Winton." I stopped the lorry. "Come on, this is where we came out."

We were half-way down the hill, and as soon as we had climbed out I released the brake and let the lorry run. "That'll distract their attention," I said, and led the way through the barbed-wire fence and into the wood that lay directly below our gun site.

Chapter Ten

SMOKE OVER THORBY

The crash of the lorry as it hit the bend seemed surprisingly loud. Automatically we halted, listening. The trees whispered amongst themselves, stirred by a faint breeze. There was no other sound. We crossed the trench where we had stumbled into each other only just over three hours ago. A ghostly pallor filtered through into the wood so that everywhere was shadow. We went stealthily, flitting from tree to tree. Reason told me that it was all right. A sentry would not leave the path without cause and, if he were anywhere near, his attention would be drawn towards the lorry. But reason could not still the flutter of my nerves. So much was at stake. We had to get back to the site without being caught. To be frustrated at the last moment by the obtuseness of a Guard's corporal would be bitter in the extreme. And I knew that the wood was the easiest part. Beyond was the slope up to the barbed wire. It was bare of all cover and would be lit by the moon. Finally there was the barbed wire itself.

We reached the path, a broad white swathe in the moonlight, and crossed it without mishap. At last the trees thinned and their leafy boughs stood out against the white of the hillside. We pushed through the low-hanging fringe of the trees and paused, gazing up at that pale grassy slope. There was the dannert wire, a dark streak against the grass, and along it a figure moved slowly. At every step the man's bayonet caught the moon and glinted white.

"Cor!" said Micky. "This ain't 'alf going to be a job."

I nodded. "I'm afraid the odds are against us," I said. "We'd better split up."

"O.K., mate. But what do I do if I get through and you don't?"

"Go to Gun Ops. and get in touch with any one in authority. Tell them what you've heard and seen. And if a sentry challenges you, don't try and get away. Good luck!" I said. "If we both get through we'll meet in the hut."

"See you in the 'ut, then."

"I hope so," I replied. And we parted company, advancing into the open and moving obliquely up the slope. The sentry was going away from us along the wire. He was the only one visible. There might be another where the wire ran into some trees to the south of our hut, but I had to risk that. Crouching low, I moved quickly up the slope, my eyes on the sentry. Once he stopped and stood for a moment gazing down into the valley. I flattened myself into the grass. The moon seemed unnaturally bright. I felt he must see me. But at length he resumed his pacing northwards along the wire.

I was now less than a hundred yards from the wire. I could just see the barbs on it. I began to worm my way forward on my stomach. My whole instinct was to make a wild dash for it. Time was so precious. But I knew that I should lose far more if I were caught. So I continued to crawl forward, laboriously slow though it seemed. I was lost among a forest of grass tussocks. I could no longer see the sentry without craning my head up and I could see no sign of Micky.

At last I was in view of the whole length of the wire from the trees on my left to a dip away to the north. The sentry was returning along his beat. I lay low, burying my face in the grass, hoping that my head would pass for a shadow. The jingle of his equipment came near and nearer, until I felt he must stumble right over me. I longed to look up and see whether he was looking at me. Suddenly I knew he was past me. The rattle of his bayonet against the rifle boss gradually receded. Then it stopped abruptly.

I couldn't resist the temptation. Cautiously I raised my head. He was standing stock-still about thirty yards along the wire to my left. The moon was behind him so that he was a dark silhouette, reminiscent of countless memorial statues to men who had died in the war to end war. It seemed an age that he stood there motionless, gazing down the slope in front of him. Somewhere on that slope Micky must be lying, waiting, as I was lying, waiting.

God knows how long he stood there. I didn't dare make the slight movement necessary to look at my wrist-watch. The smell of the dried grass reminded me of the lazy peace of summer under an oak tree or the still quiet of the Sussex downs. The familiar scent brought an ache of longing to my heart for the days that were gone. At last he moved on, but only to stop a few yards farther on to gaze again down the moonlit slope. My heart began to thud against my ribs. Surely he must have seen Micky. His bayonet caught the moon and the steel of it shone white.

I thought he never would move on. Time was passing. and time was precious. Already I thought I could sense a slight lightening of the sky that was not due to the moon. Dawn would soon be here.

But at last he turned and resumed his measured pacing along the wire. He did not pause again, and finally disappeared into the little stretch of wood through which the wire ran. This wood was not more than fifty yards away to my left. Had time been less pressing, I should have waited until he came back along his beat and was walking away from me to the north. That would have been the safest thing to do. I could then have made certain that his back was towards me. But my watch showed the time to be already three thirty-five. If I waited until he returned it might easily be another quarter of an hour before I could cross the wire. I dared not wait that long. I had to chance it.

I raised my head up out of the grass. There was no sign of any other sentry patrolling the wire. I rose to my feet and, crouched low, made for the wire.

There was no retreat now. I reached the wire and parted the near side of a coil with my gloved hands. I did not even glance in the direction of the wood. If he were standing there watching me, there was nothing I could do about it. My whole attention was concentrated on getting through that wire in the quickest possible time. Had the slope been down instead of up, I am certain I should have risked jumping it. As it was I had to follow the more laborious procedure of climbing through it. And the angle of the slope made it more difficult.

I slipped into the gap I had made in the near side of the coil and then, pressing the farther side apart, swung my right leg high over the wire into the gap.

"Halt! Who goes there?"

The challenge rang out clear and startling in the stillness. I froze, the barbs of the wire cutting into the flesh between my legs. Instinctively I looked in the direction of the wood. But before my eyes had seen that there was no one there, I had realised that the challenge had come from the opposite direction. As I turned my head I heard the sound of a man running. He was coming along the wire, up out of the dip, as fast as his equipment would allow him. His rifle, its bayonet gleaming, was held at the ready.

For an instant panic seized me. I wanted to run. But I was still astride the crossed coils of the wire. Before

I could get clear he would have ample time to pick me off. I waited. There was nothing else I could do. The sweat broke out on my forehead with the sense of frustration that overwhelmed me. There was the hut and the gun pit. They were not more than fifty yards away and so plain in the moonlight that I could almost believe myself there. Just fifty yards between success and failure. It was heart-breaking. But perhaps Micky would get through.

"What are ye doing?" The man had halted a few yards from me and I saw his thumb on the safety-catch of his rifle. He was a Scots Guard, big and heavily built, with a flattened nose and large hands.

"Trying to get through the wire," I said. "Do you mind if I get my other leg over. It isn't very comfortable in this position."

"All raight. Bun dinna play ony tricks. If ye du I'll no hesitate to shoot."

"I won't play any tricks," I said. I pressed the wire down and swung my other leg over. I managed it better this time and did not lose my balance.

"Why are ye creeping into the camp like this?" he demanded.

"I broke camp," I replied. "That's my gun site over there. I had a good reason for doing so."

"Och, mon, it willna du." He shook his head. "Ye've got yerself in a awfu' mess."

"Look," I said. "Be a sport. I had my own reasons for breaking camp."

"Ye canna wheedle me. I know my duty. Ye're under arrest."

Out of the corner of my eyes I saw Micky creeping up on the wire. I moved a little farther along so that the sentry had to turn away from Micky in order to keep facing me. "Stand still!" The rifle jerked threateningly.

"Give me a break," I said. "We've been in this place more than a month without leave. We haven't even had any local leave." Micky was at the wire now.

"I had to see someone. It was urgent. The only way I could do it was by breaking camp. I bet you haven't been long in this place. You'd understand if you had." I was scarcely thinking what I was saying. Anything would do so long as it kept his attention away from Micky, who was now clambering through the wire.

"That sort o' talk willna get ye onywhere." The man was ruffled. I felt he would like to have let me go, but he didn't dare. "Ye'll have to see the corporal. Ye might be a German parachutist for all I ken. Come on, now. Get going."

At that moment there was a dull thud along the wire. Micky had lost his balance and fallen flat on his face.

The sentry swung round. Instantly his rifle was at his shoulder. "Halt!"

Micky had just got to his feet again. His head jerked quickly in our direction. His face looked very pale in the moonlight. I could even see his eyes. They were narrowed and shifty-looking. His momentary hesitation was obvious. In a flash my mind wondered how often he had looked at a policeman in that same indecisive manner. Suddenly he dived forward. He looked like a little rabbit scuttling to cover towards the hut.

"Halt, or I fire!" The sentry's thumb pressed the safety-catch forward.

I jumped forward. "Don't fire!" I said. "He's my pal. Don't fire!"

Micky might think he had a chance, but he was not a fast runner and he was not attempting to zigzag. To a good marksman he was an absolute sitter.

"Micky!" I yelled. "Micky! Stop!"

He glanced over his shoulder. I waved to him. "Come over here," I called. "Quick!" And in practically the same breath I said to the Guardsman, "Hold your fire. He's all right—only scared of being caught."

Micky had stopped, doubtful what to do. "Come over here!" I called to him again. Reluctantly he began to walk in our direction.

The sentry lowered his rifle. He turned to me. "Will ye tell me what's going on here? Are there ony mair of ye?"

"No," I replied. "There's only the two of us. And I didn't break camp to meet my girl friend. We broke camp to get certain vital information from men we knew to be Nazi agents."

"It willna du." He shook his head. "Ye'd best tell the truth when ye see the corporal. Come on now. March!" By changing my story I had lost his sympathy. It was a pity. But it couldn't be helped. Pray God the corporal wasn't a fool. The sentry fell in behind me. "Gang straight for that pill-box oop yonder."

Micky joined me. He was still panting slightly. "Why the hell did you call me?" he demanded gruffly, as he fell into step beside me. "I could 'a' made it."

"You could not," I told him.

"I thought this information was important. It was worth the risk, wasn't it?"

"It wouldn't have helped to have you shot," I said. "He couldn't have missed at that range."

He didn't reply to that and we walked on in silence. We climbed the final slope of the hill. The pill-box, which was about a hundred yards to the north of our hut, looked squat and menacing in the moonlight.

"Corporal! Corporal!" called our guard as we approached the low concrete and brick structure. "Corporal!"

The corporal in charge came out, crouching to get through the low entrance of the pill-box. He blinked the sleep out of his eyes as he came up to us. He was short for a Guardsman, and he had reddish hair and a sharp, rather bitter face. This was going to be difficult.

"What's all this?" he demanded. There was only the faintest trace of a Scotch accent.

"A' caught these two getting into the camp over the wire, Corporal." Our guard nodded in my direction. "First this laddie says he broke camp to meet his lassie.

Then when I challenge the other laddie he says they broke camp together in order to get some information aboot Nazi agents. They say they belong to the gun over yonder."

The corporal looked us up and down. His eyes were sharp and close-set. "Name and number?" he demanded.

"Hanson," I said, and gave him my number. Micky also gave the information he wanted. He then checked our papers and aerodrome passes.

"Right," he said. Then, turning towards the pill-box, "Guard, turn out!"

They tumbled out, bleary-eyed and half awake, putting their tin hats on as they came.

"McGregor and Baird, march these men down to the guardroom."

I cleared my throat—I felt nervous. "Excuse me, Corporal," I said, "but——"

I got no further. "Anything you have to say, say it to the duty officer when you come on charge in the morning."

"I would like to see my sergeant before going to the guardroom."

"I will see him. If you really belong to the site, I will let him know that you have returned."

"But I must see him. It's of vital importance——"

"Don't argue. March 'em away."

"God in heaven, man," I cried, "do you want the Germans to land on the 'drome without any one having a chance to prevent them?"

"Speak when you're spoken to, Gunner," he barked. "You're under arrest. Try to remember that. You'll have a chance to think up all your crazy excuses for breaking camp in the guardroom. You," he said to the two Guardsmen detailed as escort, "take 'em away."

I broke free of them as they closed in on me. My sense of frustration was so great that I lost control of myself. "Listen, you fool!" I began.

"Don't adopt that tone with me," he cried.

"Shut up." I spoke quietly. And perhaps because there was a ring of authority in my voice, he did not interrupt

187

me this time. "If you don't let me see Sergeant Langdon, I can almost certainly guarantee that you will pay for your denseness with your life. At dawn this morning this and other fighter stations are going to be invaded from the air. Normally a landing on the 'drome wouldn't succeed. At this moment three, possibly four, R.A.F. lorries manned by Nazi agents are approaching Thorby. They carry smoke containers. The wind is north-east." I glanced at my watch. "The time is now three-fifty. At any moment now those lorries will enter the camp and drive along the tarmac here. They will take up a position somewhat to the north of us. A smoke screen will then be laid across the 'drome. Under cover of that smoke-screen troop-carriers will land. And under cover of that smoke screen the ground defences will be stormed."

I had shaken him. I could see it in his face. In my desperation my voice had probably carried conviction. "And how would the troop-carriers land if the runways were screened by smoke?"

"They will land blind," I said. "The start and finish of the runways will be marked by captive balloons flown at a definite height. Probably they will carry lights. There's very little time if the other 'dromes are to be warned. That's why I want to see my sergeant."

"Why don't you want to see the ground-defence officer—eh?" He was still suspicious.

"Because by the time I had got him out of bed and convinced him that I wasn't crazy, it might be too late to stop the smoke screen." I didn't tell him that I was afraid the ground-defence officer might not believe me and that I wanted sufficient proof to leave him in no doubt of the position. "All I want to do is to have five minutes' talk with Sergeant Langdon. That's not an unreasonable request, surely?"

He hesitated. "Well," he said, "it can't do any harm." Then, with a resumption of his previous sharpness: "All right. March 'em over to the hut yonder. Lance-Corporal Jackson, take charge."

We were half-way to the hut when I heard the sound

188

of engines approaching from the direction of the square. A sudden excitement surged through me. An instant later the first of four R.A.F. lorries appeared from behind the low bulk of the hut. They lumbered past us along the tarmac, dark, cumbersome shapes against the moon. I turned to the corporal . " That's them," I said.

" They look all right to me," he said. But I could see that he was impressed.

I went in by the back entrance of our hut, the corporal following close on my heels. The door of the sergeant's room was on the right. I went straight in. A hurricane lamp turned low stood on a table beside Langdon's bed. I shook his shoulder. He mumbled and turned over with his eyes tight shut. I shook him again. " What is it?" Unwillingly he opened his eyes.

" Good God, Hanson !" He sat up in bed with a jerk. " Where the hell have you been? Is Micky with you?"

Before I could say anything the Guards' corporal said : " This is one of your men, is he, Sergeant?"

" Yes."

" We caught the two of them entering the camp over the wire just below your site."

" What's going on here?" It was Bombardier Hood's voice. He pushed past the corporal into the room. " Oh, so you're back, are you? I just came in to wake my relief and heard voices in here," he added by way of explanation. He was fully dressed with gas mask at the alert and he carried a rifle and bayonet.

" Sergeant Langdon," I said.

" Yes?"

" I want you to give Bombardier Hood instructions to get every one up and dressed as quickly as possible."

" But why?"

" What the devil are you talking about?" cut in Hood. " Do you realise that you've done a very serious thing, breaking camp. Your absence was reported to Mr. Ogilvie."

" There's no time to waste," I told Langdon urgently.

"There's going to be an air invasion of the 'drome at dawn. Four lorries carrying smoke containers have been got into the camp. They passed the site just before I woke you. The smoke will screen the landing."

"What the hell are you talking about?" demanded Langdon, swinging his feet out of bed. "How do you know this?"

"I've just watched Vayle superintending the loading of the lorries and issuing his instructions. It was at an isolated place called Cold Harbour Farm in Ashdown Forest. They caught us, but we killed two of the guards and got away." I pulled the revolver I had taken from our guard out of my pocket and tossed it on to the bed. "There's a revolver we took off one of them. I'll give you the details as the others are getting dressed."

Langdon hesitated. His face wore a puzzled frown. Suddenly he glanced up at Hood. "Have four lorries passed the pit?"

"Yes, just before I came in to wake my relief," he replied. "But they were perfectly ordinary R.A.F. lorries. You're surely not going to take any notice of this ridiculous story. Personally I think Hanson is trying to screen his own rather peculiar activities. You remember, just after he arrived here there was that business of a plan of the ground defences being found on a Nazi agent. Then he talked with that German pilot and later he was identified——"

"Give a 'Take post'," Langdon cut in.

"But it's a ridiculous story. R.A.F. lorries with smoke containers! It's——"

"Give the 'Take post'," Langdon ordered. "We'll soon find out if there's any truth in it."

Hood went out sullenly. A second later came his shout of "Take post." It was followed almost immediately by the sound of men scrambling out of bed and into their clothes. The thin partition wall only slightly muffled the noise, and the hut itself shook to the sudden burst of activity.

"Now then, tell me the whole story," said Langdon as he slipped his trousers on over his pyjamas.

Briefly I outlined the events of the night, with some reference to the things that had led up to them.

"And what do you suggest this detachment does?" he asked when I had finished.

"Surrounds the lorries," I replied. "No officer is going to send out an urgent warning to all the other fighter 'dromes unless this ridiculous story of mine is backed up by some concrete evidence. If you find those lorries are harmless, I don't care what happens to me. Anyway, I know they're not harmless."

"All right. We'll do that. Are you willing to leave these two men in my charge, Corporal? I'll make myself personally responsible for them."

"Very good, Sergeant."

"Oh, just a minute, Corporal," said Langdon as the other was leaving the room. "Hanson here expects the lorries to be parked somewhere on the north-east side of the landing field. Will you notify all Guards' posts along this side of the field that in the event of rifle fire being heard they are to close in on four R.A.F. lorries. The personnel of these lorries are dressed in R.A.F. uniforms."

"Verra good, Sergeant. I'll do that."

As he went out, Micky appeared in the doorway, looking rather sheepish. "And I'll bet you didn't go out after fifth columnists," said Langdon as he put on his battle top.

Micky looked uncomfortable, but said nothing.

"All right. Go and get your rifle," said Langdon.

A sudden glint of eagerness showed in Micky's eyes. "An' baynet, Sarge? Cold steel! That's the stuff to give the bastards."

"All right." Langdon turned to me. "I don't know whether it has any bearing on the position, but Squadron-Leader Nightingale drove up to the pit at about twelve-thirty. There was an alarm on at the time. He asked for you. When I told him that you were missing, he ran back to his car and drove off at a terrific lick. He had that Waaf of yours with him."

"He knows the situation," I said. "He got in touch

with a fellow on my paper for me. He may have got some fresh information."

Bombardier Hood came in. "Well, they're all dressed, Sergeant. And I've kept them in the hut." His tone conveyed his complete disagreement with the arrangement.

"All right. Come on, then, Hanson. And I hope to God this doesn't prove to be a fool's errand." Langdon led the way out of the room and into the hut, where one hurricane lamp was all that lit the gloom of the blackout.

Everyone was crowded round Micky. They fell silent as we entered. Every face was turned towards us. "Get your rifles," ordered Langdon. "Issue twenty rounds per man, Bombardier Hood. Fuller, you will remain as sentry." Whilst the rounds were being issued, Langdon said: "Hanson has returned to camp with a story of an air invasion at dawn. Four lorries have arrived on the landing ground which he says are manned by fifth columnists whose job it is to put a smoke screen across the 'drome at the appropriate moment. I intend to investigate these lorries. We will surround one of them and I shall go forward and examine it myself. It will be your job to cover me, and if there's any truth in Hanson's story I shall rely on you to cover me properly. Micky, Chetwood, Helson and Hood, you will carry hand grenades. You'll find them under my bed. Right, let's get going."

Outside the moon, though low in the west, was bright by comparison with the gloom of the hut. A faint pallor showed in the eastern sky. I glanced at my watch. It was past four. "Dawn will soon be breaking," I said.

"Will they attack before it's light or after?" Langdon asked me.

"I don't know," I replied. "I should think about half light. They would want to get the troop-carriers in before it was light enough to make them an easy target for our fighters."

As we passed the pit, the stocky barrel of the three-inch lifting darkly against the moon, Langdon said: "Helson, my bike is over there. Will you bring it along? I may want you to act as runner if anything happens."

"O.K., John. Shall I bring the gun as well?"

The laughter that greeted his remark was derisive. Kan's rather high-pitched laugh and Chetwood's deep bellow rang out clear above the others. I glanced back. The detachment was following us in a ragged bunch, and I noticed that Kan and Chetwood were walking on either side of Hood. He was talking and they were listening intently. I couldn't hear what he was saying, but for a second his eyes met mine, and I knew that if by any chance the lorries turned out to be harmless it would go ill with me.

Half unconsciously I quickened my pace as we reached the tarmac edge of the landing field. Langdon and I walked in silence. For myself, I began to feel uneasy, almost frightened. The events of the night seemed more like a dream than the reality I knew them to be, and now that I had persuaded Langdon to action I had an unpleasant feeling that I might be wrong. All my self-confidence seemed to have been expended in my effort to obtain this positive action. Langdon, too, was anxious. If I was wrong, he would look a fool in the eyes of his detachment and would have some awkward questions to answer when I came up on charge in the morning.

We passed the dispersal point to the north of our site. We were half-way to the next dispersal point when Hood joined us. "Where are your lorries?" he asked.

The question was pertinent, but the way he put it was almost exultant. In that moment I came as near to hating any one as I have ever done. Dimly I could now make out the trees and scrub at the north end of the 'drome. The tarmac roadway, a ribbon of white in the moonlight, curved away to the left as it followed the perimeter of the landing field. Nowhere could I see any sign of the lorries. I felt a sudden sinking sensation inside me. The gravel pit by Cold Harbour Farm seemed so far away and unreal. I felt scared. "We'll cut down behind the next dispersal point," I said. "They've probably spread out along the slope in order to cover as much ground as possible with the smoke."

Hood grunted. His disbelief was quite unmasked. I sensed that Langdon was feeling uncomfortable and ill at ease.

We struck off the tarmac on to the dry, coarse grass. We passed the crumbling sandbags of what had once been a Lewis gun pit. In places the grass gave way to bare, baked earth. The grass became thick and more plentiful, however, as we reached the slope and passed behind the great bank of the dispersal point. We threaded our way between two bomb craters, relics of Friday's raid, stumbling over heaps of loose clay that were hard like bricks.

At last we came in sight of the wire that stretched like a dark snake across the grass half-way down the slope. Two men moved along it, carrying a heavy cylindrical object between them. They were in R.A.F. uniform. I touched Langdon's arm. I had a sudden feeling of triumph. My relief was so great that I could hardly speak. "That looks like one of the smoke cylinders," I said.

We had stopped, and for a moment we watched the two men moving along the wire with their burden. The others crowded up behind us. They had stopped talking, sensing some development. "All right," Langdon said. "Leave your rifle, Hanson, and come on with me. The rest of you get down in the grass and don't make a sound."

Langdon and I went forward alone. We did not attempt to conceal ourselves. We walked diagonally along the slope and at every step more and more of the wire came into view. Two more men in R.A.F. uniform appeared, carrying another cylinder between them. And then at last we sighted an R.A.F. lorry parked against the wire at a crazy angle. Four men were busy unloading the cylinders from it. One of the Guards' sentries was leaning on his rifle watching them.

"Good enough," said Langdon. "So far as it goes you're right."

. We turned and retraced our steps. "What do you mean—so far as it goes?" I asked.

"Well, I've got to satisfy myself that they shouldn't be doing what they are doing."

"But surely you believe what I have told you now?"

"Yes. But it's just possible you may have been mistaken. God knows, I hope not for your sake. But it is possible that they may be R.A.F. and that they may have orders to put those cylinders out along the wire. You see my point?"

"What are you going to do, then?" I asked.

"Try and bluff them into showing their hand."

We had reached the others now. "Get back to the road as quickly as possible," Langdon ordered. "Go quietly and keep low."

I picked up my rifle and followed him. As soon as we were out of sight of the wire he broke into a trot. We rounded the end of the dispersal point and reached the tarmac. On the roadway we increased the pace. After doing about three hundred yards at the double, Langdon stopped. When the whole detachment had come up with us, he said: "There is an R.A.F. lorry almost directly below us down the slope of the hill. That is our objective. I want you to spread out about twenty yards apart in a long line. We will then move forward. As soon as you come within sight of the lorry, get down and try to creep forward without being seen. I want you to finish up in a big semi-circle round the lorry. That means the two flanks will close in. Your final position must not be more than two hundred yards from the lorry. You'll have five minutes from the time we move forward to get into position. I shall then go forward on my own. You will not open fire until either I give the order or they open fire. If I give that order or if they fire on me, I shall rely on you to take the lorry in the quickest possible time. It will mean that they are there for the purpose of assisting an invasion of the 'drome, and there will be very little time to spare. Is that understood?"

No one said a word. "All right, then. Spread out on either side of me at the double."

As soon as the detachment had spread out in a line along the edge of the roadway, Langdon waved his hand and started forward. Langdon, Hood and myself were together in a little bunch. Micky was twenty yards to the left of us, and Helson, who had left his bike on the edge of the roadway, was on our right. The line was not very impressive, there being only four men on either side of us. But it advanced with some pretensions of a line, and as a result looked reasonably like an infantry section in extended order.

We soon topped the brow of the hill, and before we had gone thirty yards down the slope we sighted the lorry. Langdon had judged it nicely. We ourselves were directly above it. We crouched down, moving forward more cautiously. The moon was low enough now for the sharper slope of the hill near the brow to be in shadow. This shadow completely swallowed up the detachment, so that, looking on either side of us, I could scarcely believe that we were not alone.

The slope gradually eased off and the shadow ended abruptly. We were less than a hundred yards from the lorry and we halted here. I touched Langdon's arm and pointed along the wire to the north. The slope spread out here in a shoulder and on it, close against the wire, was parked a second R.A.F. lorry. Here, too, men dressed in R.A.F. uniform were carrying cylinders along the wire.

Langdon looked at his watch. "The five minutes is up," he said. "I'll go and see what they're up to."

"It's suicide," I said. "If you force them to show their hand you'll get killed. This is too big a thing for them to have any scruples."

"Well, at least I shall have died to some purpose," he said with a boyish laugh which sounded brittle and false to my sensitive ears.

"Let me go," I said. "It's my show."

"No, this part of it's mine," he said. "You've done
196

enough." His tone was quiet and final. He was, after all, the detachment commander.

"Well, whoever you talk to, see that you don't get in my line of fire. I used to be something of a shot when I was at school. I'll keep him covered the whole time."

"Thanks." He rose to his feet and went down the slope, his slim figure suddenly showing up in the slanting light of the moon. Beyond him the eastern sky was paling.

It all seemed so strangely ordinary. And yet there was a difference. The slope down which John Langdon was walking and the line of dannert wire—I knew it all so well. In the stillness of the evenings I had walked along this hillside. And my rifle! It had just been something to take on night guards. Now all these familiar things took on a new significance. This hillside might suddenly become a miniature battlefield. My rifle was suddenly a weapon. And yet there was no visible indication of a change. Everything looked much the same.

Langdon had reached the lorry now. A man in the uniform of an R.A.F. sergeant jumped out of the back of it. Langdon moved slightly so that he did not screen the man. Quickly I cocked my rifle and raised it to my shoulder. It seemed rather unnecessary. The man was unarmed. I could see no sign of hostility.

Hood probably sensed my feeling, for he suddenly said: "Mind that thing doesn't go off. You don't get away with murder just because you're in uniform."

I made no reply. I felt distinctly uncomfortable.

The Guards' sentry had continued on his beat. Langdon was alone. Two men were watching him from the tail-board of the lorry. I wished I had brought a pair of glasses with me. Langdon nodded in our direction. The R.A.F. sergeant glanced at the slope above him.

Then suddenly the whole atmosphere of the scene changed. The man had produced a small automatic from his pocket. I saw it glint in the moonlight as he waved Langdon towards the back of the lorry.

Automatically my forefinger had taken the first pressure

on the trigger. Langdon moved slowly towards the lorry
The man covering him pivoted but did not actually move
The foresight came up into the U of the backsight. I
squeezed the trigger. The recoil was pleasantly reminiscent
of the ranges at Bisley. There was no sense of killing. The
man was just a target. He jerked forward with the force
of the bullet's impact, stumbled and slowly crumpled. I
reloaded automatically without removing the rifle from my
shoulder.

Langdon hesitated for a second, watching the man fall.
It was like a "still" from a film. The two men on
the tail-board of the lorry gazed at their leader, fascinated,
momentarily incapable of action. Then men carrying the
cylinders along the wire halted.

Then suddenly, like puppets, they all came to life.
Langdon dived for the slope. The men along the wire
dropped their cylinders and ran for the lorry. The two
men on the tail-board disappeared inside. They reappeared,
a second later, with rifles. Two more came out from
behind the lorry, they also had rifles.

Langdon had reached the steepest part of the slope.
He was running hard and zigzagged at the same time.
I fired at the men on the tail-board. As I reloaded I
heard the crack of Hood's rifle just to the left of me.
I fired again. Sporadic fire had now developed along
the whole of our short line. One of the men on the
tail-board toppled to the ground. The other disappeared
inside. I turned my fire on the four men who were coming
up along the wire. They were spread out, and though little
spurts of earth were shooting up all round them, they
made the lorry without being hit.

"They've got down behind the wheels of the lorry,"
Hood said. Little spurts of flame showed in the dark
behind the bulk of the lorry. I could hear the thud
of bullets as they lashed into the grass at Langdon's
feet. I concentrated my aim on the pin-points of flame,
firing rapidly. Others were doing the same. I don't know
whether we hit any one, but our fire seemed to put

them off their aim, for Langdon reached the shadow and jumped down beside us, panting heavily.

I stopped firing. I had only six rounds left. " What do we do now?" I asked.

" Send a runner back," Langdon replied breathlessly. " Helson !" he called.

" Yes, sergeant," came his voice from the right of us.

" Get on that bicycle. Ride to the pit and 'phone Gun Ops. Tell 'em what's happened. We want reserves to put these lorries out of action. Tell 'em to issue an Attack Alarm, have all ground defences manned—to prepare for an air invasion of the 'drome within the next half-hour. O.K.?"

" Right." Vaguely his form loomed up out of the grass as he scrambled to his feet and started back up the slope.

" What about the armoured car over by Station H.Q.?" said Hood. " It's just the thing for this job."

" You're right. When you've done that, Helson," Langdon called after him, " go down to Station H.Q. and rout out the R.A. lads who run that armoured car. Bring it back here."

" O.K." He disappeared from sight, merging into the shadow of the hillside.

" They're getting a Bren gun out," Hood said, and his rifle cracked. One of the men, who had appeared on the tail-board again, ducked. I raised my rifle and fired. I had the satisfaction of seeing his legs give under him. But he still continued to hand down first two guns and then four boxes of ammunition. I fired again at the men on the ground. Fire crackled out along the hillside once more. But they got the two guns into cover behind the lorry.

" Hold your fire !" Langdon yelled.

There was no alternative. Every one's ammunition was getting very low. We had to keep some reserve until reinforcements came up.

Langdon nudged my arm. " The Guards are coming

up, along the wire. See?" Two men were running along the wire with bayonets fixed and others were moving along the slope of the hill in extended formation.

I suddenly felt sorry for the poor devils behind the lorry. They were doing their job as they saw it, just as we were doing ours—and they hadn't a hope, unless the time fixed for the landing was very near indeed. The sky was perceptibly lightening. I glanced at my watch. It was nearly four-twenty. I began to feel anxious. There were those other three lorries. So far we had done nothing about them. And though the cylinders which had been carried out along the barbed wire to the south of us were useless, this lorry could still contribute to the smoke screen with the cylinders that had not yet removed from it.

"We must do something about those other lorries," I said to Langdon.

"Yes, but what?" he replied. "The armoured car is the only thing that will fix them."

"But that may be too late."

"Yes, but what the hell can we do? We'll have to wait for that."

The paling night had become quiet again. It seemed like the lull before the storm. How long would this quiet last? I had a vision of those big Ju 52's coming in through the smoke, disgorging their hordes of field grey. Two a minute, we had been told, was the speed at which they could land. Something had to be done.

The quiet was shattered by the ugly clatter of a Bren gun. The fire was not directed at us, but at the line of Guards advancing along the slope.

In a flash inspiration came to me. "My God!" I said to Langdon. "The Bofors. Number Five pit has a field of fire right down the slope. It should be possible to bring it to bear on one of the lorries at any rate."

"You're right, by God," he said. "Take charge, will you, Hood. Hanson and I are going up to Number Five pit."

"Wait," Hood said. We checked, half standing.

"Christ! he'll never make it." Hood's voice was a tone higher than usual in his excitement.

We both crouched, breathless. I felt a horrible sick sensation inside me. At any moment I expected that small figure to double up and pitch headlong down the slope.

It was Micky. He had jumped to his feet and was running down the slope like a mad thing. His rifle, complete with bayonet, was slung across his shoulders. "What the hell is the fool up to?" I muttered.

The Bren gun was chattering away. But its fire was still concentrated on the advancing Guards. Apparently they saw Micky too late, for when they checked their fire in order to train their gun on to him, he was already at the foot of the steep part of the slope and within some thirty yards of the lorry. He suddenly stopped and swung his right arm back. For an instant he stood poised like a javelin thrower. Then his arm came forward and a small object curved lazily through the air. At the same instant the Bren gun set up its rat-a-tat again, and Micky checked and staggered.

I lost sight of the Mills bomb he had thrown. But it must have been well aimed, for he had barely fallen to the hail of bullets that bit into the turf all round him, when there was a sudden flash beneath the lorry, followed by the sound of an explosion; not loud, but sharp. The lorry rocked slightly and several pieces of wood were flung into the air.

Complete silence followed the explosion. Then quietly, menacingly, smoke began to rise out of the back of the lorry. At first I thought it must be on fire. But the stuff began to pour out in a great cloud, thick and black like funnel smoke. Then I knew that the smoke cylinders had been hit.

Micky was on his feet again now and running rather jerkily towards the lorry. He made it just as one of the Bren gunners staggered out from behind it. Micky had unslung his rifle. The fellow tried to dive back into the lorry. But Micky was on him before he could turn. I saw a flash of steel in the moonlight and the man fell, pinned to the ground by the force of Micky's lunge. The last I saw of Micky as the smoke enveloped the lorry, he was tugging to get his bayonet out of the poor wretch.

The smoke lay close to the ground like a thick amorphous blanket, gathering volume with every second. In an instant the lorry was lost to sight as the breeze rolled the smoke up the slope towards us.

"Come on," said Langdon. "Let's get to the Bofors."

We scrambled up the slope and struck northwards along the brow of the hill. As we ran I asked Langdon what had made the fellow he had spoken to produce a gun. "He said he was acting under instructions from Winton," Langdon replied. "They were going to test smoke as a means of defending the 'drome against heavy air attacks. I asked to see his instructions. When he said that they were given to him verbally, I told him he would have to get the cylinders back into the lorry and return to Station H.Q. for written instructions. We argued for a bit, and when I made it clear that I suspected him and that I was determined to prevent the cylinders from being set off, he showed his hand."

We were now in sight of Number Five pit. The slender barrel of the Bofors showed above the sand-bagged parapet. Tin-hatted figures were moving about inside the pit and other members of the team were standing about outside their hut, fully dressed. The pit was perched just on the brow of the hill. One of the lorries was almost directly below it and another was just visible about seven hundred yads farther north long the wire.

When we arrived at the pit the sergeant in charge was at the 'phone. We were challenged, but the guard recognised Langdon and let us enter the pit.

"Sergeant Guest." Langdon's interruption was met by a silencing wave of the hand. Langdon went over to the fellow and tapped him on the shoulder.

The sergeant turned impatiently. "Keep quiet," he said. "This is important. They're expecting an invasion at dawn."

"I know, I know," Langdon said. "Its' one of my fellows reporting to Gun Ops. Put that 'phone down and listen a minute."

Guest handed the receiver to his bombardier. "What do you mean—one of your fellows? What's happening? There's been firing——"

"That was us," Langdon interrupted. Briefly he outlined the situation.

When he came to the point of our visit—that the Bofors should open fire on the two R.A.F. lorries visible from he pit, Sergeant Guest said : "I can't very well do that without an officer's permission. I mean, how am I to know that they aren't really R.A.F. lorries?"

"Well, get your men on to tearing down the sandbags so that we can lay on the lorries while we talk the matter over," Langdon said.

We had barely convinced him of the need for opening fire by the time sufficient parapet had been taken down, and then it was only with great reluctance that he gave the order to load and lay on the lorry immediately below the pit. He didn't like it. I must say I couldn't blame him. He had only our word for what was going on. I don't think he would have done it at all if he hadn't seen the dense blanket of smoke creeping over the brow of the hill to the south and spreading across the landing field.

"All right," he said at last. "Layers on. Load! Lay on that R.A.F. lorry. Vertical zero, lateral zero."

"On, on," came from the two layers.

"Set to auto. One burst. Fire!"

The pit shook at the sudden utterances of the gun— Umm-pom, umm-pom, umm-pom. The flame guard belched fire and the barrel thrust backwards and forwards at each shot. The tracer shells flew through the air like little flaming oranges chasing each other to the target. They hit the lorry square amidships and burst with soft plops. Five shots and the lorry had disintegrated into a great billow of smoke that poured out from its shattered sides and, began immediately to creep up the hill, hugging the ground.

"By God, Langdon, you're right," cried Guest excitedly. "It is smoke."

"Get that other lorry," shouted Langdon. "This stuff will be on top of us in a moment."

The gun traversed left. More sandbags had to be removed from the parapet before the layers could get on target. The smoke rolled up the hill, thick and black and strangely menacing. The vanguard of it topped the hill to the south of us, putting a dense screen between ourselves and the dispersal point below which we had attacked the first lorry. It was clear we should miss the bulk of it, but the fringe of the wretched stuff was only a few yards from us when the layers reported. "On, on."

A moment later the Bofors spoke. It was like the sound of tom-toms in a mountain gorge, steady and angry. The first two little balls of fire hit the slope in the foreground. The layers elevated slightly and the fourth shell registered a direct hit on the cabin. Two more shells and Guest ordered "Cease fire!" The last shell so shook the wreckage that it slowly toppled over on to the wire. Great volumes of black smoke poured lazily from it as it had from the other two.

"Nice work," I said. I had a horrible feeling of exultation. "Now there's only one left and the armoured car ought to be able to deal with that."

"If it can get through all this smoke," said Langdon.

"No matter," I said. "One lorry won't make much of a smoke screen."

"Yes, but supposing they came over now." He looked anxious. "The whole field will be covered with smoke. The ground defences couldn't do a thing."

"It doesn't matter," I replied. "They couldn't land. Don't forget the whole thing depends on their having balloon markers at each end of the runway to guide them in. Besides, they won't come yet. It must have been worked out to an intricate time-table. The cylinders wouldn't have been distributed for at least ten minutes. And they would have had to allow some slight margin.

I should say we have got another quarter of an hour. But we must warn other aerodromes."

At that moment the Tannoy sounded faintly from the depths of the smoke, wisps of which were beginning to curl over the pit: "Attention, please! Attention, please! Attack Alarm! Attack Alarm! All ground defences to report immediately to their action stations. Crews to stand by at dispersal points. All other personnel to take cover. Anti-aircraft defences will be fully manned. All personnel throughout the camp will put on gas masks immediately." The message was repeated.

And then: "Tiger and Swallow-tail Squadrons to readiness immediately."

"Thank God for that," I said. "Helson has persuaded someone to take action."

The phone rang. Sergeant Guest answered it. Then he put his hand over the mouthpiece and turned to us. "It's the C.O. Thorby on the 'phone. He wants to know if any one in this gun pit has any accurate knowledge of what's going on."

"I'll talk to him," said Langdon.

He took the receiver. "Sergeant Langdon here, sir. The position is this: There was a plan to land troops on the aerodrome at dawn this morning under cover of a smoke screen. Four R.A.F. lorries entered the camp at roughly three-fifty hours carrying smoke cylinders and manned by fifth columnists in R.A.F. uniforms. Gunner Hanson of my detachment saw a large number of these lorries being loaded up in a gravel pit in Ashdown Forest. Mr. Vayle was in charge. Yes, Vayle. The four lorries that entered Thorby distributed themselves along the wire to the north-east of the landing field—that is, to windward. My own detachment dealt with one of them and two more have just been destroyed by Bofors fire from Number Five pit. Yes, sir, as far as we know it's only smoke. Gas would hamper their own troops as much as ours. Well, the cylinders must be fairly well shot to pieces. It shouldn't take long to clear. No, they were to be guided in by balloons flown at a fixed height at each end of the runway.

The last one must be practically at the north end of the 'drome. The wind is north-east, you know. Yes, the runner who reported to Gun Ops. has gone on to get the armoured car. You'll come out with it, sir? Very good. I'll wait here at Number Five pit. Well, we think in about quarter of an hour. Can you send an urgent warning out to all 'dromes in the south-eastern area? Yes, there isn't much time. Very good, sir. I'll be here."

He put down the receiver. "He's sending out a warning to other stations right away," Langdon told me.

"Is Winton coming out here?" I asked.

"Yes—and the ground-defence officer."

"Aren't you two going to put your masks on?" came Guest's muffled voice. He already had his on, and I suddenly realised that the whole of his detachment had put gas masks on. The smoke was curling into the pit and it smelt acrid and dirty. I had a moment of panic as I discovered that I hadn't got mine with me. Langdon hadn't got his either. In the excitement of the moment I don't think any of our detachment had taken their masks with them. Langdon sniffed in the air and then shrugged his shoulders, as much as to say, what will be will be. We examined the pit gas detectors. They were unmarked though the smoke was thickening all round us. To the north it was still light, but visibility was too bad for us to make out any details. To the south, however, it was pitch black.

It gave one an unpleasant feeling of being choked. At the same time I began to feel that expectant void in my stomach. Time was slipping by. In a few minutes it would be zero hour. I began to wonder what would happen. They might not have the smoke screen to help them, but that did not necessarily mean they wouldn't land. And if they landed—well, on paper it should be a massacre. But—I wasn't sure.

"I think we'd better get out of here whilst we can still see our way," Langdon said to me. "Winton will never get as far as the pit in this stuff. We'll meet him on the road."

Smoke from the lorry to the north of us was now pouring over the brow of the hill and rolling in a thick, low-lying cloud across the landing field. It didn't spread much, however, so that there was quite a well-defined lane of pale light, part moon, part dawn, between this bank of smoke and the one behind us. The latter was already beginning to thin out, for the cylinders, having been shattered, had not much staying power.

We had barely reached the roadway when a pair of headlights nosed out of the smoke. At first I' thought it was the armoured car. But when it cleared the smoke, it turned out to be a small sports car. As it drew up alongside us I recognised it for Nightingale's. Three people were sitting in it. They looked strangely impersonal, for they had gas masks on. The two in front were in Air Force uniform. But the one behind was a civilian.

I knew who the two in front were before they removed their gas masks. The driver was Nightingale, and it was Marion who sat beside him. "Where have you been, Barry?" Her voice was quiet. For a moment I thought her eyes looked reproachful, anxious. But there was a smile on her lips—a smile that made my heart race—and it spread from her lips to her eyes. Her whole face was suddenly lit up by that smile.

It was an exquisite moment, shared between us there in the pale light of the dawn with the trappings of war all around us. It was an oasis in that grim, exciting desert of useless action. All that she had to offer a man was in her eyes as the smile overwhelmed the anxiety in their depths like sunlight. And both were for me. I felt pain in my heart, pain that was yet pleasure; pain that I had found beauty, but could not grasp it firmly for all time; pain because our moment was fleeting. Life is full of this ache for moments that cannot be held. War makes it greater, but because there is a futility and not an inevitability about the immediate cause of one's inability to hold one's moments.

I am sure I should have stood staring at her long oval face framed in her dishevelled page-boy's hair and those sweet smiling eyes with no other thought till the troop-carriers came flocking to the 'drome. But the spell was broken by the civilian in the back. " Well, you old dog, Barry—what have you been up to?"

I jerked my gaze from Marion. The fellow had removed his gas mask. It was Bill Trent. "What the hell are you doing here?" I said. I fear my tone was bleak. He had broken the spell. And any one who breaks the spell of that first discovery of love given and offered freely must surely expect a cold welcome.

"I got back here from a forced landing near Redhill to find him waiting for me," John Nightingale explained. "He had tried to see Winton without any luck."

"He's proved that Vayle's a spy," Marion cut in, her voice sounding surprisingly matter-of-fact.

"How do you know, Bill?" I asked.

"Because he's not Vayle at all, old boy," Bill Trent replied. "Vayle was last seen in Dachau concentration camp in 1936. That was two years after the Vayle who is a librarian here returned to England."

"Yes, but how do you know?" I asked.

"After I'd got your message I did everything I could to find out Vayle's background. I got details about the family, but all his relations seemed to be dead. I could unearth very little information about him prior to 1934. In desperation I combed through my refugee acquaintances. I knew a man who was one of the very few to escape from Dachau. He said he had been with Vayle for nearly two years in that camp. I knew he was telling the truth because he gave me Vayle's life history, which tallied with what I had been able to discover. He said that when he escaped Vayle was still there, slowly dying of T.B."

"I got Winton to see Trent," John Nightingale put in. "It was a bit of a shock for him. Vayle is a very brilliant man and he has done a great deal for Fighter Command in working out tactics. A guard was sent to bring him in for questioning. But he had left the camp. That scared me. I told Winton everything that you had told me. He sent me out to your site to fetch you. It was then past midnight.

You were missing. Miss Sheldon was on night duty at Ops. She told me which Cold Harbour Farm you had picked."

"And we went there and we found a dilapidated old farmhouse and a dear old gentleman in a night-cap and gown," Marion put in. "But you weren't there. He spoke of two soldiers he'd given a meal to. We came back here. We were in Ops. when all this started, and then Winton spoke to your sergeant. What happened to you, Barry? You did find something, didn't you?"

Briefly I told them of the gravel pit and the lorries—and Vayle. I explained the plan to them. And I was just beginning to tell them how we had destroyed the three lorries when out of the thinning smoke came the armoured car, followed by two R.A.F. cars. Langdon stepped forward and waved to them. They drew up just short of us.

Winton jumped out of his car, and Major Comyns and Ogilvie got out of the other. They had just taken their gas masks off and they were stuffing the face pieces into their haversacks as they came up to us.

Langdon stepped forward and saluted. In a few words he explained the situation. When he had finished, the C.O. turned to a young artillery lieutenant who was standing by the open door of the armoured car. "Ross," he called. "There is an R.A.F. lorry somewhere along this wire to the north. It must be put out of action at once. If possible, I want it captured intact. And I want prisoners. I'll be at Ops."

"Very good, sir." His voice was muffled in his gas mask. The iron door of the armoured car clanged to, and the great lumbering vehicle roared off along the tarmac and disappeared into the smoke to the north of us, which was also beginning to thin out now.

Winton turned to me. "Good work, Hanson," he said. "I'll not forget it. I'd like you to stay with me. Sergeant Langdon, get your detachment together and your gun manned as quickly as you can. Gun Ops. will keep you informed."

"Yes, sir."

As Langdon disappeared, Winton nodded to me, and I followed him to his car. He paused with one foot on the running-board. "Mr. Ogilvie, will you go round the gun sites. See that everything is all right, and above all see that they all know what their fields of fire are for action against 'planes landing on the 'drome. They must stick rigidly to those fields. I don't want them duelling with each other across the landing field. Comyns wil take you in his car. You'll be going round the ground defences, Major, won't you? Excellent! Good luck!" He climbed into the driving seat. "Come on, Hanson, jump in."

I got in beside him and the big car shot forward, dipping sharply as he swung it round. The smoke was no more than a few thin wisps now, and in front of us the familiar shapes of the station showed dimly in the cold grey light of dawn. We made a half-circle of the landing ground and swung in at the barbed-wire gates of Operations. Winton had driven fast, and all the time he plied me with questions. But as we descended the ramp to Operations he was suddenly silent.

His was a big responsibility. And in the minutes that followed I came to admire him greatly. He was conscious of the weight of that responsibility. It was a weight that could not be carried lightly. But he carried it calmly and without fuss. I think he was one of those men who are at their best in action. He was cool and he used imagination.

The first thing he did on entering Operations was to order two Hurricanes to be loaded with smoke and to send a dispatch rider to the meteorological tower for two balloons. "Tannoy!" he called. "Give the All Clear for gas."

Faintly from somewhere outside that big subterranean room came the echo of a voice that spoke quietly into a microphone in one corner: "Attention, please! Gas all clear. You can show your faces again, boys. It's all clear for gas."

The room was confusing at a first glance. There were

so many girls sitting at telephones and so many officers and Waafs standing about, apparently doing nothing. And everything centred on a large table, the top of which was a map of south-eastern England and the Channel.

I suddenly found Marion at my elbow. She squeezed my arm and I looked down to find her eyes bright with excitement. "It's all yours," she said. "Your show. I hope it goes well."

"Where's Nightingale," I asked.

"Gone to dispersals. In a few minutes he'll be leading his squadron up."

"And Trent?" I asked.

"Oh, I left him at the entrance. He's trying to get permission to come in here." She squeezed my arm again and crossed the room to a vacant desk on which was a telephone and a pad.

I stood there, bewildered and alone. I felt conscious of my dirty oil-stained battle dress, so out of place here where there was nothing but Air Force blue. I wished I could have been going up with a squadron to fight invasion. Action! I wanted action; to be on the gun—anything rather than the suspense of waiting with nothing to do.

Winton called me and handed me a message. On it was scrawled: "Mitchet report four smoke lorries captured." After that, one by one, the fighter 'dromes of the south-east reported lorries containing smoke either captured or put out of action.

All at once my sense of bewilderment vanished. I no longer felt out of place down here in this strange room. It was like being suddenly transported back to journalism. Here was action and I was watching it. My brain would record impressions of it, and some day I'd use this material. God! What wouldn't some Fleet Street boys give to be on the inside of this story. I felt the thrill of pride that comes of achievement.

A Waaf came up to Winton. "Mr. Ross reports lorry captured intact, sir," she said. "He's got seven prisoners."

"Good. Tell him to fetch the lorry and the prisoners down here at once."

So much for Vayle's attempt to help German troops to land at Thorby. I remembered how he had sent those lorries off. He had been so calm and so assured. Well, he had had every right to be. It had been a clever plan. His luck had been out, that was all. And what would he do now? It seemed such a strange anti-climax for him to be arrested and shot as a spy. Yet that was what would probably happen. And Winton would, of course, have to be present at the court-martial.

Telephone buzzers sounded. The Waafs at their desks began writing furiously. Others took the slips of paper to the table. The whole room suddenly sprang to life. Everything was confusion; but it was the ordered confusion of a job being carried out.

Little wooden markers with arrows began to appear on that section of the table that represented the Channel. All the arrows pointed one way—towards the south-east coast. And the wooden markers had swastikas on them. They also had numbers. There were several thirties and one or two forties and fifties plotted within the space of a few seconds. Each marker meant a formation of enemy planes. I counted three hundred and forty plotted already.

"Get both squadrons up," Winton ordered. And a moment later came the faint sound of the Tannoy: "Both squadrons scramble! Tiger Squadron scramble! Swallow-tail Squadron scramble! Scramble! Off!"

I heard a Waaf on a telephone just near me saying: "Several large formations of hostile aircraft approaching from the south-east. They are believed to be troop-carriers with fighter escorts. Heights range from fifteen to twenty thousand feet. Guns are to hold their fire."

The movement of the enemy air attack began to take shape as the markers were moved steadily forward with every observation report that came in. Other markers also apeared. These had the red, white and blue roundels of the R.A.F., and they were mainly inland from the coast.

The young artillery officer, Ross, came in. He went

straight up to Winton. They conversed in low tones. Suddenly the C.O. said: "Balloons? With lights? Excellent. A green at the start of the runway and red at the end, eh?"

"No, the other way about, sir. And it's a red light and a white light."

"Sure the fellow isn't trying to put one across you?"

"I don't think so, sir. He's pretty badly hurt and very frightened."

"What height are they to be flown at?"

"I don't know, sir. I didn't ask him."

Winton turned to me. "Do you know what height these balloons are to be flown at, Hanson?"

"Vayle said fifty feet, sir."

"Good. That means about thirty feet above the smoke. Get the balloons blown up and the lights attached. The red light will be above the hangars just east of Station H.Q., and the white one above the main gates. Fly the balloons at eighty feet. Can you get them in position in five minutes?"

"Yes, sir."

"Very good. I'm giving orders for the smoke screen to be laid right away. It will be between thirty and fifty feet. See that the balloons are up by the time the smoke screen is finished."

"Yes, sir." He dashed out of the room.

Winton went over to the switchboard. "Give me Number Two dispersal," he told the Waaf telephonist. "Hallo! Marston? Are those two Hurricanes ready with smoke? They're to take off at once and lay a smoke screen along the eastern edge of the 'drome from the Thorby road to the north edge of the landing field. The smoke must not be loosed at less than thirty feet or at more than fifty feet, and they must cut off at the limits given. They will continue until the smoke is exhausted or they receive instructions to cease. Right. Tell 'em to scramble."

Winton had a number of ground-staff officers round him now. He was issuing orders to them in a quiet, precise voice. I only caught a few words here and there.

From above ground came the faint murmur of engines revving up. On the table the swastika markers had moved forward over the coast. The attack was taking shape. Formations of about fifty bombers and a hundred fighters were closing in on each of the fighter stations. Two of these formations were heading in our direction.

An officer came to the telephone just beside me. " Gun Ops.? Warn the guns that the two Hurricanes just taking off will be laying a smoke screen about fifty feet above the drome. They are only to fire on enemy 'planes landing on the field. They will not open fire at aircraft that crash. Any survivors will be mopped up by ground defences."

Before he had finished speaking the Tannoy announced: " Attention, please ! A smoke screen is being laid over the 'drome by two of our own machines. Hostile troop-carriers may be expected to attempt a landing. Some of these will probably crash. Ground defences will ensure that no hostile troops are allowed to take offensive action after their 'planes have crashed. Care should be taken to avoid getting in the field of fire of the guns which have instructions to open fire on any hostile 'planes that succeed in landing on the 'drome. Off."

" Hanson !" It was Winton calling me. " I think you had better report back to your gun site now."

" Very good, sir."

" Any points that have not been covered?"

" I don't think so, sir."

" Right. Thank you for your help—and good luck."

" And to you, sir." I saluted and hurried out of Operations. Bill Trent was outside. " Look after yourself, Barry," he said. " I'll want a story out of you when the show is over."

" You'll be lucky if you're allowed to print it," I said. And jumping on the first bike I saw, I rode up the ramp and out on to the tarmac. I could just make out our gun pit almost on the other side of the 'drome. It stood out against the dull glow of the eastern horizon. The moon had set and the flying field looked pale and flat and cold. Tin hats—blue and khaki—showed above the ramparts of the ground-defence trenches. Soldiers stood waiting, their rifles ready, at the entrance to pill-boxes. There was an unpleasant atmosphere of expectancy.

As I crossed the tarmac in front of the hangars one of the Hurricanes made its first run along the eastern edge of the field. It was just a vague, shadowy thing in the half light, and it flew so low that I felt it must pile itself up on the first dispersal point. And it left behind it a thin line pencilled across the dull grey of the sky. The line spread and grew, a dark, menacing cloud. It ceased at the northern edge of the 'drome. I could just make out the shape of the 'plane as it banked away for the turn.

By the hangar nearest to Station H.Q. men were busy about a balloon that looked like a miniature barrage balloon. Just below it was fixed a red light. As I passed the hangar the balloon rose gently and steadily into the air.

Soon I was cycling down the roadway on the eastern edge of the field. It was getting very dark now. The smoke was overhead, a great billowy cloud that moved slowly south-west over the station. It was so low that I felt I must be able to touch it by putting my hand up. Here and there a stray wisp reached down to the ground, curling gently, and as I rode through them my nostrils filled with the thick, acrid smell of the stuff. As I passed the dispersal point just to the south of our pit the second Hurricane zoomed overhead. It was so close that instinctively I ducked. Yet I could not see it. The darkness increased as its smoke trail merged with the rest, and I almost rode past the gun site.

As I entered the pit my eyes searched the faces that I could barely see : Langdon, Chetwood, Hood, Fuller. But Micky wasn't there. Nor was Kan. " What's happened to Micky?" I asked Langdon. " Is he . . ." I hesitated.

" No," he said. " He's got a bullet through the shoulder and another shattered his wrist. It's a light let-off, considering the risk he took. We got him to the sick bay."

" What about Kan?" I asked.

"Dead," Langdon said. The baldness of his statement shocked me. "He leapt up to follow Micky and took it in the stomach."

He didn't add any details and I didn't ask any. I could well imagine how he had died. I could see him swept into the maelstrom of a fight by his sense of the dramatic. He would have leapt to his feet, a young Raleigh, a Hotspur, a d'Artagnan, imagination cloaking him in the swaggering fineries of the Chivalry. And then a searing pain in his stomach, making him stagger and collapse as he had so often staggered and collapsed heroically for an audience. Then the sordid reality of blood on hard unyielding earth, of pain and finally of death. Poor Kan.

The silence in the pit that had followed Langdon's words was shattered by the roar of a Hurricane as it passed just over our heads laying its smoke screen. The wind sang past it's wings. It was unpleasantly close, yet we could see no sign of it. Over us was nothing but a dark fog of smoke, and every now and then a wisp curled into the pit, making us cough.

"What the hell is the smoke for?" Bombardier Hood asked me.

I started to explain, but the Tannoy suddenly blared out: "Mass formation attack alarm! Mass formation attack alarm! Two large formations of troop-carriers, escorted by fighters, are approaching the 'drome from the south-east."

The telephone rang. Langdon answered it. When at length he had put back the receiver, he said: "They're mostly Ju. 52's. They're at eight thousand feet and coming lower. Gun Ops. say that fifty are expected to attempt a landing on the 'drome."

"Fifty!" said Chetwood. "Good God!"

There was a stunned silence.

Then Hood exclaimed: "How the hell are we expected to fire on them when this blasted smoke screen has made it so dark that we can barely see the hut over there?"

"You don't need to for the moment," I replied. "The

idea is that they pile themselves up against the hangars."
And I explained about the balloons and how they should
mislead the Jerries.

"Yes, but suppose they do manage to land?" Hood
insisted.

The 'phone rang. I shrugged my shoulders. I didn't
know the answer. That worried me. I hadn't realised
how dark it would be after the smoke screen had been
laid over the 'drome.

Langdon put down the receiver. "That's the answer
to your question," he told Hood. "As soon as they start
coming in the searchlight on Station H.Q. will be switched
on."

"Won't that give the game away?" asked Chetwood.

Langdon hesitated. "I don't see why it should. After
all, suppose this was their own smoke and they were feeling
their way in, they would surely expect us to try and pierce
the smoke with what lights we had available."

"Listen!" cried Fuller.

For a second all I could hear was the steady drone of
the two Hurricanes. The drone grew to a roar as one of
them swept over us. The noise of its engines gradually
lessened. Then suddenly behind that noise I thought I
heard a steady throb. For a moment I was not sure. The
other Hurricane swept over the pit. And when the sound
of its engine had dropped to a distant drone, I knew I was
right. Faint to the south was a low throb, deep and
insistent. My inside seemed to turn to water. The
moment had arrived.

The sound grew till it beat upon the air, drowning
the engines of the Hurricanes except when they were
very close. Like the ripping of calico came the sound
of machine-gun fire. Two bursts. The sound of the
German 'planes seemed to fill the heavens. I had a horrible
sense of claustrophobia. I longed to tear that curtain of
smoke away so that I could see what we had to
face. More machine-gun fire. Then the high-pitched
drone of a 'plane diving to the east of us. It rose to a
crescendo of sound like a buzz-saw. And when I thought

the noise of it could not rise any higher there was a tremendous crash.

"Attention, please! Attention, please! Troop-carriers are now circling to land. They will come in from north to south. Gi' 'em a reet gude welcome, lads. Off!"

The throb of their engines had passed right over the 'drome. But the sound had not then gradually faded. It seemed to split up. All round the 'drome was this deep, persisting pulsing. I must admit I felt scared. I think we all did. The menace was unseen. There was only the sound of it. And the sound was all about us.

The gun was laid on the landing field. Chetwood and Red were in the layers' seats. Two sandbags on the parapet marked the limits of our field of fire. Shells fused at a half and one stood ready in the lockers behind the gun.

One particular engine became noticeable above the general throb that filled the air. It was coming in from the north. "Right. Fuse a half. Load!" Langdon's voice was clear and calm, and I recognised that boyish note in it that had struck me before.

The searchlight on Station H.Q. flickered and blazed into life. The great beam produced a queer effect. It was diffused by the smoke so that the landing ground was lit by a sheen of white and not by a beam. It was rather like the moon seen through thin cloud. And above it the banks of rolling smoke looked inky black.

The throb of the approaching plane drew nearer. The beat of it was slower now, and I could almost hear the screws ploughing their way through the air. The throb became more and more sluggish. The sound crossed the 'drome in front of us. It seemed as though it was feeling its way through the smoke.

Then suddenly landing wheels and a vague spread of wings showed white through the smoke. The moment of its appearance in the light of the searchlight seemed an age. It was dropping gently, searching with its wheels for the runway that should have been there. The whole 'plane was visible now, like a huge silvery moth flying into the light of a street lamp on a misty night. There was an iridescent unreality about that great winged thing, so cumbersome, yet so fairylike.

It came out of the smoke flying straight for B hangar. Too late the pilot saw the trap. Poor devil. He was feeling for a landing in thick smoke. Suddenly he had dropped right through the smoke, and in the dazzling light the dark shadow of a hangar loomed up in front of his cockpit.

The sudden frantic revving of the engines made the 'plane buoyant. It lifted slightly. For a moment I thought he would clear the hangar. But his undercarriage caught the edge of the roof, and the great 'plane tipped slowly up on to its nose and then over on to its back. There was a splintering crash and it disappeared from sight as the roof of the hangar collapsed.

The next one was already coming in. Above us the bursts of machine-gun fire were becoming more and more persistent. Somewhere up there in the cold light of the dawn a dog-fight was in progress. The next 'plane was coming in to find its landing now. It was crossing the landing ground, feeling its way as the first one had done. Because I wanted a visual impression of the pit in that moment I glanced round it. All eyes were fixed, fascinated, on the white glare of the searchlight, waiting for the instant when the plane would become visible as it dropped gently through the smoke. I imagine the gaze of every one around the landing field was fascinatedly fixed on the bright belly of the smoke above the hangars.

The Tannoy broke in upon our expectancy. "Ground defences south of B hangar to cover exits from the hangar. Cover exits from B hangar. Off."

I hardly heard it. All my senses were concentrated on watching the 'plane that was coming in. No one in the pit stirred. No one spoke.

One moment there was just the smoke made white by the searchlight. The next, the 'plane was there. It looked just like the other, monstrously big and all silvery. I felt rather than heard the slight gasp as we saw it. It was dropping faster than the other. The pilot never seemed to see the hangar. The great 'plane simply drifted straight into it. The wings crumpled, and as it fell in a shattered wreck to the ground we heard the crash of it. Several figures staggered out. They seemed dazed. There was a burst of machine-gun fire. And then another. The figures crumpled.

I suddenly realised that it was getting lighter. The fog of smoke above our heads was thinning out. The Hurricanes had finished laying the smoke. Another Ju. 52 was coming in. Above our heads the sounds of machine-gun fire had become almost constant, and behind the throb of the circling troop-carriers was the high-pitched drone of fighters diving and twisting and climbing. A pale light filtered into the pit. And in a moment I could see the eastern sky all flushed with the light of the sun, which had not yet risen above the horizon. The edge of the smoke, banked up in dark-brown billows, rolled away from the pit like a curtain, revealing a cold sky tinged with bluish green. To the east of us I could see a dozen or more big Junkers flying round and round in a circle, nose to tail for protection. It was not light enough yet to see the fighters, scrapping high overhead. But I could see one fighter diving on the formation of Junkers, letting rip with his guns and zooming away again.

" Look !" Langdon nudged my arm.

I swung back to the landing field. The breeze had freshened and the bank of smoke was rolling back fast. But it still covered two-thirds of the field. The light of the searchlight seemed fainter and farther away now that we were standing in daylight. And it showed another troop-carrier below the smoke. It had come through the smoke sooner than the others, and the pilot had time to see the danger. The roar of his engines as he revved seemed to shake the pit. But he scarcely lifted at all. Only his speed increased. He banked and his wing hit the hangar. The whole scene looked unreal. It was like watching a show. The presence of the smoke seemed to put a barrier between ourselves, who were standing in daylight, and the 'plane and the hangars, which were in artificial darkness and lit by artificial light. Rather a similar effect to that of the footlights in a theatre.

The plane crumpled up much as the others had done. But there was a sudden explosion and a great sheet of flame was puffed up into the smoke. In an instant the flames had spread to the hangar. The belly of the smoke glowed red. It was a fantastic sight—the twisted, blazing wreckage and the flames licking up the battered side of the hangar. I thought I heard screams. It may have been my imagination. But I knew men were dying in that inferno, dying a horrible torturing death. The thought sickened me. I had not become sufficiently imbued with the bestiality of war to feel exultant, though I knew they were dying because they had come to destroy us. It was either them or us. I knew that. But it didn't prevent me from feeling a direct responsibility for their death.

The next 'plane coming in was frightened by that red glow. Its engines revved up and the sound began to come towards us. Suddenly it appeared out of the smoke, its wings balanced at a crazy angle as it banked. It was coming straight for us.

"'Plane!" yelled Langdon. "On, on," came the voices of the layers. And the barrel of the gun began to follow the target as it banked round and away from us. Langdon waited till it was side on to us and then ordered, "Fire!"

The gun cracked and before the flames of the charge had ceased to spurt from the barrel, it seemed, the shell had exploded. The noise of it was almost as loud as the noise of the gun. At that range it was impossible to miss. Langdon had judged the fuse range nicely. The shell burst just in front of the 'plane. The wings folded down and the whole 'plane seemed to disintegrate. The fuselage split in half. I saw men falling out. The wreckage strewed itself among the trees in the valley.

The smoke had rolled back now and exposed the whole aerodrome. It lay on the south-western edge of the 'drome like a low cloud. It was getting really light now and the high cloud above us was tinged with a delicate pink. Against that lovely colouring little dark dots darted in and out amongst each other like flies.

All round the 'drome big cumbersome Ju. 52's circled and circled incessantly like vultures waiting for their prey to die. And amongst them the fighters droned like angry hornets. To the north-east of us there were more over Mitchet.

What would they do now? They were full of troops, not bombs—thank God! I half expected them to sheer off homeward now that their plan had failed. But they continued to circle. I wasn't sure whether they were undecided or whether they were waiting for something.

But we were not left long in doubt. Some twenty German fighters, who were still flying in formation well above the dog-fight, went into a dive. It was Langdon who first pointed them out to us. He had been searching the sky with his glasses.

They came right down to the north of us. Only when they were at about two thousand did they flatten out. Then they began to circle, and one by one they dived out of their new formation and came straight for the 'drome.

I had no doubt of their intention. Nor had Langdon. "Take cover!" he yelled. And we flattened ourselves in a bunch against the parapet nearest the approaching fighters. He crouched down too, but he kept his head just above the sandbags so that he could see what was happening. There was a sharp burst of machine-gun fire and a second later an ME. 109 shot over us. The Bofors pit to the north of us had taken the full force of the first attack. From the other side of the 'drome came the sound of a similar attack.

Then came the high-pitched drone of another German fighter. The staccato chatter of guns. The cinders on the floor of the pit kicked and little holes appeared in the sandbags opposite where we lay. One of the sandbags above me fell on my tin hat, covering me with sand. Zoom!

The 'plane flashed overhead. All round the 'drome Lewis guns and Bren guns opened up, adding to the confusion.

"Layers on," Langdon shouted above the din. "Fuller ammunition. Chester number six. Remainder stay under cover."

I peeped over the parapet as the three men detailed sprang to their posts. A troop-carrier was just coming in to land. "Fuse one. Load. Fire!" The drone of another Messerschmitt approaching could be heard even above the noise of the gun. We must have fired at practically the same moment as the other three-inch. There were two bursts just in front of the 'plane, mixed up with streams of tracer shells from the Bofors. I saw it plunge. Then I ducked as the pit was sprayed again.

By the grace of God no one was hit, though Langdon got his face cut by a bit of flying cinder.

Three times this happened. Each time we destroyed a 'plane. The fourth time I found myself laying. Red had been killed outright, a bullet through his head. This had happened as we destroyed the second Junkers. The third time it was Blah who was hit. He got a bullet through his arm. Fuller got one in the foot.

Three twin-engined 'planes appeared out of the north. At first we thought they were Me. 110's. But suddenly Langdon cried, "They're Blenheims."

And Blenheims they were, thrown in as fighters to make weight in the emergency. They came in at about two thousand feet. And high up we saw a squadron of Spitfires dive on the Messerchmitts that had been worrying us.

Then suddenly Junkers and Messerchmitts turned for home, the latter circling the troop-carriers to cover their retreat. It was all over in a few seconds. One moment the sky was full of Jerries and the din of battle. Then the sky emptied. The throb and drone of 'planes died away. A great quiet settled on the Station, in which the crackle of the flames at B hangar was the only sound. I leaned back against the gun. Peace at last. It was over.

passed out then. I didn't faint. It was jus
reaction left my mind a blank. I wasn't consciou
sound or sight. I came to to find Langdon getting th
casualties to the sick bay. And the Tannoy was announc
ing: "All clear! All clear! All ground defences and
gun teams will remain at the alert. All clear! All clear!"

THE END